Dragon Knights

The Captain's Dragon

BIANCA D'ARC

This book is a work of fiction. The names, characters, places, and incidents are products of the writer's imagination or have been used fictitiously and are not to be construed as real. Any resemblance to persons, living or dead, actual events, locale or organizations is entirely coincidental.

No part of this book may be used or reproduced in any manner whatsoever without written permission, except in the case of brief quotations embodied in critical articles and reviews.

Copyright © 2019 Bianca D'Arc
Published by Hawk Publishing, LLC

Copyright © 2019 Bianca D'Arc

All rights reserved.

ISBN-13: 978-1-950196-20-3

Captain Liam O'Dare is hunting pirates over land with a trio of unlikely allies - a sea dragon, a mysterious virkin, and a woman who is altogether too intriguing. The path they must follow is full of danger, but working together, they stand a good chance. Can they find Fisk and serve up the justice he so richly deserves? Liam and his friends will do everything in their power to make it happen.

DEDICATION

For my dear ol' Dad who continues to be a source of light and joy in my life in his 94th year on this planet. I'm hoping and praying he gets to stick around for many more!

CHAPTER 1

Captain Liam O'Dare stood at the helm of his ship, watching his crew do their jobs. They were in pursuit of the pirate Fisk, who had not only been responsible for the death of Liam's wife years before, but who had resurfaced and stolen a vital page out of an ancient book. Not just any book. No, this book belonged to the last of the wizards of old, Gryffid, who had been living in seclusion these many years on his island populated by near-immortal fair folk and the gryphons he had created eons ago.

That Gryffid had come out of hiding recently was still shocking news to everyone in the lands inhabited by men and dragons. That he had allied himself with the royal family of Draconia was another surprising move, though not altogether unexpected. The royal lines of Draconia were said to be descended from Gryffid's former ally, the great wizard, Draneth the Wise. Draneth was long gone, yet Gryffid remained, and Draneth's descendants were still ruling Draconia with a fair hand, from all accounts.

Liam O'Dare had made his home on the southern coast of Draconia for many years, as he'd made his living running trade routes between the major port cities on the coast and other far-off lands. He'd spent more time at sea these past two decades, allowing his daughter to remain at home with trusted retainers as she grew into a woman. She'd gradually taken over the land side of the business, running the trade rooms and warehouses with precision. Liam was proud of Livia, so like her mother it was hard to look at her, sometimes. She'd grown into a smart, beautiful young woman.

Just recently, though, she had befriended a dragon, of all things. Liam had not known when the blind dragon, Hrardorr, had come to the Southern Lair, that he would lead Liam's daughter into danger and romance. She'd fallen in love with two knights—which was the way Lair marriages worked, for some reason—and gone off with the two men. One of those men partnered with Hrardorr, and the other was knight partner to Hrardorr's mate, the dragoness, Genlitha. The men and dragons all worked together and the five of them—three humans and two dragons—now lived together as a family unit.

From what Liam had been able to learn since Livia's interest in the men and dragons had come to light, any offspring of either the dragon pair or the human trio would be raised with two sets of parents—one dragon and one human. The whole thing seemed damned odd to Liam, but Livia was beyond the reach of his discipline, now. She was a grown woman and had chosen to tie her future to those four beings.

He'd never seen her happier, but he also didn't pretend to understand it all. He'd never had many dealings with dragons or their knights. He left the business end of his trade to trusted employees on shore for the most part, while he did the sailing. He'd lost his wife. There was little left to tie him to the shore, except the daughter who looked more like her mother's ghost with each passing year.

He loved his daughter, but his heart had never really recovered from the loss of his wife. He wasn't sure Livia understood, but the time to make things up to her was over, now. She had her own life with two strong men and two mighty dragons. He hoped she'd be happy and live a good, long, productive life with them up at the Lair. He thought perhaps they'd made some progress in mending fences, but he couldn't spare any more time for family matters. The safety of the land—of all lands—was in jeopardy, and Liam had to do what he could to fix things.

A book had been cunningly stolen from the wizard Gryffid. Not just any book. No, this was a book of high magic. An ancient book. A *dangerous* book. Livia and her mates and the dragons had recovered the book itself, and it had already been returned to Gryffid. All except for one page. That one damning page, which contained a spell that might shake the very foundations of the Citadel itself.

The Citadel was a mythical place way up North where the last of the ancient wizards lay encased in ice. They had been trapped there during the last great battle of wizards when the fate of all the other races was being decided. Those that had been trapped in the Citadel were the worst of the worst. Those powerful beings saw humans, fair folk, dragons, gryphons and all the other sentient races as merely toys for their amusement. They didn't care how many had died in the wars. They didn't care about anything but their own power.

In the ancient days, when the race of wizards had walked the lands, there were those among them who championed the lesser races. Gryffid and Draneth the Wise had been two of many who had fought for the lives of men and fey, dragons, gryphons, and all the others. But Draneth was gone now, and Gryffid was the only wizard left free. If the Citadel was unlocked and those ancient ones poured forth, there would be no force strong enough to oppose them. Gryffid couldn't battle all of them on his own, and the lesser races had never developed the kind of power the wizards of old had wielded.

The sanctity of the Citadel must be preserved at all costs. Which was why Liam had gone racing off after Fisk as he escaped with that single, damning page.

Or, at least, one of the reasons.

O'Dare had been looking for Fisk for two decades. Liam wanted justice for the woman he'd loved and lost. He wanted

Fisk to pay for killing her. In short, he wanted Fisk's head on a pike. Nothing less would satisfy the smoldering rage and boundless sorrow that had engulfed Liam after his wife's death.

"Captain, there's something in the water, following us." Benyon, his first mate, came up to him, handing over the spyglass.

Liam scowled and took the cylinder, extending it out to its fullest length. He held the device up to his eye and looked out over their wake to the waters beyond. They were making fast time toward the last known direction of Fisk's ship, and Liam didn't have any patience for diversions.

Fisk was hard enough to follow, considering he had some kind of magic fouling his trail. It would be all Liam could do just to find his long-time enemy, again, but he would do it come hell or high water.

Liam looked hard at the water, waiting to see what Benyon was talking about. His patience was rewarded when he caught sight of something flashing darkly just under the water's surface. But the object was much closer than he'd expected. He only saw it because it was actually *in* the ship's wake.

Great. Just what he needed. A sea monster come to harry his ship.

"I see it," Liam grumbled as he handed the glass back to Benyon.

"What do you think it is, Captain? One of them sea dragons?" the man asked.

Liam's eyes narrowed. Perhaps his daughter had sent one of her new friends to follow him. If so, he was going to have a few things to say about that.

Liam strode to the back of the ship and strained to see the dark shape he'd glimpsed from above. He was much closer to the water here and able to see the wake. Sure enough, within moments, he saw the flash of scales once more.

That wasn't any fish.

Liam knew that dragons and their knights communicated through their thoughts. Draconic mouths were not made to speak the words of men aloud, but they had some sort of magic that allowed them to be heard in their chosen companions' minds. Livia could do it. She'd befriended the blind dragon all on her own, meeting the men well after she'd already established a friendship with the dragon.

Liam shook his head at the thought. Where had he failed that his daughter had taken up with *two* men? He'd thought she was the image of her frail, ladylike mother, but Livia had proven by her recent antics and the choices she'd made for her life that she had a wild streak... Just like her father.

She might look sweet and delicate on the outside, but she was an O'Dare through and through. She'd even gone off to hunt pirates alongside her men—something Liam would never have allowed. Maybe it was a good thing she now had two husbands. One man wouldn't stand a chance curtailing her high spirits and keeping her safe. Maybe two—and their two dragons—would have better luck.

He was still shaking his head as he caught a flash of color approaching much closer. The damned thing was nearly under his ship.

"If you can hear me..." Liam thought as hard as he could toward the shape just under the water. *"You can just go back to my daughter and tell her to leave well enough alone. I don't need a babysitter."*

A rumbling chuckle seemed to sound through Liam's mind, making him start. Then, the chuckle turned to words, and something was speaking directly into his mind.

"I was not sent by your daughter, Captain. I follow you because you follow Fisk. I would assist in regaining the vital page of Gryffid's book, if you have need of dragonish help."

"But you're a sea dragon," Liam said aloud, shocked into speaking, rather than limiting his observation to his thoughts. Luckily, there was no one near enough to hear him.

"I am, but what has that got to do with anything?" came the voice in his mind.

"You owe no allegiance to Draconia. As far as I know, your kind lead lives well away from the affairs of men. Why do you want to help?" Liam kept talking aloud since it seemed the dragon could hear him either way and there wasn't anyone nearby enough to hear his side of the conversation.

"Several reasons, but the most important being that the page in question could destabilize more than just Draconia. If the Citadel is breached, all the lands—and all the seas—will suffer. I have decided to pledge our help in preventing that from happening, if at all possible."

"*You* pledged the help of all sea dragons?" Liam paused a moment. Who was this creature that he could commit all the sea dragons to the cause?

"*It is my right as their Lord to do so, but once my brethren became aware of what that stolen spell book page meant to the safety of everyone, they really had no objection. The recent mating of one of our group to a land dragon and the discovery of Hrardorr and his mother, who was lost to us many years ago, has reminded the sea-based dragon community that there is another world above the waterline and that we can be part of it, if we wish. Many of my kind, as you put it, are curious about the land and are eager to visit Draconia and meet other dragons who prefer the land. To ensure that we can do so, we need to step up and help prevent the Citadel's breach. It's in everyone's best interest.*"

"Forgive me, milord, I didn't realize who you were," Liam backtracked, knowing most dragons preferred respect and formality from humans. If this one was used to being in charge of all his brethren, it was probably best to be extra respectful. After all, if he took offense, he could easily capsize Liam's ship or poke holes in it from below. Neither was a good idea.

"*How could you, when you can barely see me below the water?*" The dragonish chuckle sounded again, in Liam's mind. "*I am Lord Skelaroth,*" the dragon proclaimed after a moment.

"And I am Captain Liam O'Dare. It is an honor to make your acquaintance, milord."

The sea dragon lord kept to the depths after their initial discussion. The crew would see him from time to time, but often, he was an invisible presence somewhere in the deep.

Liam didn't mind that. He was more comfortable with the dragon at a distance than up close and talking to him, at this point.

Liam still couldn't quite believe it. He'd actually had a conversation with a dragon. And not just a regular dragon, but one of the fabled sea dragons. And not just any sea dragon, but the leader of them all. It felt unreal, at times.

Then again, he could still hardly believe his own daughter had taken up with two knights and their dragons and was forming a family with them all. He didn't understand it. In fact, he preferred not to think about it. In his mind, his little Livia was still a toddler, or a shy teen. The image of her sainted mother. Perfect, and definitely *not* interested in boys. Much less two of them at once!

He still felt a little ill thinking about her being married. To them both. He knew that was the way of it in Lairs. All of Draconia knew about the strange arrangements the Lair families had, but the details were thin on the ground. Mostly, the Lair families kept to themselves because the Lairs were generally situated well away from the towns. Dragons required special accommodations, and their human counterparts went to live where the dragons would be happy, not the other way around.

Liam's mind was drifting, which was a clear sign that he needed sleep. He sent word to Benyon to take command for a few hours, then went to bed. It was the middle of the night anyway, and most of the men were already asleep. The night watch could take care of things for a little while.

*

"Captain?"

Benyon's voice came to Liam from just outside his stateroom door. Liam had already been up for a while, but he'd postponed going on deck to consult his maps.

"Yes, Mr. Benyon," he replied without moving from his study of the map he was currently looking at.

"Sir, you really need to come out here."

The note of panic in Benyon's voice struck Liam as odd. He made sure he had all the weapons he habitually wore on his person and headed cautiously for the door. The sight that met his eyes as he stepped through into the sunshine made him stop short.

There, on his quarterdeck, stood a compact black dragon with a black leather pack affixed to its back. He was no expert, but this did not look like a juvenile, though it was on the small side compared to the dragons he'd seen before. This dragon looked fully grown, just…smaller, and much less colorful than other dragons.

Liam took in the way his men all stood back from the beast. There was a lot of fear and curiosity on his ship at the moment, and he didn't blame them one bit. Liam strode forward to meet the dragon head on.

"As you were, Mr. Benyon." Liam snapped out the order, and his first officer seemed grateful for permission to get back to his station near the helm, leaving the dragon problem to his captain.

Liam moved to face the dragon, waiting to see what would happen next. The dragon's neck bent sinuously as its head lowered and maneuvered so that it was directly opposite Liam.

"Can you hear me?" came a decidedly feminine voice in Liam's mind. *"Your daughter has the gift, so I'm betting you do, too. I am Rivka. Can you speak with me, Captain O'Dare?"*

"Lady Rivka, I have neither the time nor patience to play games. What are you doing on my ship?" First Lord Skelaroth and now this. Was this voyage to be plagued by dragons?

The long neck jerked back in surprise. *"You can hear me! I knew I was right about you."* The female dragon seemed genuinely pleased, then her tone changed. *"There isn't much time,"* she told him. *"I know you're chasing Fisk, but he has put ashore in Tipolir. The Jinn are doing their best to keep him in their sights, but he is a tricky one, and he has some sort of magic that allows him to foul his trail. Our one advantage is that he seems to believe he went ashore undetected."*

"But you saw him, somehow," Liam said almost sarcastically. Was he to ask *how high* when this unknown dragon said jump? He thought not. His daughter was the one who had tied her fate to dragons, not him.

"Not me. The sea dragons. They stationed themselves all along the coast and have been physically watching every dock and every port. They spotted him and passed the information through the Jinn."

"And you got it how?" Liam challenged her further, though he was beginning to appreciate that this lead might actually be a good one.

"I am Jinn," she told him. "I am Rivka of the Black Dragon Clan."

"I have, of course, heard of your Clan, but I thought the name was just a euphemism," he said quietly, knowing many eyes were upon them. He trusted his men, but this seemed like sensitive information, and he didn't want to be party to revealing something he shouldn't. He wouldn't like to have the Jinn hunting him. They were said to be relentless.

"It's not," she said rather curtly. "Look, I don't have time to waste here. Will you make haste for Tipolir or do you give up the search?"

"I will never give up on the justice I seek from Fisk," he answered truthfully.

"Then, you'd better head for Tipolir. We believe he is going to go overland from there, but if he turns about and heads out to sea, again, it will take a fast ship like yours to follow him."

Liam frowned, thinking through his options. Up to this point, he'd been spinning his wheels and had found no traction on his search. Perhaps this un-looked-for help was just what he needed to move forward on his quest. He made a snap decision.

"Mr. Benyon, make our course for Tipolir at top speed," he shouted to his first mate.

"Aye, Captain. Tipolir at top speed," Benyon repeated, then turned to the helmsman and reissued the orders. He then got the mates moving to unfurl the mainsail and get the ship moving as quickly as it could.

Satisfied that his crew were hopping to it, Liam turned back to the black dragon. "Will you remain with us or go aloft, Lady Rivka?" he asked politely.

Rivka seemed to sigh. She looked tired to him. *"If it's all the same to you, Captain, I would like to stay on your ship. Do you have a hatchway large enough for me to squeeze through? I have been flying in the sun for some time, and I am rather overheated. The scales reflect a lot of the sunlight, but black still absorbs a great deal of heat in these Southern climes."*

Liam thought fast. Where could he put her that was nice enough? One didn't just toss a dragon in the hold of a ship with the crew. Dragons were special. Respected. Scary, when they felt insulted. Even Liam recognized the need to tread lightly.

"The doors to my rooms are large," he told her, trying his best to sound gracious. "Perhaps you could duck down a bit and fit through there?" He pointed to the back of the ship where his room took up most of the stern on this deck. "I can have water delivered. We have plenty of fresh water since we resupplied not two days ago."

She seemed to be judging the size of the double doors, her head tilted to one side. *"I believe that will be adequate. Thank you, Captain. If you'll just open the doors, we'll see if I fit."*

CHAPTER 2

Liam went himself to the doors and opened them wide. The dragon crouched down and just fit inside the large room. When she was in, she turned to look at him.

"Please close the doors and do not allow anyone entrance, except yourself. I am prepared to have you know some of my secrets, but no one else," she told him rather mysteriously. Liam scowled as he closed the doors and signaled for one of the hands.

He instructed the man to deliver a basket of fruit and several pitchers of water to the side of the entryway, but not to come inside. The young man rushed off to do his captain's bidding, and Liam took a moment to check that his orders regarding their speed and heading had been carried out. By the time he'd satisfied himself that everything was running as smoothly as possible on his ship, the young man had returned with the water and fruit. Liam thanked him and sent him away, then he turned to his own door and knocked politely.

"You can come in now," the dragon's voice came in his mind.

Liam picked up one of the pitchers of water and looped the basket handle for the fruit over his arm, using his free hand to open just one of the doors to let himself in. He expected to find the dragon curled up in the middle of the floor. Instead, he found a lovely woman wearing form-fitting black leather armor, unstrapping a set of swords from her back. She turned as he opened the door and smiled. She had lustrous, dark wavy hair and deep green eyes, and her smile lit up the entire room. For the first time in a long time, he noticed how attractive this woman—any woman, in fact—was, and it disconcerted him a bit.

"Close the door, Captain. You're letting the flies in." Her spoken voice was as soothing as her words in his mind had been, for he had no doubt that the woman and the dragon were one and the same. He didn't know how he knew it, but he was certain of it. Especially since the dragon was gone and the woman was in his quarters.

"That is some magic trick you have there, Lady Rivka," he said, entering his cabin and closing the door behind him.

"It's not really magic," she told him. "It's just the way I was born. I am half and half. The descendant of one of the children of Draneth the Wise."

"Like the royal line of Draconia," Liam said, thinking aloud. "Do you mean to tell me that the king and his brothers are all dragons under the skin, as well?"

Liam was having a tough time getting his footing back after being hit with the whammy of having a beautiful woman in his cabin rather than the dragon he'd seen enter. His instant attraction to her was something he hadn't expected at all. It had been a very long time, indeed, since a pretty lass could capture his attention. Not since Olivia, in fact. That his interest should rouse now seemed...inexplicable.

"How else do you think they can so easily rule both humans and dragons? They are both. Our kind were born to bridge the gap between the two races," she said, taking a seat in front of his desk. She seemed to relax a bit, as if very tired. "Can I have some of that water, please? I wasn't kidding about the sun. I'm not originally from such a warm climate, and it's a bit of an adjustment."

"Certainly." Liam snapped to attention, realizing he'd been standing there, staring.

He moved into the room and put both the pitcher of water and then fruit basket on his desk. He then went around the desk to the sideboard and retrieved two crystal goblets and his bottle of port. He needed a drink of something stronger, even if she didn't.

By the time he returned to the desk and took his own seat behind it, she was munching on an apple. He poured her a glass of water first, watching as she drank it down in one long series of gulps. Just the subtle action of her throat seemed to shake something to life inside him that he didn't fully understand, but recognized as lust. Shaking his head at his own strange reaction, he then offered her the port by simply raising the decanter questioningly. She reached for the water pitcher instead, answering his query just as silently.

When she had ingested about half the pitcher of water and the entire apple, he sat down opposite her, the desk between them. He watched her carefully, calmly assessing what he'd learned. It wasn't all that shocking to discover that the rulers of Draconia were even more special than he'd thought. What was surprising was that they'd been able to keep their secret for so long.

"Now, Captain," Lady Rivka said as he waited to see what would happen next. "We need to make some plans. How are your men set for fighting on land? Hard travel? Taking a prize ship?"

Liam frowned but answered her questions. "All of my men were chosen because of their fighting skills. This ship, in particular, out of the fleet I put together, is the best of the best. Most of my men were soldiers. Honorable mercenaries or guardsmen. Some are reformed pirates, used to fighting on sea and land. All grew up near the shore and have no fear of water. They learned to sail at a young age, for the most part, and are naturals on land or at sea."

"That is excellent," Rivka replied, sitting a little forward on her chair. "I ask this because there are several possibilities lying before us on this path. First, Fisk's ship. We must stop it, if we can, to prevent him from taking to the sea, again. He's got some kind of magic on that ship that makes it nearly impossible to spot from the air or follow at sea, as you have experienced for yourself. If at all possible, we must deny him the use of that ship."

"Which is why you asked about taking a prize. Well, I won't dissemble," Liam told her. "We've done it before. I'm not a pirate…exactly. But I have taken ships that were up to no good. My men are well versed in the necessary techniques, and there are enough men here to form a prize crew to remove the captured ship to another port where I have more sailors and resources."

"As I had hoped." Rivka seemed pleased with his answer. "The thing is, there is no clear way to sail much closer to the Citadel."

"The Citadel?" Liam repeated, wanting to know more about what this fascinating woman had to say about that magical and dangerous place.

"Well, that's where Fisk has to be heading," she said. "That page of the book contains the spell that can break the ice that holds the enemies of all mankind and dragonkind at bay. I, and many others, believe that is Fisk's goal. To free the dark wizards imprisoned in the Citadel and return chaos to the world. It's an insane notion, but I suppose Fisk thinks he'll be looked on with favor by those evil beings of power and rewarded for freeing them. From all I have been taught, he's more likely to be squashed under their feet as they make their escape."

Silence reigned for a moment as they both thought that through. "It cannot be allowed to happen," Liam said finally, in a somber tone.

Rivka's flashing green eyes met his. "Exactly why I have come to you, Captain," she told him. "I believe you know Fisk best, and I know you have a personal reason to hunt him. I believe you have the best shot of either capturing him or hounding him into a position where our allies in Draconia and elsewhere can capture him and retrieve the page of the book." Her voice dropped to a more grave tone. "I am sorry for what happened to your wife, sir," she told him with all formality.

Liam looked up sharply. "What do you know of it?" Not many people knew the truth of what had happened to his dear Olivia.

"Fisk killed her," Rivka said quietly. "You have my deepest sympathy."

"Not many know the truth of what happened that day," Liam said, surprised by both her knowledge and circumspection. He wanted to know more about what she knew and how she knew it.

"We Jinn have our own sources of information," she replied, sitting back in her chair. Her body language was closing up, and he suspected he wouldn't get much more out of her on this topic.

"I have run across your people from time to time, of course, but I know little of them. Few Jinn sail the high seas."

"True enough. We prefer the land routes," she agreed.

"Recently, it seems, many of your kind have gathered in Draconia. Why?" He figured the oblique angle wasn't working, so he'd go for a direct question.

"The prophesied time came to pass," she said, surprising him. "Many of us in the Black Dragon Clan are direct descendants of Draneth the Wise. We belong to Draconia, first and foremost. When Arikia was found and became our queen, we knew that was the time to return to the land of our origin. Almost all Jinn have been recalled and are building homes around Castleton."

"Truly? I had heard rumors, of course, but we are a long way from the capital here," Liam observed, shocked by what Rivka was revealing. Perhaps direct questions were the best way to deal with this beautiful Jinn Lady, after all.

"Oh, it's all true. Riki is our queen, and the Prince of Spies is our king. Rather fitting, I thought, since we Jinn, at our heart, are a nation of spies. We still have operatives all over, and will continue to send out caravans, but our home base is here, now. We finally have been able to come home."

Liam hadn't known any of that and was taking it all in. He wondered if he could help with intelligence gathering, once his task with Fisk was finally complete. He had built up one of the biggest fleets on the high seas with one purpose in mind. Now that the purpose—catching Fisk—was at hand, he had started to think about possible futures for his fleet of ships.

"If some of your brethren wish to go to sea after this is all over, I have many fast ships that call on foreign ports on a regular basis. I think the Jinn—and the crown—might find that sort of thing useful," he said carefully.

Rivka smiled. "Once this task is done, I believe we could come to some arrangement. No sense letting a network like the one you've built go into decline. Not when the kingdom and all our peoples will still need protectors and sources of information for those protectors."

Liam smiled for the first time in a very long time. He liked the way this woman thought. She was quick-witted and challenging. Something he'd seldom encountered in the fairer sex. Of course, since his wife had died, he hadn't been in port much, and there were no women on any of his ships.

"My thoughts exactly," he agreed, allowing himself a moment of enjoyment, thinking of a future that had not yet come to pass where he was free to be just another citizen of Draconia, not a man hell-bent on vengeance and bringing a certain piratical bastard to justice.

Liam left his rooms, leaving the fascinating Rivka inside. She was weary from her journey, and she had graciously offered to let her sleep in his bed. They had talked about the particulars of what would, or could, happen when they reached Tipolir, but she had been yawning toward the end, and he'd taken pity on the woman and left her to rest. There was plenty he could do on deck to prepare his ship and crew for what was to come.

A small creature, about the size of a cat, hopped up on the rail beside Liam as he looked out on the deck below. Liam didn't jump. He'd become used to the virkin's presence aboard his ship. Better than a ship's cat at catching and devouring vermin of all kinds, the virkin had joined his crew in Elderland, on Liam's last trading voyage there. The creatures were said to be intelligent and even capable of basic communication once they matured, but this little one had been newly hatched when it climbed up Liam's pant leg to settle on his shoulder.

He didn't know enough about virkin to know when she might mature enough to communicate, but he talked to her, regardless. He knew only vague rumors about virkin, and nobody aboard hailed from Elderland, though they all enjoyed the benefits of having such a fierce hunter aboard to keep the vermin down. Since the virkin—whom he called Ella—had joined the ship, there had been no rats or even spiders, in fact. She was a master hunter, and nothing escaped her claws.

Ella was shy, though. She most often slept in Liam's cabin, but had been conspicuous by her absence when he'd let Rivka enter there. Ella had been hiding, and he figured she might be afraid of the dragon. Virkin had wings, too, but they were tiny compared to a dragon. Ella was a miniaturized version of the sea dragons he'd seen. Colorful and without flame. Scaled in jewel tones but, somehow, sleeker than their land counterparts.

Liam held out his hand, allowing Ella to decide whether or not she would allow him to touch her. In that, she was much like a cat. She butted her head into his hand in a way he had come to recognize meant she wanted a scratch behind her ears and the little horns that protruded from her forehead. Her scales were soft to the touch, but tough enough to protect her little body.

"Where have you been hiding, my lovely?" Liam crooned to the creature in a quiet voice as he scratched and stroked her scales in the way she liked. Soon, he could feel the rumble of her purr under his hand, and her eyes closed in what looked like virkin-ish bliss.

She gave him a little chirp in her near-sleep. Ella made the cutest sounds, sometimes. He wasn't sure if virkin were supposed to communicate verbally or through body language. Not for the first time, he wished he knew more about the species. He hadn't ever expected one to choose him for its companion, but now that she had, he couldn't imagine sailing without her aboard. She was both useful and comforting to a man who had lost almost everyone that had ever mattered to his heart.

"Were you afraid of the big black dragon?" he asked Ella, rhetorically, still stroking her scales as she drifted to sleep on the rail. He thought about the fact that the dragon was a shapeshifter. A lovely shapeshifter, at that.

If his mind drifted to the oddity of having a woman in his bed for the first time since he'd lost his dearest Olivia, he didn't let it dwell there long. Rivka was absolutely nothing like dear, sweet Olivia. For one thing, Rivka was a warrior. Those swords she'd had strapped across her back were not just for show. They gave every appearance of long acquaintance and hard use.

Rivka had flashing dark eyes that held secrets and mysteries all their own. Olivia had possessed the clearest blue gaze that could hide nothing. Rivka was tall and muscular where Olivia had been petite and the softest welcome in the world to a man who had lived a hard life on the sea.

There really was no comparison between the two women. What's more, Rivka was not only a Jinn, but a *dragon*. That was something completely outside Liam's experience. She was royalty…or the next best thing to it. She was magical and mysterious. Liam didn't even know if she had a husband among the Jinn or if people who could turn into dragons somehow behaved differently than regular people.

"Why am I even thinking about it?" Liam muttered to himself as he stood at the rail, stroking Ella and peering outward into the gloom.

"I beg pardon, Cap'n?" Benyon asked, coming up beside Liam.

"Nothing," Liam replied, sighing heavily. "Make your report, Mr. Benyon."

*

Rivka slept in the captain's bed, uncomfortably aware of the scent of him in the cabin. She hadn't expected him to be so devastatingly attractive. Tall, handsome and younger than she had imagined, Liam O'Dare was too attractive for his own good. He had tanned skin from all his time spent sailing the seas under the sun, and he had the fit body of a man who pitched in with the physical labor of running his ship, not sitting back ordering other folk to do the hard work.

His blue eyes were as deep as the sea, and the golden lights in his dark brown hair made her want to run her fingers through it. She was fighting a very visceral attraction to the handsome sea captain. Something she hadn't expected or prepared for, but something that was very real, regardless.

She had been told of his tragic past, of course. How he had lost his wife and dedicated his life, from that point on, to bringing the pirate Fisk to justice. When she'd heard the story, at first, she'd scoffed about how long it was taking Captain O'Dare to get Fisk, but then, she'd retracted her scorn as she'd learned more about Fisk and the magical means by which he'd been concealing his trail for so very long.

Once she had realized the true depths of what Liam—she could no longer think of him by any other than his first name, now that she had slept in his bed—was up against in chasing Fisk, she had changed her opinion. She realized he must have loved his wife dearly to spend so much of his time and effort to bring her killer to justice. The fleet Liam had managed to build was a thing of beauty that had already come in very handy in protecting the land of Draconia from Fisk and his kind.

It had been thanks, in part, to Liam's fighting fleet that only the single book had been stolen from the wizard Gryffid's tower. And that book had been returned, thanks again to Liam's support of the recovery efforts. Just that single page remained abroad to threaten all good people, everywhere, and Liam was working harder than anyone to retrieve it. She admired his single-minded focus. Not many men would dedicate themselves to a quest and follow it through, no matter how long it took. She liked that about him, too. In fact, she was discovering there was a great deal to admire, and not much to complain about, where Liam was concerned.

Finding the missing page would also mean finding Fisk. Rivka knew that was probably a large factor in Liam's motivation, but when it came down to it, Rivka didn't think it mattered *why* Liam was doing this…only that he *was* doing it. He was risking greatly for the chance to fulfill his own quest while aiding in protecting everyone from the horrors that might be unleashed if that page and its spell was used where it could do the most harm.

She would chase Fisk all the way across Draconia and the Northlands, if she had to. She was a warrior of her people, and she had sworn to this quest. She would see it through, no matter what. Right now, that meant partnering with Captain O'Dare. He was the closest anyone had come to finding Fisk, and he knew the pirate and his habits better than anybody.

She had hitched her wagon to Liam's and would remain with him as long as the partnership proved worthwhile. That she would be spending a great deal of time with the handsome and attractive captain was something she'd just have to deal with.

*

"Cap'n, there's a ship on the horizon," the man in the crow's nest called down to Liam on deck where he'd been talking over their next moves with Mr. Benyon and his mates.

Liam immediately pulled out his spyglass and concentrated on the distant horizon. They'd been chasing the sun all day, heading westward toward the great port city of Tipolir. Sure enough, far in the distance, he saw a ship—not under sail but, seemingly, at anchor, far from shore. Strange.

Liam compressed the spyglass back into the smaller cylinder he habitually carried in his coat pocket and turned to Benyon. "If it is Fisk, he's anchored in a strange place." The implications troubled Liam. He would have expected Fisk to dock in Tipolir, not anchor his ship far away from any support from ashore.

"Have the watch keep an eye on that ship as best we can until the sun sets. We'll make for it and prepare the men for a possible hostile boarding," Liam ordered.

"Aye, aye, Cap'n," Benyon replied briskly and set to work dispersing Liam's orders to the right people.

Liam busied himself on deck until suppertime. They slowly gained on the ship, and the closer they got, the more it looked like Fisk's *Thorny Nettle*. Liam had always thought the ship was aptly named because it had been a thorn in his side for decades. Others just called it the *Nettie*, for short, but Liam knew better.

Liam went back to his cabin when supper was served, instructing his steward to leave the tray outside while he checked on the *dragon*. He knocked at the door gently, not wanting to disturb Rivka, but also wanting to offer her the evening meal. She answered his knock with a soft *come in*, so he opened the door and went in, carrying the tray.

The cook clearly hadn't known what to do about a dragon on the ship, so he'd simply sent up two large portions of the captain's grub. Tonight, he'd been served a small game hen with sides of potato and roasted peppers. The same dish had been prepared for the guest, which would probably have been totally inadequate for a dragon but seemed to suit Rivka, in her human form, quite well.

"Oh, that looks delicious," she enthused as Liam set the large platter down on his desk and lifted the covers off everything.

He served her first, clearing a spot on the opposite side of his desk for her to use. She didn't seem to mind the makeshift accommodations, for which he was grateful. He knew women liked, and often expected, certain niceties which were scarce on a ship like his.

Liam filled her in on the ship they were approaching over the meal, and she asked pointed and intelligent questions about his plans and contingency plans. She decided she would take her dragon form to *help*, as they neared the ship. In fact, she decided she would take a short flight over, to look at the other ship, just after dark.

"Is that wise?" Liam asked, not wanting to argue with a dragon, even if she was in human form, right now, but compelled to point out the possible dangers. "We know Fisk has blades that can pierce dragon scale."

"If I wait for full dark, it will be very hard to see me," she insisted, dipping her spoon into one of the slices of pie that had been included on the tray for their dessert. "And I'll be careful."

Liam didn't like it, but when it came down to it, she wasn't under his command. He had no say in what the female dragon shapeshifter did or didn't do. The best he could do was support her should she come to harm.

It was quite a change from the way he was used to dealing with females. Women, in his experience, had always been more fragile, in need of his protection. Rivka, by contrast, was well able to take care of herself and look after her own safety. She was more the protector than the protected. She was a warrior, in her own right. A magical being with powers he probably could never fully comprehend.

But she was also a beautiful woman. Something about her appealed to him on almost every level, which hadn't happened to him in more years than he could count. Not since his wife had he met a more intriguing female. And that was a thought that made him pause in his steps.

After losing the love of his life, he'd thought he would never meet another woman he could find the least bit attractive. Then, Rivka flew into his life and upset all his notions about attraction and the kind of woman he could find himself drawn to. Something about her stirred him in ways he hadn't been stirred in too long a time to countenance.

It was impossible, though. Liam would never love another, and aside from the attraction, he knew he would not shame his wife's memory with some loveless encounter with a substitute female that could never be his Olivia. He'd vowed never to love again, and he was old enough to appreciate that sex without love was merely a physical act without meaning. He'd had the best. He would never go back to mere passion. That would dishonor both himself and the memory of his lost love.

No. No matter how attractive he found the lovely Rivka, Liam would not indulge his baser instincts. What would such a woman want with him, anyway? He was merely human, whereas she was a shapeshifting dragon, for star's sake. Such a mismatch wouldn't stand a chance and, Liam knew, neither would he. Thanks be to the Mother of All.

He wasn't in the market for a fling, or even a roll in the hay. Such things were over for him, now, and he was better off without all those passionate emotions getting in the way of his true mission in life: to kill Fisk.

Retrieving the page of the book was a new mission, but it dovetailed nicely with his *raison d'etre*. Get the page, kill Fisk. It was all one purpose, now, since Fisk had the blasted page.

"Don't scowl so, Captain," Rivka's voice came to him, reminding him that he wasn't alone.

Had he spent so much time stewing in his own thoughts, of late, that he no longer knew how to keep up his end of a conversation? Yes, he realized. That was probably the case.

"My apologies, milady. I was thinking about our shared mission." He hoped she'd accept that at face value and let it be.

Rivka eyed him warily for a moment, but then just shook her head gently and looked down at her plate. He realized they had consumed the meal, and he should probably take the plates away. Normally, he would ring for a steward to clear the table since Rivka was a guest, but nobody but Liam knew she was a shapeshifter. He merely collected the plates himself and placed them back on the tray he'd brought them on. He'd take it with him when he left the cabin, again. For now, there were plans to discuss.

CHAPTER 3

Discussing his plans with anyone sat odd with Liam. He'd been on his own for so long. Master of his own fate…or doom. He hadn't consulted with anyone on his course since before he'd lost his wife. He'd worked long and hard to become his own man, beholden to no one on his ship or in his business.

He'd turned over a lot of the authority for the business on land to Livia and certain trusted managers in various ports of call, but on the high seas, Liam sought no one else's counsel. He knew his ship, his capabilities and his mission better than anyone, but he was forced to admit, Rivka, by her very nature, knew more of magic and magical things than he did.

Fisk was using magic, the blaguard. Liam would have to learn—or seek counsel of those who understood such things in ways he could not—if he was to catch the murderous bastard once and for all. Rivka had come into his life at just the right time, it seemed. She was a magical being who might have more of a chance of finding Fisk's trail than Liam did, he was sorry to admit. She was also a ranking member of the secretive Jinn Brotherhood. She had connections on land that he lacked. Particularly inland.

Liam's own network was thick on the ground in port towns and even along the coasts of other countries, but he had never bothered to build connections inland anywhere. Liam was a man of the sea, after all. Fisk was a pirate. A seaman, as well. Never had Liam imagined Fisk would flee over land where Liam could not easily track him. He'd assumed the chase would be from port to port or over the waves, not over mountains and through farmlands and deserts.

Liam hated land. Horrible things had always happened to him on land. But, if a land chase was his fate, then so be it. Liam would do everything he had to do to catch Fisk.

"The ship lies at anchor here," Liam told Rivka as they sat together after he'd cleared away the dishes. He pointed to a spot on the map he'd unfurled and lay across the table. Liam had spent many years perfecting and modifying it with his own hand.

"It seems an odd place," she said, looking thoughtfully at the map. "What are these lines?" She pointed to a feature he'd drawn in blue ink.

"Prevailing currents, as far as I could detect them. I've made a study of the shoreline all the years I've been at sea," he explained.

Rivka paused, looking up at him. She seemed impressed. "I had no idea you could detect such detail from the surface, but then, I've never spent much time on or near water. Except the occasional lake, of course." She smiled, her final words playful, and Liam found himself almost grinning. One corner of his mouth lifted, and it was an odd enough sensation that it startled him. It had been a very long time, indeed, since he had smiled.

"I have spent almost my entire life at sea," he said, hearing the gruffness in his own voice, but he couldn't help it. "Such things are important, particularly when storms come," he finished, knowing he sounded a bit abrupt, but damned if he could change it. He wasn't good with people, anymore. And, furthermore, he didn't really *want* to be.

"There appears to be no real advantage to anchoring his ship in this spot," Rivka observed astutely. "Why do you think he's done it?"

"It doesn't make sense. It's too far for easy access to the mainland by boat. It's not near anything in particular. He's also on the edge of a shelf that drops off into very deep water. It's about as far from shore as he could go and still get a solid anchorage," Liam said, frowning at the map. What was Fisk up to, now?

"How close are we?" Rivka asked, still studying the map.

"We will not be near enough to see much before nightfall," he admitted.

"Perfect." She looked up at him, a daring glint in her green eyes. "I'll go out after dark and take a look."

Liam grimaced and her gaze narrowed even more. "I know I have no right to tell you your business, but Fisk is well known to use diamond-bladed bolts and arrows. It's not safe for you—even under cover of darkness."

Rivka shook her head, smiling slightly. "I appreciate your concern, but I assure you, I know how to be careful. The Black Dragon Clan is full of spies, you know."

*

Rivka had enjoyed teasing the handsome captain. She thought about their earlier discussion as she winged her way under cover of darkness toward the faint silhouette of a tall ship, not too far distant. Liam's ship was still sailing this way at top speed, but he would not arrive for an hour or more. That gave Rivka time to investigate on her own.

Although, she suspected that she wasn't completely alone. She caught the occasional glint of light off highly-reflective dragon scales beneath the water below her, keeping pace with her flight easily. It looked like those sea dragons could really *move*, when they wanted to. She'd sensed a sea dragon nearby most of the day.

The sea dragon in question hadn't made any attempt to communicate with her, so she assumed it was following Liam's ship out of curiosity. She didn't know if Liam was aware of the sea dragon or not. She hadn't asked, and he hadn't volunteered the information, if he had it.

Still, if this sea dragon was going to investigate Fisk's ship with her, perhaps she would introduce herself. First, though, she had to see what she would find at the ship. If things stayed quiet, she would observe and perhaps have time to talk to the sea dragon about any observations it could make from below. If she flew into a hail of arrows, she would fly right back out, again. Anything else, she'd deal with as it came. She was prepared for just about anything.

Except finding the ship completely abandoned.

Rivka circled the ghost ship, unable to detect a single living soul on board. Finding it safe to land, she perched on the crow's nest, high above the deck, peering cautiously downward as the sea dragon's head rose from the water.

"Greetings, milady. I am Skelaroth, leader of the sea dragons in these waters."

Well. At least he had good manners. "*I am Rivka of the Black Dragon Clan. It is good to meet you, Lord Skelaroth,*" Rivka addressed the colorful and huge sea dragon below.

"*This ship reads as empty from below,*" Skelaroth said without further pleasantries.

"*It seems empty from up here, too,*" Rivka agreed.

She leapt down onto the deck in her dragon form, then changed swiftly to her human guise, quickly drawing the twin curved blades she carried on her back. She neither knew nor cared how the magic worked, but whatever she was wearing in human form went with her into her shifted form and came back when she shifted back. She had been wearing her blades, along with other weapons still secreted about her person, when she had taken flight to find Liam.

"I'm going to look below," she said out loud to the sea dragon. He didn't reply, merely nodding his massive head as he tread water beside the ship.

Rivka made short work of her search. She looked into each compartment and the hold, finding everything empty. Not even a ship's cat or the rats they were meant to chase was left on board. It was odd in the extreme. She went back to the main deck to find Skelaroth still there, watching from the water.

"The ship is completely empty. Not a bail or button left in the hold. Not even a mouse," she reported.

"*This seems highly improbable,*" Skelaroth mused. "*Humans always leave something behind, in my experience.*"

"Yes, we do. But this…" Her thoughts trailed off.

"*This seems almost like magic was used,*" Skelaroth said in her mind.

Rivka blinked, then blinked again, looking up at the mighty sea dragon. "That's not beyond the realm of possibility. We know Fisk has used magic in the past to foul his trail. But why leave his ship anchored here? If he was intent on leaving it for good, why not cast it adrift?"

"*Perhaps he does not want to let it go entirely. Maybe it remains here, as a backup plan,*" Skelaroth said, craning his long neck out of the water to look over the rail to the deck, inspecting the ship closely.

"That's got to be it," Rivka agreed. "It's the only thing that makes sense, but I have to say, it's damned spooky."

The sea dragon chuckled, but unlike his land counterparts, no smoke rings billowed up from his nostrils. Sea dragons did not generally flame the way land dragons did. The laughter, without the accompanying tendrils of smoke she was accustomed to, brought home the differences between land and sea.

This dragon was mighty by any standard. Much larger than herself, of course. In general, black dragons were the smallest of all dragons, but they were also the only dragons that could shapeshift into a human form. They were, quite literally, half and half. Half human and half dragon. Born of the great wizard, Dranneth the Wise's line, to rule over both humans and dragons, in harmony.

Rivka wasn't an historian. She didn't really know where the sea dragons fit in. She supposed someone, somewhere, must know the full story about how land and sea dragons came to be, but that wasn't really important to her, right now. No, what mattered most, at the moment, was whether or not this particular sea dragon—Lord over all the dragons who swam these seas—would lend his aid to her quest. Not one to beat around the bush, Rivka asked Lord Skelaroth straight out.

"I seek the page from Gryffid's book. It is why I approached Captain O'Dare. I believe he has the best chance, right now, of finding it. Will you help, Lord Skelaroth?" She looked the dragon straight in the eye.

He chuckled, again, surprising her. *"I, too, approached the good captain, not long before you landed on the deck of the ship. I have already pledged myself to this quest. I'm surprised Captain O'Dare did not speak of this to you."*

So was she. "Perhaps he thought it was some kind of secret. Liam likes to play his cards close to his vest, I've noticed."

"Liam, is it?" Skelaroth gave her the side eye. *"Perhaps you were too busy discussing other things, eh? You two are of an age, are you not?"*

Rivka shook her head, hoping her cheeks were not turning pink. She was a warrior woman. She didn't generally have time for romance. Such things were not part of her usual activities. She was far too busy seeing to the safety of her Clan. And, besides, Captain O'Dare was still famously mourning the death of his wife. He'd been on a personal vendetta to bring Fisk to justice for many years. His heart was not free, even if Rivka allowed herself to feel for him. That was a no-win situation. Better they remain colleagues in pursuit of a common goal. That, she could handle. That, she could do.

"I think you'll find that such things are not so simple above the water's surface, or among humans, for that matter," she told Skelaroth.

"But you are at least half dragon, are you not?" he asked with seeming innocence.

"And half human. That complicates matters," she

admitted, giving Skelaroth a stern look.

"*Shame,*" was Skelaroth's comment. "*He seems a good man, but he has a lonely soul.*"

"Perhaps that is his choice," Rivka said, hoping to end this conversation. "He will be here shortly. I will go and tell him what we've found."

Rivka shifted into her dragon form and took a running start down the deck of the ghost ship, her wingtips skimming the tops of the waves until she gained some altitude. Skelaroth stayed behind, guarding the ship and perhaps looking it over more closely while she went back to Liam to advise him of what they'd found. She was also going to have a word or two to say about keeping his alliance with Skelaroth a secret, but she knew she couldn't be too angry about that. Heaven knew, she was keeping secrets from Liam, as well.

That's what she did. She was, after all, a Jinn spy. One of the best. She learned things and kept secrets, revealing them only when necessary, and when the safety of her people hung in the balance. She had many secrets she would never divulge about a myriad of things, but she thought Liam probably should have told one dragon about his discussions with another. It just made sense.

She landed on the rail of Liam's ship, catching her balance with her wings before hopping down onto the deck as the men made room for her. She nodded her head at them, thanking them silently and also apologizing a bit for startling a couple of them. It couldn't be helped. She was black against a night-dark sky. They hadn't seen her approach until the very last minute.

Her claws clicked against the wooden deck as she made her way closer to Liam. He was already on his way to her side, as well.

"*The ship is abandoned,*" she told him quickly, using her mind to speak with him in her dragon form. "*Lord Skelaroth is guarding it from below, but I checked the decks, and there's absolutely nothing left there. Not even a mouse. Lord Skelaroth thinks Fisk used magic to erase all traces of his presence from the ship and left it anchored here as a backup."*

"That makes sense," Liam said aloud as they walked toward his cabin. "So, logically, we should remove his ability to use that ship. Do you think it is safe for a small portion of my crew to board and take her elsewhere?"

Rivka thought that was a good idea. Better, even, than sinking the ship outright. There could be something learned from the ship, given time to study it. *"It should be, and it would deny Fisk that avenue of escape."*

"Mr. Benyon!" Liam shouted to summon his second-in-command. They stood overlapping watches, and Benyon would be readying himself and the crew for the night watch in not too much longer.

Liam consulted with Benyon on the personnel who would be best at manning Fisk's ship and taking it away. Where to take it seemed obvious. Liam ordered that it be sailed back to Dragonscove where his daughter, Livia, could take charge of it.

"Do you have anyone you can trust in Dragonscove that knows of magic?" Rivka asked as Benyon left to gather the crew he'd need. *"We might learn something from the ship, or the kind of magic used on her."*

"There are several options," Liam replied, choosing his words carefully. "Livia has contacts at the Southern Lair, of course. Some of them—especially the new leaders, from what I gather—may be useful. Also, I have made a friend or two among the folk of Gryphon Isle who are here, on the mainland. They can also examine the ship. If need be, Livia can sail her to Gryffid for closer inspection. If there's anything to be learned from her, we will have it."

"Excellent." Rivka ducked to enter through the doors Liam had opened for her that led into his rooms.

He wasn't surprised, this time, when she shifted shape to her human form, as soon as he had closed doors behind them. She sat in the chair in front of his desk and stretched out her shapely legs. He couldn't help but notice the way the supple, tight leather she was wearing hugged her calves and thighs. For a moment, he got a flash of those luscious legs wrapped around him in passion that made him shake his head.

This wouldn't do. He had no business fantasizing over the woman. She was the next best thing to royalty...and he was still on a quest to gain justice for a dead woman. A woman he had loved with all his heart. There simply wasn't anything left in his chest to give to another woman.

Apparently, his loins felt differently, but that was something he would just have to ignore. He wouldn't further complicate an already complicated situation by adding lust to the equation. For the first time in years, he had to tamp down his baser impulses. What was it about this dragon-woman that brought out the animal in him? He didn't dare pursue that line of thought. Better, for all concerned, not to find out.

Desperately trying to clear his mind, Liam walked over to the sideboard where a decanter of port and some glasses were kept securely fastened to the table. He poured a drink and asked Rivka with a silent gesture if she wanted some. At her nod, he handed her the first glass and poured another for himself.

She toasted him silently before taking a sip. Olivia had never liked port, but Rivka seemed to truly enjoy the fine vintage he had purchased on one of the last *regular* merchant voyages. He hadn't been doing any real trading in the past few months, but Livia was getting most of their ships back to the trade routes, and profits would again begin to flow into the coffers of his trading empire. Of course, all those diamonds had helped tide them over.

Livia and her dragon friend, Hrardorr, had appropriated the diamond-tipped weapons that had been used so dreadfully against dragons and gryphons, and had stripped the blades. She had lined up gem cutters to turn the blades into harmless, sparkly baubles and sent them off with trade caravans to several different kingdoms. There were always nobles and jewel smiths looking for precious gems.

The sea dragons had no use for such sharp, dangerous items. They had gladly helped Hrardorr harvest the bolts from the sea floor and the holds of the many ships they had sunk. Livia had been scrupulously fair in dividing the spoils of their recent battles. The Lair got its share, as did the people of Gryphon Isle and Dragonscove, but there was a lot of loot. So many diamonds cut from so many blades. There was plenty to go around.

She had advised caution in seeking to sell the jewels, as well, which meant that everyone who had received a cut would be selling off only as many as they needed at the moment, so as not to glut the market. There would be a diamond supply from those sources for many years to come, which meant a little ended stability for those people who had been attacked by Fisk's fleet, for the foreseeable future.

The diamonds had kept Liam's empire afloat…literally. But they had killed and maimed. Such icy, cool gems had been used for their lethal purpose by evil people. But never again. They'd been neutralized, and Livia had seen to it that they could never be used to hurt anyone, again. He was as proud of her as he could possibly be, even if he still wasn't completely convinced about her choice of mate. Make that *mates*—plural.

CHAPTER 4

Liam had never thought his little girl would grow up to become partner to *two* knights. He'd always hoped she'd attract a nice, stable young man from a good family. He had wanted her to have an easy life. Coddled. Pampered. Not living in the dragon's Lair with two warrior men and a set of fire-breathing dragons.

He shook his head. She seemed to like it, but he despaired of her future. He had never had much to do with dragons, even though he had lived most of his life in Draconia. He'd spent a good portion of his time at sea, and until recently, dragons were seldom to be seen in, or near, water. Oh, there had been tales of sea dragons, but few ever saw them, and they'd never had much to do with men.

All that had changed recently.

"So," Rivka's voice came to him, shaking him out of his out of his reverie, "when were you going to tell me about your alliance with Lord Skelaroth?"

Liam was surprised by her words but didn't let it show. He walked to the chair behind his desk and sat down, making her wait for his reply. It also bought him time to figure out what he was going to say.

"Should I have?" he finally asked in reply. He didn't wait for her to answer but went on almost immediately. "Frankly, I have only spoken with him once. I thought I saw him following us, but I couldn't be completely sure. I don't know much about dragons, milady. I may be a man of the sea, but sea dragons are still a bit of a mystery to me."

Rivka eyed him as if she was considering his words. At length, she nodded and leaned forward to place her empty glass on his desk.

"They are a mystery to us all, Captain," she admitted, startling him a bit. "I don't know much about them, myself. Lord Skelaroth surprised me when he revealed himself, but I believe he is dedicated to the alliance with you. Dragons—land dragons, at least, though I see no reason why sea dragons would be any different—seldom make promises they don't intend to keep. In fact, I have never seen a dragon do so. They are truthful beings—mostly because nobody can do much about it if a dragon doesn't want to do something." She chuckled at her own words.

"What about dragons who are also human?" Liam asked, watching her closely.

Rivka sat back and eyed him from under half-lowered lids. Why he found the pose so seductive, he didn't know, but he shrugged the thought away, wondering what she'd say next.

"I'll admit, the human side does influence our dragon side and vice versa. But the dragon part has a need for truth and honor that doesn't let our human side stray too far from those ideals. Of course, I'm Jinn. I might be lying to you, right now, just to play with you." She grinned at him, and he had to shake his head.

"I don't know much about the Jinn, either," Liam told her, "but I suspect you have a wicked sense of humor, milady."

"I might have heard people say that a time or two," she admitted, still smiling. Then, she sobered a bit. "Now, what have you got planned after you secure the ship?"

"I want to go aboard and see the state of it for myself, first. Then, I'll post the skeleton crew to sail her to

Dragonscove. I'm going to write up very specific instructions for my daughter on what to do with the ship, but I trust Livia to improvise, if necessary. She's proven herself incredibly resourceful of late, much to my surprise."

"Well, she is your daughter, after all," Rivka offered.

Liam shook his head. "I'd always thought she took more after her mother than me. It would have been so much easier if I'd been right."

"Perhaps," Rivka allowed. "But, from all I've seen and heard, your Livia is a remarkably capable young woman. I'm glad she is the way she is. Her mates are also forces to be reckoned with. We need them all in this fight."

Liam's gaze narrowed. "You've met?"

Rivka nodded. "All of them. I was chasing after Fisk's trail when your daughter and her mates retrieved Gryffid's book of magic. All, but that one damning page." She grimaced. "My father was Livia's contact at the inn. He's a bard."

"Of course he is." Liam shook his head again, ruefully this time. "The more I hear about the Jinn and how involved they've been in Draconia's affairs for so long, the more I wonder if our King and his family really rule this land."

Rivka sat upright. "We're not some kind of shadow government. We just help. Quietly. From the sidelines."

"Not really," Liam countered. "Not anymore, at least. You're out there, in the open, now. Doubling the size of Castleton, last I heard, with more Jinn flooding into the country every day."

Rivka tilted her head, as if considering his words. "Your news is a bit outdated. The influx has slowed to a trickle. Most of our brethren who are moving here, have already done so. Some will remain abroad, to keep our information networks intact. We may be out of hiding, so to speak, but our intent was never to take over the country. We are allies. Brothers-in-arms. Family. We're not going to oust Roland. We're here to support him."

Liam was still skeptical, and it probably showed on his face. Rivka sighed.

"Many of us in the Black Dragon Clan are direct descendants of Dranneth the Wise's youngest son. We know we were never meant to rule, but to be supportive of the children of Dranneth's oldest. They are the rightful rulers of this land. We were born and bred to be their helpers. Hidden, for a long time, but now coming back to the homeland to fulfill our destiny." Her words had a ring of truth that Liam could not deny. "There was a prophecy, you see. A sacred trust. When Arikia and Nico came to us, it was fulfilled. We knew, then, it was time to come home."

"That was the only sign? Seems kind of shaky to me. What if you're wrong? Or what if the prophecy is bogus? Have you considered that?" Liam couldn't help but play devil's advocate.

"Their arrival was far from the only sign the prophecy was coming to fruition," she told him. "There's all this interest in the Citadel—people actively trying to free the trapped wizards. The lunatic that rules Skithdron. The appearance of gryphons in Castleton. The fact that Gryffid has rejoined his island home to the rest of the world and begun active discussions with the rulers of Draconia. There's more. Believe me. Much more. This *is* the prophesied time. Much as I could wish it were not."

"I take it, then, that the prophecy isn't all wine and honey?" Liam asked, his gaze narrowing.

Rivka shook her head. "Far from it. Struggle and strife, mostly. And the Jinn standing ready to aid in coming battles and helping avert potential disasters."

"Like the one we face now, if that page of the book gets to the Citadel?" Liam challenged.

"Exactly like that," Rivka agreed.

A knock sounded on Liam's door in the pattern he had requested Benyon use to signal that they were getting close to their target. Liam stood from his desk and stowed the empty glasses.

"We're there," he told her succinctly, his mind on the ship as he went about his tasks.

"I'll shift and come out on deck with you," she replied, standing and moving to the open area of the room in which her dragon form would fit.

Liam stood by the doors, waiting for her to change so he could open them wide for her exit. It struck him again, how odd his life had become in just a short while. Suddenly, there was a sea dragon following his ship in the water, and a mysterious woman warrior who could turn into a compact black dragon at will, in his life. He, who had always avoided dragons.

It made him wonder why he'd been so keen to avoid them all his life. Most children in Draconia were fascinated by the creatures and dreamed of being knights. Not little Liam O'Dare. He'd wanted the sea all his life, and he'd worked hard to make it happen. He hadn't allowed himself to be distracted by dreams of dragons.

And then, he'd met Olivia. Dreams of her left no room for anything else. Of course, by that time, he was well on his way to starting what would become his trading empire. Olivia had been impressed by both his business and his status as a ship's captain. Olivia had taken up all his thoughts and ambitions for the few years they were married, and then, after she was gone, the driving need for vengeance had filled in all the empty places.

But dragons had wormed their way into his life. Somehow. When he hadn't been paying attention. He shook his head slightly at his own thoughts. He'd avoided them for so long, and now, it seemed, he couldn't get away from them.

Not that he wanted to get away from the luscious Rivka. Far from it. His body wanted to be near her, even as his mind tried to reject the idea. She wasn't Olivia. She was about as different from his lost wife as a woman could be. It didn't matter. He saw something in her that aroused his baser instincts as no woman had ever done before.

He would have to maintain caution around her. He didn't want entanglements—especially not with a *dragon*, of all things. Liam wasn't sure why he was so dead set against dragons, and always had been. Perhaps, somewhere in the back of his mind, he had always known that they would complicate his life and derail him from achieving his chosen directions.

If he'd been the starry-eyed dreamer, fantasizing about dragons and knights, he would never have accomplished his goal of becoming one of the youngest-ever sea captains in the trading fleet. He would never have been able to establish his own trading company or build it into the empire it had become. And, for certain, he would never have been able to collect his fighting fleet of ships, warrior captains, and soldier seamen to aid in this ongoing battle against evil.

That only proved, in his mind, that he'd been right to keep dragons out of his life. Dreaming about them could only have interfered with everything he had accomplished, so far. He wondered how teaming up with them now, would affect his future, but there was just no way to know. Perhaps the Jinn had a prophecy about that, too, he mused. Maybe Rivka would tell him, if he asked.

"Ready," came her voice in his mind. He had stood facing the doors so as to give her privacy in which to shift shape. Not that she needed it. She went from human to mist to dragon pretty quickly, but he wanted to show respect and not gawk at her changing form, again. He wasn't sure why. It just seemed like the right thing to do.

He threw open the double doors and strode out of his cabin, the black dragon that was Rivka following behind. Someone would close the doors for him, he was sure of that. His crew knew not to leave any hatches unsecured. They were good men of the sea.

Liam went straight to the rail to see how close they were to Fisk's ship. Very close, indeed, he discovered almost immediately. He started issuing orders for the approach and checked over the men Benyon had collected to crew the empty ship. He was busy for a while and, when he looked up again, Rivka was no longer on his ship but waiting for him— or so it seemed—on the empty deck of Fisk's ship.

He ordered the boarding, and it went off easily on relatively calm seas. He went over with the first of his crew and tasked them to make a thorough search of every crevice. He had more than just the crew that would take the ship in the initial boarding, just in case. They were a platoon of seasoned fighters, as well as the technical experts who had been chosen to take the ship to Dragonscove. A young officer named Keen would captain the ghost ship. It would be his first command, but Liam had been watching him and had every confidence in the young man.

Liam took his own tour of his enemy's flag ship, paying special attention to anything that might have been left behind in the captain's quarters, but there was nothing. Not even a speck of dust marked the living space of the former captain of this vessel. Very odd, indeed.

"It had to have been magic, right, milady?" he asked Rivka as he joined her on deck. "No way could someone clean out a ship this spotless otherwise."

Her dragonish head bobbed in agreement. *"I believe there are spells that could accomplish something like this, though, of course, I am no mage. Jinn traditions note many cases in which magic has obscured evidence of someone's existence, or passage, in the days of old."*

"In the days of magic, you mean," Liam said gently, though his jaw clenched. He didn't like magic or wizards or anything to do with the evil that have been kept secretly, all these many centuries, locked away in the impenetrable ice of the far, far North.

The dragon nodded, once again.

"Sir!" Captain Keen's baritone voice came from behind Liam. He turned to meet the young officer's gaze. "All hands report the ship is clean as a whistle. Nothing left behind."

Liam could see the confusion in Keen's eyes and decided to take pity on the young man. After all, Keen would be the one sailing her back to Dragonscove. He should rightfully know what he might be up against.

"Lady Rivka and I have been discussing this," Liam told Keen. "It is her considered opinion that Fisk may have, once again, used magic to cover his tracks. There's just no other way a working sailing vessel could have been made this clean or empty. It's like it just came out of the shipyard, except for the aged color of the wood." Liam put his hand on the rail. "It's the damnedest thing."

Keen frowned. "Do you think the magic he used might cause us problems on the voyage, sir?"

Liam looked up at Rivka.

"I can't see how," she told him. *"Whatever happened here, it was done as they left the ship. I don't sense any curses lingering, or anything that could make this vessel dangerous to a new crew. Still, I advise caution, and a fast passage to their destination. After which, the ship should be checked over very carefully by more expert folk than I."*

Liam nodded respectfully to the dragon. "As you wish, milady."

He relayed her words to Keen and, only then, realized that the secret of his ability to hear the silent speech of dragonkind was well and truly out, now. Not that it was that big a secret. Liam didn't see how such knowledge could be used against him, so he tried not to think about it too much. His men would believe what they would believe, and he had little to say about it. It was known now, that his daughter could converse with dragons, so it wasn't too much of a stretch to think that she had inherited her ability from Liam.

Keen gave the signal, at Liam's command, for those who were not staying aboard to go back over to Liam's ship. He and Rivka were the last two to make the crossing. He left Keen with words of encouragement, and advice, confident that the young man would do well.

Liam ordered his ship to make best time for the nearby port city of Tipolir. There had been no trace left behind on Fisk's ship as to where he and his crew might have gone, but it only made sense that they had to have made for land. For one thing, the longboats had been conspicuously absent from the ship. The men had rowed ashore. That was the simple explanation.

Of course, they could have offloaded to another ship and

gone somewhere else, but there was no way to know that for sure. Plus, Liam didn't think they'd had enough time to coordinate all that. Regardless, Liam had to make a search of Tipolir. Fisk had been too close to the port not to consider that he'd gone ashore there to either take or send the precious page of Gryffid's book north, overland to the Citadel.

Since they were so close, Rivka stayed in dragon form, and Liam stayed on deck with her. He watched as Keen set sail behind them, heading out toward Dragonscove. He'd gotten underway without any apparent problem, so perhaps he'd have an uneventful voyage. Liam certainly hoped so.

Liam realized something at that point. "Milady, have you seen Lord Skelaroth? Do you know where he is?"

Rivka's head cocked to the side. *"I'm not sure. Let me check."* She was silent in his mind for a few minutes, then reported back. *"He sent a few of his fellow sea dragons to escort Fisk's ship back to Tipolir. He was organizing that while we were on the ship."*

"If I'd known, I would have warned Keen," Liam said, watching the other ship grow smaller in the distance.

Rivka snorted, sending smoke rings upward through the rigging. *"I think all three of us are not used to consulting others when we make decisions. Perhaps, we'd better start improving communications now, before any real action starts. If we're working on our own plans, we could easily run afoul of someone else's and mess everything up."*

Skelaroth surfaced next to the rail, swimming easily to keep pace with Liam's ship. He blinked at them as his voice came into both of their minds. *"Too true, milady. I apologize for not alerting you both to my plans. I have sent three young sea dragons to act as underwater escort for that ship. They will help your men get it safely to Dragonscove—and beyond, should the decision be made to sail for Gryphons Isle to seek the wizard's counsel."*

"Thank you, my lord," Liam said formally. "Perhaps we should discuss what we each plan to do when we reach Tipolir, since we will be there in less than an hour."

"I will take to the land and, thence, to the sky," Skelaroth announced. *"I have been enjoying the sky swimming lessons your land dragons have been giving at the Island Lair. I will look for patterns from*

above and can easily watch the roads heading away from the city."

"*If you've got the high-guard, then I will take my human form and work with Liam on the ground. There are many Jinn in the city, and I will be able to contact them for information,*" Rivka put in.

"I will set some of my men to searching the shoreline for signs of recent passage," Liam told them. "It is possible that the longboats Fisk had could have put ashore at several different spots along the coast. I will have my people check, just in case he avoided the city, itself. As for me, I will head straight for the docks and my warehouse here. There are standing orders in every port where I do business that any sightings of Fisk or any of the vessels known to cooperate with him, are to be noted, and agents are to be followed and observed. If my people are on the ball, we might be able to run him to ground that way. Or, at the very least, know a bit about where he came ashore and where he went from the dock."

Rivka nodded slowly. "*Your people watch the waterfront. My people have eyes all over the city. We run several inns and taverns, and our minstrels play in almost all of the others. If you know which direction he went from the dockyards, then I can ask the right questions of my kin and find out where he went from there.*"

"*This sounds like a very good plan,*" Skelaroth offered.

"Agreed," Liam concurred. Heaven help him, he was about to go into partnership with not one, but two dragons. Would wonders never cease?

Tipolir was a grungy city at its heart. Rivka had never liked it. She'd come here on Jinn business, a time or two, and knew several of the other Jinn working in this city, but it wasn't a place where she felt comfortable. There were many factories, for one thing. Smoke from the forge fires shrouded the city both day and night. Nearby iron mines meant that smelters worked round the clock, refining the ore and creating iron bars and bricks for transport to other parts of the world where the iron wasn't so plentiful.

The brisk trade in iron meant there was a lot of money among the merchant classes, and many, many workers to man the forges and smelters. A few *haves* and many *have nots*. This occasionally erupted in violence or work stoppages as workers sought to gain fairer wages or more protections against injury.

Rivka had been in the city, several years ago, when a team of workers had been killed by faulty equipment. The riots after that terrible tragedy had lasted for a week. But the demand for more safety measures had been met, in that instance, and there had not been a repeat of that particular problem ever since.

That seemed to be the pattern here. A tragedy, followed by a protest, followed by a remedy and continued work. Rivka had often thought that it was also unnecessary. If only they would design the equipment with more safety in mind, from the beginning, a lot of death and unrest could be avoided. But the people here seemed to thrive on conflict, and so, the pattern repeated, over and over.

Rivka had left Liam at the docks, after night had fallen. She'd flown away to an inn she knew, where she could shift into her human form in the privacy of the barn. Nobody had seen her in the dark of the night, and she was able to talk to the innkeeper, who was also a member of the Black Dragon Clan. What she learned there made her frown.

Nevertheless, she went on to her next source of information and learned what she could. She had of arranged to meet with Liam at her next destination, a tavern of Jinn ownership that had excellent food. They were going to meet for dinner, if at all possible. Of course, plans could change quickly if either of them learned something that needed immediate action.

So far, though, everything she'd gleaned had been days old. She needed something more current before she would know her next move. Perhaps Liam or Skelaroth had fresher information, she thought as she made her way to *The Smiling Dragon*. The sign above the door had a fanciful purple-winged serpent carved into it, the mouth of the strange-looking beast curved upward in a toothy grin. She just shook her head as she opened the door and went in.

CHAPTER 5

Liam spotted Rivka the moment she entered the tavern. His heart gave an unexpected flutter, which made him frown. Why should he react so strongly to a woman he'd only just met? A *warrior* woman, so totally unlike the fragile flower of womanhood that had held his heart for so many, many years. It didn't make sense. Rivka was not the kind of woman he usually found attractive. She didn't need protecting or cosseting in any way. She was a fighter—an actual *dragon*, for goodness sake—who could well take care of herself.

Yet, he was undeniably attracted to her. The sudden tightness of his breeches was proof enough of that. Perhaps that's all it was. A physical attraction to a stunning woman. He could almost forgive himself for that, even though he had not been so powerfully attracted to a female since his wife had died. His hardness abated. Even this base physical attraction felt like a betrayal of his beloved Olivia's memory. He cursed himself under his breath as he watched Rivka scan the room.

She caught his eye and nodded coolly, indicating with a slight jerk of her head that she was going to talk to the barman and would be right over. He acknowledged her message with what he hoped was similar coolness and drained the last of his ale, suspecting she would bring a refill as part of her pretense for talking with the barman.

The tavern was crowded, and Rivka's entrance had been noticed by many of the men. She was a handsome woman, after all. But, when she'd subtly indicated she was here to meet Liam, most of the room had gone back to their own pursuits. This beautiful female would likely not be interested in anything the single men in the room had to offer. Not if her attention had already been captured elsewhere.

Liam had to admire her actions. She'd just subtly let all the men who'd been watching her down easy, without saying a word. He stared at the fire in the massive fireplace a few yards away from his table and thought through all he had learned. He hoped she would have further information to clarify some points, but even if she didn't, his next steps were becoming clearer as he thought through his options.

A short while later, a new flagon of ale was placed on the table before Liam. He looked up to find Rivka, holding her own flagon and smiling in greeting.

"The landlord was most accommodating," she told him. "We can have a private dining room for the next hour. Our meal is already being prepared and the table laid. Shall we?" The veiled invitation in her eyes made his toes curl. He had to remind himself this was a show she was putting on for the benefit of anyone watching them too closely. "They have shepherd's pie tonight," she added, grinning.

The quirk of her chin invited him to mischief, and he wondered what it would be like if the coy act she was putting on for the men in the common room was real. Then, he caught himself. He wasn't here to flirt with a pretty girl. He was here to catch a pirate, recover a wizard's dangerous stolen artifact, and finally get his revenge. That thought settled him as he stood, taking his flagon with him and following where she led.

The private dining room was at the back of the tavern, well away from the hubub of the common room. Liam realized there were several private rooms back here, and most were in use. He caught a flash of other diners as the doors opened and closed to admit servers.

"*The Smiling Dragon* is known for their private accommodations," Rivka told him as they walked. "Many a deal has been brokered in these rooms over their excellent food."

She didn't say anything further, and she opened the door to the farthest private room. She led the way in, seeming unsurprised to find someone already inside as Liam paused only briefly in the doorway before stepping in and closing the door behind him. This tavern had to contain one of her contacts, and for whatever reason, she was allowing Liam to sit in on their meeting. He liked that. It indicated a certain level of trust.

"This is Min," Rivka said quietly, introducing the girl who was standing by the table. She was dressed as a server and had likely just brought in the meal that was already laid out for them.

Liam greeted the child in a subdued tone, offering her a smile. She responded shyly but looked to Rivka for her lead.

"It's okay, Min. This is Captain O'Dare. He's my partner in this quest. You can speak freely in front of him," Rivka told the girl, who seemed to sag a bit in what Liam thought was relief.

"It's like this," Min said. "Two days ago, I was serving a party in the largest of our rooms. They were a rough sort. Sailors. Fighters. I dare not go into the room on my own, in fact, lest one of them try something I'd have to shout over." She made a face, loosening up as she told her tale. "I was helping Jem, the kitchen boy, clear up the mess when one of the men mentioned the name Fisk."

Liam tried to control his instinctive reaction. It wouldn't do to scare this poor girl, but he knew from the way her eyes widened that she could probably see his clenched jaw and fists.

"Go on, Min," Rivka encouraged the girl. "You're doing great."

"Well, I knew to listen. Papa told us all to keep our ears

open for that name or anything to do with a book or a paper. We watch everything, anyway," the girl rolled her eyes, "but what we're told to look out for changes from time to time. We're used to that. It all depends on what's going on, and what the Clan most wants to know."

Clan? Liam realized this girl must be Jinn. So, the secretive brotherhood had even their children spying on people. It was appalling, in one way, and brilliant, in another.

"Min and her family are part of the Wind Dancer Clan," Rivka told him as the girl paused. "They are closely related to my own Clan but live mostly in Elderland, though Min and her immediate family have been here in Tipolir for three generations, now."

Liam reached into his pocket and withdrew a coin, flipping it toward the girl. Min caught it with quick little fingers. "That's from Elderland," he told her kindly. "See the image?"

The girl peered down at the coin with wide eyes. "It's a virkin!" She looked up at him, again. "You've been to Elderland, sir?"

"Many times," Liam replied, warming to the girl, who had to be only about ten summers old. She reminded him a little of Livia, though he'd seen his daughter very little over the years as she grew.

"Have you ever seen a real one, sir? A virkin?" Min asked, still wide-eyed.

Liam nodded. "Yes. As a matter of fact, there's one on my ship, but she's very young and very shy. Her name is Ella. Best mouser I've ever had. Not a speck of vermin survives long on my ship, and when she's eaten them all, she dines in my cabin, with me."

The girl giggled, and he noticed Rivka was looking at him strangely. Perhaps she hadn't thought he could unbend enough to be kind to a little girl. He'd hoped to put her more at ease, and it looked like it had worked.

"Papa said to listen for the name Fisk and remember all we heard. Well, the meal was over, and the men were leaving, but three were the last out of the room. One said something about Fisk, and the other two quickly hushed him, saying that he knew better than to use the master's name. They'd all been drinking heavily, you see. Papa says three flagons of ale will loosen just about any tongue—and brain, too." She giggled at what must have been an oft-repeated saying in her family. "The man scoffed at his friends, saying it didn't matter, anyway, because the master was already far from here and the rest of them would keep pursuit at bay, chasing ghosts for days and days."

Liam nodded. This meshed well with what he'd been able to learn. The girl had little more to tell them, but Rivka questioned her until she had a good description of each of the men who had been in the room. Liam listened with half an ear while his mind examined the facts, as he knew them.

When Rivka told Min she could go, the little girl came over to Liam, her palm open with the coin still in it, offering it back to him. He stifled his surprise and smiled at the girl.

"It is yours, Min," he told her. "My gift to you for your service."

Min's eyes lit up as her little hand closed over the heavy silver coin. "Thank you, sir!"

She practically bounced out of the room, so great was her joy. Liam thought she was happier with the image of the virkin than the silver itself. Trinkets were important to children at that age, he recalled. He used to send all sorts of things home for Livia while he was on his travels.

"That was well done," Rivka told him as she joined him at the table. Min had left the room, closing the door behind herself.

"It's not hard to be kind to a child," he said, a bit put out that she might've thought he'd be curt or mean to the little one.

Rivka said nothing as they both sat down at the table. They ate quietly for a while, hungry from their labors, apparently. Liam thought through what Min had told them and how it meshed with what he'd been able to learn. Once he had it straight in his mind, he spoke.

"My people say Fisk's crew has split into many smaller groups," he told her.

Rivka looked up, surprise in her gaze. "That jives with what Min told us—if that group was one of the smaller components of his crew."

"I believe it was. Fisk is taking the page North, but he's confusing his trail so we won't know who to follow." Liam could have cursed but refrained.

"Unless all these groups going out over land are just a decoy and Fisk doubled back to the coast," Rivka said, adding complexity to an already complex situation.

"Lord Skelaroth should be able to tell us more about that possibility," Liam replied, reaching into his pocket for a scroll of parchment he'd received from the manager of his Tipolir warehouse. "My people have narrowed the search. They followed as many groups from Fisk's crew as they could and eliminated many of the false trails from consideration, but we simply didn't have enough agents to chase down all of them. Still, this helps considerably. According to my people, there are three strong possibilities left for the route Fisk may have taken."

He unrolled the small scroll and placed it down in the spot Rivka hastily cleared on the table between them. She paused to examine the map on the scroll in detail before speaking again.

"I can get the Jinn to help with this," Rivka said after a few moments, looking up to meet his gaze. Her green eyes flashed in the soft glow of the lamps that lit the small room. "But first, I'll go aloft and see what I can before morning. We should consult with Skelaroth, as well, before we pick a direction."

They had arranged to meet at the pier where Liam's ship was docked at midnight to consult with the sea dragon lord. That left Rivka a few hours after dinner to do her own aerial reconnaissance. Not that she didn't trust Skelaroth's instincts, but he was a sea dragon, unused to flying over land, and he might not be familiar enough with the way things looked on land from above to know exactly what he was seeing. She wanted to check the possible trails for herself.

Where Skelaroth's expertise would come in handy was in examining the shoreline. If Fisk had doubled back and gone back out to sea to put ashore somewhere else, Skelaroth would be their best shot at following such a trail. But Rivka's instincts were telling her that Fisk wouldn't have abandoned to ship and dispersed his crew, unless he were planning to make a run for it over land.

Rivka left the tavern, promising to meet up with Liam, on his ship. She had things to do before she would see him again, and they were things he could not help with. Rivka found a dark alley that was big enough for her to change in and allowed the shift to come over her. She walked out of that alley in her dragon form, with only the Jinn tavern keeper as witness, and took to the sky.

She had always found flying an incredibly liberating experience. She loved taking to the air. But, somewhere in the back of her mind, she was all too aware that she'd left Liam behind on the ground. He could never follow her here. He could never be part of the world of the air that she loved so much. The thought saddened her, though why it should was a bit of a mystery.

Sure, she was attracted to the dashing sea captain, but that was no reason for her to feel this way. None of her past lovers had been black dragons. They couldn't have flown with her either, and she'd never thought twice about it. She'd been courted once or twice by distantly related dragon shifters but had never felt attracted enough to them to take them up on anything they might have been offering.

It was incredibly rare that two dragon shifters teamed up, even for a temporary liaison. For one thing, they were all related to some degree. Sure, over the centuries, the bloodlines had veered away from each other, but ultimately, they all could trace their ancestry back to one of Dranneth the Wise's offspring. Black dragons were rare, and most of the time, they mated with humans. The inheritance was strong, though, and most of their children turned out to be shapeshifters, which was why the number of black dragons in the Clan had been steadily increasing—slowly, to be sure, but still increasing—over the many years the Jinn had lived in self-imposed exile from what should always have been their homeland of Draconia.

So, it wasn't abnormal for Rivka to be attracted to a human. What was strange was just *how* attracted she was to Liam O'Dare. The pull to him was strong. Very strong. And she'd never had thoughts about wanting to share the sky with any of her lovers. That was different and made her wonder just how deeply she was falling for a man who was still in love with his dead wife.

The reminder of Olivia O'Dare, paragon of womanhood and ghost that seemed never able to lay to rest, was downright depressing. Rivka knew all about Liam's obsession with avenging his wife's murder. Her investigation of the captain before she had ever approached him told her all she needed to know about his unfailing devotion to the petite lady who had been all things womanly and graceful.

So unlike Rivka, herself. She knew she could never compete with a female like that. Olivia had probably never known strife or conflict during her sheltered life. Not until the end, at least, Rivka thought grimly. How difficult must it have been for such a pampered lady to be accosted by pirate scum like Fisk? Poor Olivia must have been horrified. Rivka felt a great deal of sympathy for the woman she had never met.

By the same token, Rivka was a bit surprised to realize that she was jealous of the devotion Olivia had inspired. The love of a man like Liam O'Dare was something, Rivka was coming to realize, that was precious and true. He was a man of honor and integrity, and his love was real. It lasted, even beyond death. Yes, she was jealous of the bond he'd had with the lovely Olivia, and Rivka despaired of ever inspiring such deathless devotion from any man. Much less the handsome captain.

She could not compete with a ghost. Especially one that was so unlike herself as to be laughable. Olivia had been dainty. Pretty and perfect. Accomplished in the womanly arts. Rivka was a warrior. The only time she sewed was to repair her armor or patch a hole. She wouldn't know one end of an embroidery needle from the other, though she did have a mean set of throwing knives always up her sleeve. Olivia would have been scandalized.

Yet, Rivka felt a strange sort of kinship with the woman she had never met. Olivia had died much too young, but she'd had the steadfast love of a man Rivka herself admired. Olivia had been blessed in her marriage and the man who kept her memory alive and uppermost in his mind at all times. Rivka could almost be jealous of the way he had clung to his wife's memory, but it broke her heart, in a way, to know that he'd loved his wife so deeply and lost her so brutally. It was tragic all the way around.

Rivka pushed all that from her mind as she approached the first of the three trails out of the city that Liam's agents had identified. It was time to work. No more time for foolish speculation about things that had been and things that would probably never be. Liam's heart was claimed for all time by a woman who was no longer within reach. Rivka could never compete with that and didn't begrudge him his memories in any case. It was clear the captain was still heartbroken. He mourned deeply and had turned that anguish into anger and a years-long vendetta that was—harsh as it was to even think—useful to Rivka in her own quest.

She could be a mercenary bitch, at times, but that was just the way things were. She'd accomplish her goal. Fulfill her quest. And she'd do whatever it took to make that happen, regardless of whoever's feelings might get in the way. Such was the way of the warrior. The way she had chosen as a youngster. Though given her dual nature, there had never really been much choice about it. She had a dragon's heart, and dragons had been built for war.

Liam went back to his ship and searched for any sign of Lord Skelaroth in the nearby waters. Unable to see much in the dark, he resorted to thinking hard toward the water, hoping to catch Skelaroth's attention with his own inexpert attempts at silent communication. He scrunched up his eyes, closing them while he tried to recapture the feeling of the dragon's words reverberating in his mind. Then, he sent out a tentative call.

"Hello?"

Liam waited. There was no answer, so after a few minutes, he tried again.

"Hello? Are you there?"

Liam opened his eyes at the sound of little claws scurrying over the deck. The virkin, Ella, had come to visit him. She looked inquisitive and alert, her little head tilting this way and that as she used her tiny wings to propel her to the deck rail right next to Liam. He put out his hand to her, and his touch was accepted as she butted her head into his palm.

He stroked her absently as he closed his eyes and tried again.

"Hello? Lord Skelaroth?"

"Helrow?"

Ella made a chirruping sound, and Liam's eyes shot open. Had she...?

"Are you talking to me, little Ella?" He'd heard all sorts of tales about virkin in Elderland that said they could communicate, but he hadn't understood how...until, perhaps, now.

"Helrow?" she repeated, in his mind as she stared up at him, big green eyes blinking innocently.

"Hello, little one!" Liam smiled, his heart full of wonder. Ella had been newly hatched when she'd attached herself to him. Perhaps she was old enough now, to speak in the way of her kind—or, at least, to try.

"M Ella," she went on to say, proving she could do more than just try to mimic what he'd been thinking.

"Yes, I know. You're Ella. And I'm Liam," he replied quietly, glad of the dark and the sparse crew on deck at this time of night. He had a bit of privacy for this first conversation with his little companion.

"Leem," she repeated happily, not quite getting the name, but he didn't mind. He'd figured of all the things people called him, his given name might be easiest for this child who was clearly just learning to communicate.

"I see she has started to speak. Hello, Mistress Ella," Lord Skelaroth's voice came clear into Liam's mind.

He turned his head and discovered the water dragon had raised his head to deck height not five feet from Liam while he'd been so preoccupied with the virkin.

"Helrow," she replied shyly, looking at the giant sea dragon out of the corner of her eye.

"You don't seem surprised to see her," Liam said, turning his gaze to meet the sea dragon's.

"Oh, I knew she was there. I did a thorough inspection of your ship before I ever contacted you." Skelaroth sounded a bit smug to Liam's mind.

"How? You can't tell me you ever came aboard without anyone noticing," Liam scoffed gently.

Skelaroth chuckled. *"We sea dragons have developed other senses that the land dragons seemed to have forgotten. Or, perhaps, it's just a case of those abilities not being applicable while out of the water. Regardless, I can sense things through the sound waves and other ripples to come to me in the ocean, about a great many things. For example, I could hear the scratching of Mistress Ella's little talons—quite distinct from cat's claws, if you know the difference—from within the hold of your ship. She is quite the accomplished huntress, for her age."*

Ella seemed to understand the gist of what Skelaroth had said and preened a bit under his praise. *"Hunt mouses,"* she agreed. *"Taste good. But even better when gone and eat with Leem."*

Liam deciphered her words to means that she enjoyed hunting whatever came aboard whenever they made port but liked, even more, when she had completed her task and took her meals with the captain. Liam would feed her tidbits from his own plate, along with a saucer of cut up meat that his cook prepared just for her. She was a favorite on the ship and well rewarded by the crew for her good work in keeping the place clear of pests.

This was all fascinating, but there was still work to do. Liam looked over at Skelaroth. "Have you any news, milord?"

"*Several false trails have been laid upon the shoreline, but no one truly left by sea. All are within the city, or on their way out,*" he reported. "*I searched from above and below.*"

This was good news, as far as Liam was concerned. "Lady Rivka is aloft, right now, checking three trails my people identified but could not follow. They already eliminated many of the false trails in the city and just beyond."

"*This is good,*" Skelaroth said with satisfaction. "*I was not aware of the extent of your resources in this city, Captain, though, of course, I knew you had connections here. This is even better than I had hoped.*"

"I built my business with two goals in mind. First, to provide for my daughter's future, though I suppose that is taken care of now that she is mated." Liam shook his head, still not quite understanding Livia's choices. "The second reason—and perhaps this was the most important—was to create a network of watchers to help me track Fisk. I have been working toward the day when I can finally bring him to justice for a very long time." Liam's eyes narrowed as cold anger rose. "I will have my revenge."

CHAPTER 6

Rivka walked down the long pier, headed for Liam's ship. She could see the faint glimmer of dragon scale on the seaward side of the rail and could just make out Liam standing there, apparently talking with Lord Skelaroth. There was a smaller creature perched on the rail that became clearer, the closer Rivka got to the ship. Could it be the virkin Liam had mentioned? She was very curious to see one of those fabled foreign beasts for herself and was intrigued by how well the creature had hidden its presence from Rivka the few times she'd been aboard.

"Permission to come aboard?" she sent to Liam as she neared the gangplank. One of his men was on watch near the wide wooden plank that connected the lowest part of the main deck.

She saw him turn to look at the pier. A moment later, he called to the man on watch on the deck below, telling him to allow her passage. His crew had never seen her in her human form. She could feel the crewman's curiosity but ignored it, giving the young man a smile as she nimbly climbed aboard.

"Cap'n says to go up, ma'am," the man told her politely, pointing to the short flight of stairs that led to the quarterdeck where she knew Liam waited. She thanked the man as she passed him.

What she found as she went up the stairs was as she expected. Skelaroth's head was still at the far side of the rail, and the little virkin was perched on the rail while Liam stroked its neck and scratched around its wing-joints. It was a cute little thing, and its eyes opened curiously and blinked at her as Rivka moved closer.

"What news?" Liam asked, straight to business. Good. They didn't have a lot of time for pleasantries.

"I'm sorry to have to say that each of those three paths your people identified are viable. Each leads out of the city, and I was able to follow the trails some distance into the countryside. A small group traveled swiftly on each of the three roadways. So quickly that I couldn't catch up with any of them by air," she told him, then turned to address the sea dragon. "Greetings, Lord Skelaroth. What have you observed?"

"*Nothing by sea,*" he told her immediately. "*Many false trails, but nothing real. I believe Fisk left many of his crew behind in the city, with the express intent of delaying us and leading any pursuit astray.*"

"Makes sense," Liam said, tilting his head slightly as if considering the situation. "He split the men that could travel quickly into three groups and left the slower people here to cause trouble for anyone that might follow."

"*Then, our problem is to decide which of the three roads out of the city to take,*" Skelaroth said to them all. "*We know where Fisk is probably heading, ultimately, but I think it wiser to try to intercept him as far as possible from the Citadel. It is too risky to allow the page to go too far North. We have no idea how close he needs to be in order to use it.*"

"Good point," was Liam's only comment.

"We're going to need help," Rivka spoke up, voicing the only solution that made sense to her.

"But from who? My people are good fighters, but none have experience with overland chases or tracking. We're all seamen, not ground trackers," Liam explained.

Rivka smiled. "That's all right. I happen to know some folks who are very good at traveling on short notice, and are experienced fighters, trackers, and spies."

"The Jinn?" Liam looked intrigued. "Will they help us with something like this? It could be a long chase."

"The Brotherhood is committed to protecting this land—all lands—from the evil that could be released if Fisk makes it to the Citadel with that page," she assured him. "They'll help. Heck, we tend to get restless when we're in one place too long. I bet there are quite a few of my brethren willing to saddle up at short notice."

"*Good,*" Skelaroth said. "*That is just what we need.*"

Liam seemed to come to a decision. "We should probably take the most direct road North. Fisk isn't usually one for subtlety, and he's got to be just as uncomfortable on land as any sailor who's spent most of his life on the water. Although he might be on one of the longer routes, just to confuse things, I would bet against it. The less time he has to travel overland, the better. That's probably the thought uppermost in his mind. I know it would be mine." Liam shook his head, the hint of a rueful grin on his lips.

"So, we'll need two parties of Jinn willing to take the outlying roads," she surmised. "That shouldn't be too difficult to arrange. My people excel at backroads travel, and I can send word to the capital where the others of my kind are gathering about the king. They can fly down to intercept."

"It wouldn't hurt to also ask the king to send some of his dragon knights, I suppose," Liam allowed, though Rivka knew he was uncomfortable with the concept of his daughter's recent marriage to two knights, from all accounts. "If you have those kinds of connections."

"Don't worry," she assured him. "We're kin, of sorts. I will send word to Nico, and the Prince of Spies will fill his brother in on everything, I'm sure. As soon as we can get word to them, they will send everything they can to intercept Fisk. Our job will be to stay on Fisk's trail from this direction, long enough for the cavalry to fly in from Castleton. That's the closest Lair, at this point."

"*But how do you propose to get word to Castleton faster than we can get there ourselves?"* Skelaroth asked.

Rivka grinned. "I will send a Jinn messenger to the closest dragon, and he or she can fly for Castleton immediately while we follow Fisk."

Skelaroth was silent a moment, his great, jewel-like eyes blinking slowly in the moonlight. *"If I knew where I was going, I could fly for Castleton,"* he said, at length. *"Unfortunately, my land navigation skills are poor, at best."* He set his jaw and shook his head. *"This is something I need to address as soon as there is time, but I regret to admit, I do not have the skills—nor do any of my kind who are close enough—to carry this most important message."*

Rivka's heart went out to the big sea dragon. "I would fly for Castleton myself, but I think it's more important that I keep watch over his trail so that we might be able to identify which of the three roads he had taken. When more winged help arrives, that will be vital."

Skelaroth sighed, looking a bit defeated. *"And we sea dragons do not have the skills to track over land,"* he said in a subdued tone before his neck straightened and he seemed to come to a decision. *"Nevertheless, I will go with you. I am bigger than you, Lady Rivka, and I can fight equally as well on land or in the ocean. I have pledged myself to this quest, and I will do what I can to see it through."*

"If Fisk left as soon as possible after putting in to port, then he has a significant head start on us," Liam said, his voice contemplative, but his expression pained.

"Yet another reason for me to go with you," Skelaroth said, conviction in his tone. *"Although I have never carried anyone before, I am willing to try, if you are, Captain."*

Liam was shocked by the sea lord's words. He met Skelaroth's eyes, nonplussed by the very idea of flying aboard this behemoth's back. He wasn't sure if he was more appalled or afraid, which didn't sit well. Liam had faced death many times, in many ways, over the years. He honestly hadn't thought anything could frighten him, anymore. Apparently, he'd been wrong.

"I'm not sure what to say," Liam hedged, playing for time to process the idea.

He heard Rivka's soft chuckle, but she was only faintly smiling when he looked at her. "That would help a great deal, my lord," she told Skelaroth. "We could make excellent time and catch up to Fisk in a matter of days, depending on how big his lead is. You're right that I am not big enough to carry a rider, though I am well familiar with tracking over land. I would be happy to explain what I'm seeing from above, as we fly along."

Skelaroth bowed his head briefly. *"I am grateful for the offer, my lady. It is kindly done, and I will take you up on it. The sooner my kind increases our skill set, the better. I will send word to the Island Lair with my fellows to seek additional training from the dragons and gryphons there. Though, of course, that will not help us at this moment."*

"Still, it's a good idea, my lord. We don't know if, or when, such skills will be needed in the future," she told the sea dragon leader. "We Jinn believe that it's always best to be prepared. Now," she turned to Liam, who had taken the few minutes while they were talking to regain some of his equilibrium, "will you fly with us, Captain? I may not be big enough to carry you far, but I promise to catch you if you fall."

The teasing light in her dark green eyes tempted him beyond all reason. Liam found himself nodding. "I will try, milady. That's all I can promise for now."

"Good." She beamed at him.

He turned to Skelaroth. "Thank you for your generous offer, Lord Skelaroth. I have never flown before, and frankly, I'm not sure how it will affect me, but I'm willing to try. If I find I cannot handle flight, I will take to the ground, and you two can go on without me. This quest is too important."

"Well said, Captain, but I believe you will do well in the air. After all, your daughter seems to enjoy it, and she takes after you, doesn't she?" Skelaroth offered him a toothy, dragonish grin.

Liam sighed heavily. "Sometimes, I wish she didn't," he said before he could stop himself. He realized he was still stroking the little virkin as Ella moved under his hand. He'd thought she'd fallen asleep, but her eyes were wide, taking in everything.

"*I go, too,*" she said when he met her gaze, surprising him. She looked around to meet Skelaroth's gaze. "*I go wif Leem.*"

Skelaroth seemed as surprised as Liam felt, but after a couple of eye blinks, he lowered his head to the rail—the level of the virkin. "*You shall come with us, if you wish, Mistress Ella, but it might be an uncomfortable journey for you. Are you certain?*"

"*Yes!*" she said, butting her head into Liam's hand. "*Go wif Leem. Hunt.*"

Liam wasn't sure what kind of hunt the little creature had in mind, but he had a feeling that, if he didn't take her with him, she would probably try to follow on her own. He didn't want that to happen. She would, no doubt, get lost in the city, and he never see her again.

"All right, little one," Liam said to the virkin. "You can come. I will bring a soft carrybag, and you can sleep in there while we fly, and you can guard our campsites when we stop for rest."

"*Yes! Guard! Can do!*" She chirruped, sounding excited. "*I help. You see.*"

The trip was arranged very quickly. Liam marveled at the way Rivka and Skelaroth set things in motion. He swam away to confer with his sea dragons while Rivka went back to *The Smiling Dragon* to enlist the aid of the Jinn. She'd told Liam to pack what he needed for himself and Ella and meet her there.

It hadn't taken him long to gather his things, but by the time he reached the tavern, it was late. Long after the time when regular folk were in their beds and the tavern was supposedly closed, but when Liam pushed open the door, he was met by a bustle of folk taking their places for what looked like some kind of briefing.

Rivka was at the front of the room, and Liam slipped into a dark corner in the back to watch while she brought everyone to order. She explained the situation as clearly and concisely as any soldier giving a report. Liam was impressed. She used a piece of chalk on the slate the barman used to write out the daily food offerings, for those who could read, drawing a rough map of the roads leading out of the city and the general direction in which they went.

She claimed the North road for herself and asked that two groups form to take the roads that were Northwest and Northeast. About twenty-five Jinn were in the room. She had them split up into three groups—two of ten, each, and one group of five specialists, who seemed to know already that they would be doing something different. The two groups of ten were given the roads they were to take, and a leader for each group was chosen from among them. They went off to different parts of the great room to confer privately within their own group while Rivka went to speak directly to the five who were left.

Liam moved closer, wanting to hear what those five would be doing. He had an idea, but he wanted to hear it for himself. Rivka didn't seem surprised when he stepped out of the shadows and joined the smaller group.

"Each of you will go in a different direction," she told the five. "Find a dragon. Get him or her to take my message to Castleton, then return here. Your task will be done, and you'll have my thanks and the reward I will arrange through my Clansmen."

Liam took that to mean that she would arrange for her Clan to send payment to the messengers after the fact. Liam could help there. He cleared his throat to get their attention.

"If you go to my ship upon your return, I will leave instructions that each of you are to be paid by my quartermaster, if that is acceptable." He bowed his head slightly to Rivka to see if it was all right with her. She nodded back and gave him a small smile.

Ella chose that moment to raise her head out of the satchel he had slung around his shoulders. The strong leather had a flap that whipped up when she popped out under his arm, making everyone aware of her presence. Liam had lined the leather bag with the softest cloth he had aboard, making a warm nest for the little virkin. She had taken to it immediately and hadn't come out since he'd opened the bag to show it to her.

"*I carry message to Benyon,*" she said. "*Then come back here.*"

Liam was stunned by her offer. Just how much of what he was doing, did she understand? The virkin was proving that she was more aware of her surroundings, and the situation, than he had ever expected.

"Are you sure you know the way?" Liam asked, focusing on the virkin and ignoring the startled glances of the gathered Jinn.

Ella nodded vigorously. "*I can always find you, Leem.*"

Huh. Now, that was an interesting idea. He hadn't realized the creature was so closely bonded to him. He had enjoyed her company these past months, and she certainly seemed to like him better than almost anyone else on the ship, but he hadn't realized how very aware she was of everyone and everything.

Rivka handed him a scrap of parchment and a quill. One of the other Jinn retrieved a small pot of ink from under the counter of the bar and gave it to him. Liam nodded his thanks and took a seat at the table, writing out his orders and signing his name. He then rolled up the parchment and gave it to Ella, who had stepped out of the bag and stood beside him on the table, watching him.

"Can you hold this or do you want me to tie it around you, somehow?" he asked, unsure of how to proceed.

Ella seemed to know exactly what to do, however, and took the roll in her fore-claws. She pushed off with her hind feet and took to the air, hovering for a moment before heading out the open transom window above the door of the tavern. Just about everyone in the room paused to watch her go. Speculative looks were sent in Liam's direction, but then, everyone returned to their planning after a moment.

"It is known that the virkin of Elderland bond only to

special people," the man who had brought the ink said in a quiet voice as he took the ink pot back and replaced it behind the bar. "We Jinn take it as a sign of your integrity that one has chosen you, Captain."

Liam wasn't sure what to say to that. He merely nodded and thanked the man again for being willing to take on the task of getting word out about their mission. He hadn't known that virkin were so choosy. He hadn't known that Ella understood so much about everything. He supposed he was probably in for a lot more surprises if he kept hanging around with Jinn temptresses, but it couldn't be helped. Not at the moment, at any rate.

Ella returned faster than Liam expected, and just in time. They were about ready to take off. Rivka wanted to fly out of the city under cover of darkness so her presence wouldn't be too visible to Fisk's men that remained nearby. Skelaroth would come in from the sea and meet them at a spot they'd picked. There was a tall hill beyond the city, over which their chosen road climbed, that even an inexperienced sea dragon couldn't miss seeing from above. He would meet them there at daybreak, and they would continue together from that point.

Liam would ride on horseback with one of the messenger Jinn to the meeting place, then leave the horse with the messenger to take with him. It was all arranged. Liam left first, with Ella safely in her satchel-nest at his side. She didn't like the jostling, but she told Liam that she wrapped herself up tight in the soft "blankie" and after that, it wasn't too bad. No worse than a storm at sea, she said in a sleepy tone. After that, she was silent, and Liam assumed she was asleep.

He wished he could rest, as well, but there would be no sleep for him, this night. Not until he met up with Skelaroth and Rivka. She had to fly under cover of darkness, so that meant that he had to ride fast for the meeting place to be there when she arrived. Skelaroth was taking a longer route, coming in from the sea. He would go ashore farther down the coast and make his way over uninhabited lands, also under cover of darkness, though he would need at least a hint of the sun in order to find the right hilltop on which to meet.

Liam planned to get to that hilltop as soon as he could, take the packs off his horse and allow the Jinn messenger to keep going. He'd find an out-of-the-way spot and grab whatever sleep he could while waiting for the rest of his party to arrive. Ella had promised to guard him, though he wasn't sure how well that would work, yet. He supposed she could at least wake him up if she saw anyone approaching. That would have to be good enough.

Ella was getting more and more vocal, now that she had started talking. He liked hearing her thoughts, even as they surprised him. She definitely had a different way of looking at the world that he had never expected. She reminded him of Skelaroth, in a way. She saw things in more dragonish terms than human, which he supposed was to be expected. Ella looked almost like a tiny dragon, though there were some differences, of course.

She communicated in the same way as dragons, as well, and seemed to be getting better at it by the hour. She learned fast and was quicker on her tiny wings than he would have expected, even having watched her hunt aboard his ship for nearly a year. She was...evolving. Or, perhaps, she was just growing up in the way of virkin. In a sudden spurt, gaining language and greater strength, all at once.

Liam and the Jinn messenger—a petite woman named Maize—didn't speak as they pushed their horses into a gallop once they were outside the more populated parts of the city. The horses were faster than any Liam had been on before. Living his life on the sea, he hadn't done a lot of riding, but he knew how to stay on, which was apparently all his horse needed him to do.

Liam clung to the saddle like a burr and did his best to move with the beast. Maize rode like she had been born in the saddle. He was no longer surprised at her willingness to be a messenger on this quest. Liam had little doubt that she and the horses were holding back from their top speed on his account, but he wouldn't waylay them much longer. Already, he could see the meeting place in the near distance. Once she dropped him off, she could make better time.

CHAPTER 7

Liam was asleep when Rivka arrived at the meeting place several hours before dawn. Ella was keeping watch. The little virkin was curled up like a cat, sitting on Liam's broad chest, but her eyes were open, and she spotted Rivka overhead and watched her descend. Rivka could see the flash of Ella's eyes following her progress.

Rivka landed on the road and then shifted shape into her human form. Ella watched the whole thing, and Rivka wondered what the little virkin must think about Rivka's ability to shift shape. She didn't have to wait long to find out.

"You fly and *walk,"* Ella said into Rivka's mind in an awed tone.

Rivka had to smile. *"I am half dragon and half human,"* she confirmed for the little creature, silently, so as not to wake Liam.

"How?" Ella's little head tilted far to one side, regarding Rivka with potent curiosity.

Rivka sat on the ground near Liam. He'd chosen a spot under a tree on the side of the road, mostly hidden from view. It was as good a place as any to grab what little sleep they would get that night. She had spotted no one on the road for miles in either direction. They should be safe enough to take a few hours rest.

"*A very long time ago, there was a great wizard,*" Rivka told the virkin as she settled beneath the tree, just a few feet from Liam and his little friend. "*His name was Dranneth the Wise, and he was one of the last of the great wizards. He was a good man who worried about the fate of his friends should he die. He became the first like me—half dragon and half human. It was part of his agreement with dragonkind, so that he would understand their concerns and be able to rule justly over the land of Draconia, where dragons and humans would live together in harmony. I am a distant descendant of Dranneth the Wise's youngest son. The king and all the royal family of this land are also like me but descend from Dranneth's eldest son. Their family has ruled Draconia in peace for many generations.*"

"*What about your fambly?*" Ella wanted to know. She'd been watching and listening, wide-eyed, to everything Rivka had told her, and had understood even more than Rivka had expected.

"*My ancestors became the Jinn. We keep watch in all the lands to learn things that will help keep Draconia—and all the dragons and people here—safe.*"

"*Spies!*" Ella said excitedly, tones of approval in her voice. Rivka smiled, even as she was surprised by the sophistication of Ella's thought processes. This little virkin was a lot more intelligent than she had guessed.

"*Something like that,*" Rivka agreed sleepily. "*But more like quiet protectors. We don't seek the limelight. We work in the shadows to help keep everybody safe. It is our calling and our honor to do this work that needs doing. Just as Dranneth's younger sons helped the elders, we serve the same purpose and always have.*"

Rivka yawned again, and settled down in her chosen spot. Ella watched her, blinking a few times as she seemed to consider Rivka's words. She was also observing everything, and Rivka was surprised by the little creature's next words.

"*You tired. Sleep. I guard. Wake if trouble.*"

"*That's very kind of you, Miss Ella. It's been a very long day…and night.*"

And, with that, Rivka dropped off into sleep. She wasn't entirely certain what the little virkin was capable of, as far as guard duty went, but at this point, she was almost too tired to care.

"Big dragon comes!" Ella's little voice sounded in Rivka's mind, even as the virkin's wings fluttered against her arm. Rivka opened her eyes to find the virkin was standing in the space between Liam and Rivka, hopping on her little feet excitedly, as her wings fanned the air around her.

Liam's eyes opened, and Rivka realized Ella must have spoken to both of them at the same time. The little creature's guard abilities seemed to be much better than Rivka would have credited. Good thing for them. Rivka had been a bit irresponsible in the way she'd collapsed at Liam's side a few hours before. Anyone could have come upon them from the road or the woods.

Thankfully, they hadn't, but it had been foolish to let down her guard. They would have to make time for sleep on their journey or she'd be useless if it came to a confrontation—which she desperately hoped it would. She wanted to be the one to catch Fisk, not only because she knew she had the skills to defeat him, but also for Liam.

Liam deserved his justice after all this time and all the effort he'd put into catching Fisk. And, after what Fisk had done to Liam's wife, he deserved all the pent-up rage and anger that must have kept Liam going after all these years. Rivka wanted to see that quest come to fruition for Liam's sake, as well as for the sake of justice. And, if she could be the one to retrieve that page of the book, she would fly to Gryphon Isle herself and hand-deliver it to Gryffid. Not for the glory but to fulfill her lifelong oath to be of service to her land and people.

She wanted to see Gryphon Isle, and she wanted to ask Gryffid a question or two—if he proved to be willing to speak to her. It was a dream of hers to see the gryphons and fly among them, but perhaps, it was a selfish dream. The most important thing was the page from that book and the danger it posed to everyone, everywhere. She would focus on that, and however it was retrieved, she would do her best to contribute to its recovery.

"Skelaroth's aloft," Liam said, rubbing his eyes as he woke up from what must have been a deep sleep. "I didn't hear you arrive. Thanks for not waking me. I guess I was more tired than I realized."

"We'd been going all day and most of the night. I'm not surprised we both crashed, but we'll have to plan better from now on." Rivka got up and walked onto the road so Skelaroth could see her. She waved, and he wheeled about, diving for land. *"Not so fast!"* she thought at him as he came in at a reckless speed. He flared his wings and slowed his descent to land with only a bit more force than necessary, on the dirt road in front of her.

"Greetings, Lady Rivka," Skelaroth said formally into her mind. *"Thank you for your advice. I am unused to landing. When I do fly over the waves, I dive into the water on my return. I see I'm going to have to adjust my habits if I am to fly overland."*

Rivka nodded then thought of something. "Even if you see what looks like a large enough body of water, do not dive. Most lakes on land are not deep enough for you."

Skelaroth's great head nodded. *"I see I have much to learn. Thank you for the warning."*

She was just glad he wasn't taking her words amiss. She didn't know a great deal about sea dragons, but land dragons were incredibly formal beings and insisted on the utmost courtesy from humans they dealt with. Of course, with foot-long, razor-sharp claws and the ability to breathe fire, sometimes, courtesy avoided a lot of misunderstandings…and unnecessary violence.

"There is no one on the road for many leagues," Skelaroth reported as Liam joined them on the road with Ella hovering at his side.

The sun was just beginning to make an appearance. The dim light of pre-dawn had apparently been enough for Skelaroth to find his way here. Rivka was glad. That meant that Skelaroth had keener eyesight than she'd feared. She didn't know what to expect from a sea dragon. She would have to observe and learn as they went along, so she could discern exactly what he could do, and what he couldn't. He would also, likely, have some abilities that she was unfamiliar with. How the sea dragons "saw" under water, for example, was something all the black dragons were interested in discovering.

Perhaps, if they passed a lake deep enough, she could ask him to demonstrate. Of course, their quest had to come first. She would not pester Skelaroth unless there was a good opportunity, and the luxury of time, to do so. She could ask him questions, though, as they flew along, unless there was something else important to talk about. She had promised to help him learn how to scout land from the air. She would tackle that first and help him become more familiar with how things on the ground presented themselves from above. It wasn't always an easy skill to master, as she knew from her own experience.

"Have you rested enough?" Skelaroth asked Rivka and Liam.

"I got about three hours of sleep," Rivka replied.

"I got more than that, but how much more, I couldn't tell you," Liam admitted. "Maybe four hours? Five? I'm not sure."

"Four and quarter," Ella put in, now perched on Liam's shoulder as if she often rested there. Her little tail was curled around his back, resting lightly on Liam's other shoulder, for balance. *"I watched good."*

Liam reached up and stroked the virkin's head with obvious affection. "Well, that answers that question. Thank you, my lovely," Liam said to his little friend.

"Did you sleep, Miss Ella?" Rivka asked the virkin directly.

"Not on watch," she replied immediately. *"Slep' in sack on way."* Ella pointed with one of her foreclaws to the leather satchel Liam had over his shoulder.

Liam cleared his throat. "I created a little nest for her, so she would be warm and as comfortable as possible on the journey," he said, opening the flap on the bag and showing the padded insides to Rivka.

She was impressed at the care he'd taken for his small companion. "That looks good," she told him, then looked at Ella again. "Do you like it?"

Ella nodded emphatically. *"Snuggly."*

Liam looked amused. "Glad you like it, Ella."

The virkin raised her head and rubbed her little cheek against his. A clear sign of affection, if Rivka had ever seen one. That virkin was half in love with Liam and would likely follow anywhere he led. Ella had fixated on him, for whatever reason, and Rivka couldn't really blame her. He was a fascinating man, she had to admit. Handsome, strong, honorable...and on a quest to avenge his lost love. Rivka had to keep reminding herself of that, lest she start following him around like poor, infatuated Ella.

"I have had no sleep this night, but I propose we fly on as far as we can for a few hours, then make camp mid-morning to sleep a bit more and reexamine our strategy," Skelaroth said to all of them. *"We can fly a bit more in the afternoon and early evening before it becomes too dark to see anything below us, then camp for the night. That should get us all back to a good place rest-wise."*

They all agreed it was a good plan, and Rivka helped Liam and Skelaroth figure out the best placement for a rider, and how that rider should climb aboard the sea dragon's back. Ella went into her little nest bag as soon as Liam was settled atop the dragon, though she kept her head peeking out the top so she could see. The virkin seemed excited by the prospect of flying with Skelaroth while her human just seemed both skeptical and nervous.

Rivka shifted into her dragon form so she'd be able to do something for Liam if he fell. Ella could always get out of the leather bag—ripping it open with her sharp claws, if she had to—and save herself. She could fly, though not as fast as a dragon, of course. But, if Liam fell, only Rivka stood between him and a very hard landing.

She spoke directly to Skelaroth, coaching him through the take-off. She leapt into the air right behind him and maintained a position below him, just in case.

"*How are you doing up there?*" she asked Liam after a few minutes of observing Skelaroth's steady flight. He seemed to be getting the hang of it rather quickly, which was a good thing for his passengers. Rivka came out from under the bigger dragon and coasted alongside so she could observe Liam's seat on the sea dragon's back.

Liam nodded at her and shouted over the roar of the wind. "Doing good!"

Rivka could see that he'd found the sweet spot where the neck joined the spine. There was a natural depression there that acted as a seat for dragon riders, which all knights knew about. Skelaroth also had conveniently placed horned ridges that allowed Liam something he could hold onto for balance that wouldn't interfere with Skelaroth's flight or cause him pain.

"*You have a natural seat,*" Rivka marveled. "*I think you'll do quite well. I'll be just below in case there's a problem.*"

She veered off and dove a little, retaking her position below Skelaroth, just to be safe. This was new to them both, after all. One thing Rivka had noticed was Ella's small head peering out of the bag on Liam's chest, looking for all the world as if she was truly enjoying her first experience of riding on a dragon's back. If virkin could smile—and Ella's mobile mouth came very close, at times—then Ella had been grinning from ear to ear.

Rivka chuckled to herself as they flew, but soon, she fell into the role of teacher, explaining to Skelaroth how to tell what they were looking at from above. She pointed out various landmarks, and when they came upon people—mostly farmers either working in their fields or driving carts or other pieces of equipment with horses, mules, ox or donkeys—she helped Skelaroth identify what they were seeing.

He was a quick study, and even though he had not seen some of the land creatures before, he was able to identify them correctly the next time they happened upon them. His eyesight was, perhaps, a bit better than her own, she discovered as the morning progressed, and when it came time to find a camping spot, it was Skelaroth who pointed out the best location.

They landed on the road but quickly moved off of it to a small stand of trees in a slight dip, just before the rise of a steep cliff. The two-legs would take cover under the trees while Skelaroth could lay down in the tall grass between the trees and the road. Thanks to the little dip in the landscape and his natural coloration, he would barely be visible, even if he was awake and peering through the grasses at the roadway.

He made himself comfortable as soon as possible and drifted off to sleep with hardly any comment. That left Rivka, Liam, and Ella, of course, to make themselves comfortable, as well. Any planning they needed to do would happen after they woke again, when their heads were clearer. Rivka was glad of the chance to get more rest. It had been a long day and night just past. She needed more rest to recuperate from everything they had done in the last twenty-four hours.

She was surprised to find that Liam had packed a small tent. On closer inspection, she realized it was made of tightly woven silk. Such fabric would block the wind, not allow insects to pass through—even the tiniest ones—and would pack down into a very small bundle, which was probably why she hadn't noticed it on him.

"What's this?" she asked, walking up beside him after shifting into her human form.

"Something I picked up in Elderland," he told her as he rose from setting the last peg in place. "I thought you might want to use it while we travel, when there's time and space to make a camp."

"Me?" she asked, nonplussed. He'd brought the tent along for her? "What about you?"

"I'm fine outdoors," he told her. "Even if I am used to the rocking deck of a ship, I can sleep just about anywhere. The tent is also waterproof, so if it rains, we could use it as a tarp to keep ourselves dry."

It was a dark gray color that would not be easy to spot in the dark—or under the shade of the trees, hidden in the tall grass. She knew from her own experience that silk of this quality had many excellent properties and honestly couldn't wait to get inside the tent and see what it was like from within. That he'd thought to pitch it for her, and to bring it along in the first place, made her feel odd. Sort of soft...inside. Touched. Profoundly.

Few men had ever taken her comfort into consideration so much. Among the Jinn, she was known as a fire breather—both figuratively and literally. She'd honed herself and her skills over the years, and few people, even within her own Clan, thought much about pampering her. She would have scoffed at them years ago, but now, as she aged, she had come to value the small comforts in life. Luscious silk like that the tent was made from was one of them.

"I..." She moved closer, holding out one hand to touch the soft fabric, then gathered herself and turned to look at Liam. "Thank you, Captain. This was very thoughtful of you."

He shrugged away her words and turned to his pack. "I have some food if you're hungry."

She waved him off. "Sleep first, then food," she told him gently, unable to stifle a yawn. "Thank you, again."

She said nothing more as she knelt to enter the low tent. It was just as luxurious on the inside as she'd hoped. Soft, supple fabric beneath her and all around, a few feet above her prone body. It was a low-profile tent, longer than it was wide. Perfect for cover and not too easy to be seen from outside. Once she sealed the flap, which folded back upon itself and tied, she knew few insects would be able to thread the needle to enter her twilight world inside the dark fabric.

And it was cool. Even though the silk had been dyed to a dark grey and woven tightly, it still allowed air circulation. It...*breathed*, for lack of a better word. This kind of fabric would be cool in the heat of the day and would retain warmth in the cold of the night. Liam must have paid quite a bit for a tent of this quality. She was glad he had thought to pack it with him, and his kindness in doing so made her feel a bit fluttery inside.

He might be focused on his quest and his revenge, but he was still a thoughtful man. That was a very attractive quality, and if she wasn't very careful, she might find herself falling a bit in love with the dashing sea captain.

Impossible as she knew it to be.

Liam woke a few hours later, judging by the position of the sun. It had gone from nearly directly overhead to a short distance down toward the horizon. Ella was standing guard, as it were, perched above his sleeping spot, on a tree branch. She'd chosen one without many leaves to block her view of both the road and either side of them. They were protected in the back by the steep cliff.

He was surprised again, at how resourceful Ella was. She had taken to traveling by land and air as well as she'd taken to sailing with him on his ship. She really was a good companion. Useful to have around, too. He had to admit he just enjoyed her company. Even before she started talking, he had always liked having her around. Another living being to share his days. She was somehow reassuring to his lonely soul. Just her presence on board his ship, and especially when she was with him, let him know he was not so completely alone.

It was an odd thought for him to have, he knew. The famous Captain O'Dare who needed nothing and no one. Who never even slept with a paid companion in any port. He was solitary by choice, and his crew knew what drove him. Many of them had been with him from the beginning, and those that had not had probably learned his story from the others.

Before he could let his thoughts slip into even more depressing territory, he heard Rivka stirring inside the tent. He was glad he'd thrown the lightweight item into his pack. She'd seemed so enchanted by it, and bemused that anyone should think of her comfort. That bothered him in some indefinable way. She was a princess among her kind. She should be cosseted and pampered, yet it was painfully clear that she had chosen another path. She was a warrior woman, with all that entailed.

Why she shouldn't also seek out a few creature comforts for herself, he didn't know. Maybe she had eschewed all finery for some aesthetic, or even religious, reason? Or maybe she didn't have the means with which to purchase them. That didn't seem right. The Jinn were well known to be traders of the first order. They were famous for their fine wagons, horses and goods. Though, of course, he wasn't sure if Rivka had ever been among those who traveled the lands, making piles of money and trading for pretty or useful things like the tent he had brought along for her to use.

He got up and retrieved the pack he had stowed in the crook of a tree not too far from where they'd slept. He didn't know exactly what kind of wildlife frequented this part of the country. If there were any bears, or the like, he hadn't wanted to take a chance of attracting them to where they were sleeping. He answered nature's call while he was out of sight and then made a bit of noise on his way back to the campsite to politely warn Rivka that he was approaching.

She greeted him with a smile and had already taken down the tent. He supposed he shouldn't have been surprised by her efficiency or skill by this point, so he didn't comment, except to thank her when she handed him the neatly folded tent, already in its little carrying pack.

"It's really ingenious, how they created the tent poles," she told him. "I've seldom seen such fine work."

"There's a little market in Elderland where you can find such things. I imported all they could supply, which weren't many, unfortunately. Each of these take some time to create, but they last for decades if cared for properly."

She grinned at him. "Your trader roots are showing, Captain."

He found himself grinning back. "It took money to build

my fleet," he replied honestly. "Once this is all over, I suppose I'll go back to trading." He sighed, almost unaware that he did so, but Rivka seemed to notice.

She shook one finger at him. "That doesn't sound like a man who wants to go back to simple commerce," she said, eyeing him with a raised eyebrow. "You've built up the finest fighting fleet this country has ever seen. I would hope you could find some noble use for it, even after your quest has been fulfilled." She turned to look at the provisions he was taking out of his pack. "Of course, that's something you should probably discuss with the king. I could help arrange that for you. Later, of course."

Liam thought about that for a minute as they chose items to eat. He took an apple while she cut off a piece of cheese and part of the bread he'd packed.

"I may take you up on that offer, milady. If all goes well on our journey."

CHAPTER 8

Rivka flew alongside and just below Skelaroth for what remained of the day. They followed the road, cutting across bends to shorten their path whenever they could. They knew Fisk's party had a long head start on them, so she didn't expect to run across any recent sign of their passage until tomorrow at the earliest. Still, she kept a close eye on the ground and helped Skelaroth learn more about aerial surveillance as they went along.

They landed just before dusk, while there was still enough light to see what they were doing, and set up camp. They'd chosen a campsite near a clear stream where they could both get a drink and wash up. Liam made a small fire that was hidden from the road by a screen of trees and bushes. He had a small metal pot with him in which he boiled water for tea, much to her surprise and delight.

She set up the tent, this time, while Liam brewed the tea and set out what remained of the provisions he'd packed in Tipolir. They would stop in a village along the way to resupply. Probably tomorrow. They were traveling light, so they were limited to what they could carry easily. Liam had traveled with the satchel that housed Ella hanging across his chest and off his right side, and the equally large pack of provisions situated on his opposite side. The bag was big enough to hold the tent, the pot and the food items he'd chosen, as well as a change of clothes, but not much else. His sword, he carried strapped to his back, with a knife at his waist. He'd also worn a dark cloak to protect himself from the winds aloft. Smart.

He looked a lot like a knight, riding on the back of his dragon. Though, of course, that wasn't the situation with Skelaroth and never would be. He was a sea dragon—lord of them all in this area—and he would not choose a knight partner. At least, Rivka didn't see how he could.

Still, they made a pretty tableau as they flew along. On the ground, after Skelaroth drank his fill from the steam and went downstream a ways to loll in the water, he returned to the campsite with two fish in his talons and gave them to Liam.

"For your dinner," Skelaroth said politely to them both.

Liam looked up at the dragon in surprise. "That's very kind of you, milord. Thanks." Liam took the fish down to the water and cleaned them, preparing them expertly before putting them on an improvised spit over the small campfire. Skelaroth settled into the grass beside him, stretching out and blending into the scenery, only his large head propped up on his foreleg joining them by the fire.

"I expect we might begin finding fresh signs on or near the road sometime tomorrow," Rivka offered as they ate what was left of the provisions and waited for the fish to cook.

Liam sat on his cloak. Rivka noticed that it was waterproof on the outside and the inside was lined in warm fabric. It would act as good barrier between him and the dewy ground while he slept.

"Will we have to go slower?" Liam asked.

"Not really, but we should stop more often and check the ground. There may be things we can see down here that won't be so obvious from aloft," she explained.

Rivka sat in front of the opening to the tent. It was closed against mosquitoes, though the smoke from the fire kept most of them away. Still, she would limit the time the flap was open to avoid sharing her sleeping quarters with bugs.

Ella shared Liam's cloak, though she had gone off with Skelaroth when he'd gone swimming…and fishing, apparently. Liam offered her a few bites of his food, but it was apparent by her disinterest and the gentle swell of her full tummy that she'd probably done some fishing of her own already.

"I am sorry, friends, but I must rest now," Skelaroth said wearily into their minds. With that, he closed his eyes and was asleep in moments.

"I suppose, going out to sea and coming around the city through less populated lands, the big guy traveled farther than either one of us today," Liam said, keeping his voice down to a low murmur as he looked at Skelaroth.

"And, mighty as his muscles are from swimming, he has never carried a passenger before," Rivka added. "He was being careful not to swerve or turn too steeply so you could stay aboard. That kind of thing—the concentration it takes to learn what's essentially a new skill—takes its toll, even on the strongest being."

Liam nodded. "He's done a yeoman's job and is certainly a credit to his kind."

Rivka looked at Liam speculatively. "So, what did you think of flying? You seemed to take to it almost naturally."

"It was much better than I feared," Liam admitted. "That feeling of the wind was almost like when I have my ship under full sail and we're making time. Flying is quite a bit faster, of course," Liam smiled slightly in her direction. "And the views…" His voice trailed off as he seemed to think back on all he'd seen. "It's like nothing I've ever experienced before."

"That's good, I hope," she teased when he didn't say more.

Startled out of his reverie, he blinked at her. "Oh, yes, indeed. Flying was marvelous. Though, I suppose it's old hat to you. It must be even better to fly under your own power. To spread your wings and determine your own path."

He was more intuitive than she'd realized. She nodded,

allowing some of the wonder that never left her when she flew to show in her expression. "It really is incredible," she admitted. "I never take the gift of flight for granted."

They sipped their tea and sat quietly, enjoying the small fire as it burned down. When she started to yawn, Rivka got up and made a final visit to the bushes before she sought her tent. Liam did the same, considerately going to the other side of the small camp to give her a bit of privacy.

When she returned to the fire, she spent a few moments banking it against the night. They'd let it burn out gradually since it gave off a bit of welcome warmth. It wasn't terribly cold yet, but they were climbing in elevation, and it did tend to get cooler the higher they went.

Rivka stood when Liam returned. He came close to her, speaking in a low tone. "Will you be warm enough?" he asked. "I have a spare blanket, if you need it."

He was such a thoughtful man. She was touched. "The tent is more than enough protection," she assured him, "but thank you for thinking of me. In fact…" She stepped closer to him, reaching upward to place a kiss on his cheek. He didn't pull away, but she could feel his surprise. "Thank you for everything. You've been the most thoughtful companion I have ever traveled with."

She knew her cheeks were heating with embarrassment over her admission, but she couldn't have kept going without expressing to him how much his small courtesies and considerate actions meant to her. She had meant to move away as soon as she delivered the peck to his stubbled cheek, but he smelled divine and radiated heat and strength. It was a heady combination.

"There is no need to thank me," he said, his voice rumbling low in a way that made her insides clench with delight. "You must not have picked very good traveling companions before, if such simple things seem extraordinary." His gentle smile invited her to smile back, and she felt the corners of her mouth lifting as she gazed upward into his eyes.

How had she not realized before just how much taller he was than her? It was rare that she was made to feel petite, but Liam was a big man, both tall and muscular in that lean way that indicated true strength. He was no idle sea captain, but a self-made man who had worked his way up to the position he now held. She admired that very much.

"I think..." She dared to put her thoughts into words in a way she never would have among her own Clan. "Because of what I am and the life path I've chosen as a warrior among my kin, most of them see me as too strong to be needful of their protection—though, that isn't exactly the right word." She tilted her head a bit, thinking it though, but couldn't express it any better than she had. She shook her head slightly. "I think they forget that I'm also a woman and I like soft things. Like the silk of your tent. And the small considerations you've made throughout the day."

Suddenly, the mood between them grew even more intimate as Liam stepped closer. "I have never, for one moment, forgotten that you are a woman, Rivka."

His words sounded almost like a warning, but it was one that she could not heed. The sudden fire in his eyes was answered by a leap of flame in her belly, and suddenly, she wanted more than just a peck on the cheek and to stand within his personal space. She wanted to plaster herself to him and feel the warmth of his body against hers.

He seemed to feel the same way as one of his hands touched her waist, sliding around slowly and tugging her closer. She went willingly, her feet moving to stand next to and in between his as her body drifted closer to his incredible warmth. His head lowered, and his cheek touched hers. She could feel the gentle scrape of his whiskers against her, and it sent a little thrill of excitement straight down her spine, all the way to her toes.

Their cheeks slid gently against apart other until his mouth hovered over hers. And then... His lips touched hers in the gentlest caress she'd ever experienced from a man. Tentative, yet commanding. Hesitant, yet needful. His mouth covered hers and held for a heartbeat before applying more pressure.

She opened for him without any hint of protest, and then, his tongue swept inside, claiming, inciting her passion, and demanding her response. She gave it freely. Enthusiastically. Rubbing her body against his, she took his warmth into her soul, enjoying the sensations she had felt only with him.

Tiny alarms went off in her mind, but she paid them no heed. Liam's heart might be inaccessible, but his body certainly seemed to know what it wanted. She felt the hard length of him against her belly, and then, suddenly... He was gone.

Head spinning, she opened her eyes to find him scowling, at least three feet away from her, cursing under his breath. Not exactly the response she'd been hoping for. If not for the tingling in her lips—and other, more intimate, places—she might almost have believed their kiss had never happened. But she knew better. And she realized, with a bit of horror, that he was cursing himself for a loss of control.

He regretted the kiss, it was plain to see, but that was something she would never agree with. She was glad he'd kissed her. Glad of the moment of insanity when she'd felt like a desirable woman and not sturdy, dependable Rivka, the fire-breather who everyone seemed to think needed no gentleness from a man.

Knowing the mood was broken—possibly forever—Rivka climbed into the tent without another word. She would hold the memory of that kiss close forever. Her only regret was that it would likely never be repeated.

Liam was still cursing at himself the next morning as they broke camp, though he did it silently. Things were very stilted between himself and Lady Rivka, but they worked together to erase signs of their camp and put things back to rights. They said little, only speaking when necessary, and then, only about general things. The route they would follow. The breaks they would take. How often she wanted to land to scan the ground.

He could handle those things. The mission had to be all-important. It was the personal stuff he found hard to deal with.

He should never have kissed her. He didn't know what had gotten into him last night. The darkness. The intimacy. The easy feeling he had when he was with her. It had all compounded into making him act in a way that he should never even have been contemplating.

They hadn't spoken of it, and he wasn't sure he had the courage to do so. If he found an opportunity later in the day, he should really apologize for his rudeness, but in the cold morning light, he found himself still too worked up to be sensible. Better to wait until his temper cooled, so he wouldn't make things worse.

Skelaroth was quiet, but he seemed to be watching both Liam and Rivka with suspicion in his jewel-like eyes. Liam didn't invite discussion with the giant lizard. He didn't want to talk about what had passed between himself and Rivka the night before, and he made that very clear with his body language.

Ella was watching him too, but then, she had seen what had happened last night. She might not understand all the nuances of male-female interaction, but she probably sensed enough to realize that things were strained between the two humans of their party. Wisely, Ella chose to stay silent this morning, simply curling up on Liam's shoulder while he went about his tasks, as if to offer comfort.

When it was time to fly, she'd gone happily into the little nest bag he'd made for her. He'd left the flap open so she could stick her head out as they flew. She'd go in when she got tired, and he'd lower the flap then, to protect her from the wind.

They got in the air with little fanfare and worked their way northward along the road. Today, they would stick to every twist and turn of the road so they would be less likely to miss it if Fisk turned off onto another path. Best case scenario—they would see him and his party from above and be able to intervene, catching him on the road, in the open.

Liam relished the idea of a straight-out fight with Fisk and his men. He wanted to kill that bastard with his own hands and had wanted to do so for many years.

Rivka was in charge of how often and where they landed. They made three short stops in the morning. Liam dismounted each time and put his rusty land-tracking skills to use while Rivka consulted with Skelaroth, telling the bigger dragon what she was looking for. Liam was happy to leave them to it. Skelaroth was a bit old—and mighty—for schooling, and Liam wasn't sure if the sea dragon was sensitive about the fact that he needed to be tutored in land-based skills or not. He thought it was safer not to find out.

It was on the fourth stop of the day that Liam's venturing off the road to search on his own bore fruit. Ella swooped down off his shoulder to the ground about five feet away. He thought nothing of it, at first, but when he heard the distinctive clink of her talons against metal, he perked up.

"What do you have there, my lovely?" he asked as he drew closer to the virkin and whatever she'd found in the grass.

"*Coin,*" she replied, in his mind, lifting the small round bit of metal in one claw and holding it up to him.

Liam took the coin she offered and examined it. One side featured a man's head in profile, wearing a crown. In Liam's experience, many lands used carved images of their monarchs on their coinage, if their metal workers had the skill to do so. He flipped the coin over in his hand and sucked in a breath at the image on that side. It was a coiled serpent. A very distinctive kind of creature. A dragon's mortal enemy, it was a skith from the neighboring, enemy land, Skithdron.

Trade with Skithdron was nonexistent. There was very little travel—in fact, none at all that was officially sanctioned—over the border, which was many leagues distant. In fact, they were nearly on the other side of Draconia. It made no sense that this coin should be found here.

The only way it could have gotten here, to Liam's mind,

was in the pocket of a person who had traveled to Skithdron. And the only people likely to have traveled there were those in league with the enemy. Fisk and his crew fit the bill. They could have easily sailed to Skithdron, or anywhere else, and spent enough time there to pick up some of the local currency.

"Lord Skelaroth? Lady Rivka?" Liam called to the two who were still examining the roadway. This was too important not to share. "Miss Ella has found something."

Ella flew back to perch on his shoulder, and he scratched her head in approval as he looked around him very carefully. There was disturbance in the way in the grass flowed in this area. As if people had walked here then done their best to hide their passage.

"What is it?" Rivka asked aloud, having shifted into her human form to follow him. Skelaroth merely craned his head over on his long, sinuous neck, joining them.

"Ella found this in the grass. It is a Skithdronian coin," he said, offering the round bit of copper to Rivka.

She sucked in a breath as the skith flashed on the back of the coin. Skelaroth's head actually reared back. Liam noted the way Rivka shrank back and did not take the coin from his hand.

"Is there something wrong with it?" he asked, cautiously examining the coin again. It didn't look dangerous to him.

"Sorry. It's the image. Dragons and skiths... We're natural enemies. I can't even look at that image without my inner dragon wanting to roar and flame," she admitted.

"*The coin itself is not the problem,*" Skelaroth put in. "*It is the...animal...depicted on it.*"

The emphasis Skelaroth put on that word—animal—seemed to be significant. As if the skiths were lower than low. Base. Animalistic. Not thinking creatures, at all. Liam supposed that Skelaroth knew more than he did about it.

Liam had avoided Skithdron, as did most reasonable people. It was an isolationist nation that didn't welcome trade with anyone other than the few criminals willing to risk their necks for a profit. Hence, there had been no reason for Liam to ever go there. He wasn't the sort of cut-throat who would deal in the illegal and immoral things that were said to be of interest to the Skithdronian king.

"I think they camped here," Rivka said, breaking into Liam's thoughts. She was walking around, placing her feet very carefully. "See the way the grass has been flattened and then righted again? And here…" She flipped over a broken tree limb with the toe of her boot. Underneath, Liam could see the remains of a campfire. The ground had been charred a bit, and there were ashes in the blackened circle. "They tried to hide it, but a fire always leaves a mark."

So says the fire-breathing dragon, Liam thought. *She probably knows what she's talking about.*

"*Can you tell anything of their numbers?*" Skelaroth asked.

"Not really," she replied. "Not with any certainty."

"I counted at least four places where the grass was disturbed enough to have been sleeping spots," Liam offered.

Rivka nodded. "I agree. But there might have been more. This was probably their campsite two nights ago. It's not fresh enough to tell us more." She sighed and shook her head.

"*At least now, we know we're on the right trail,*" Skelaroth put in.

"Well," Liam didn't want to be too contrary, but had to be realistic, "we know we're on the trail of someone who has been to Skithdron. Logic tells us that must be someone from Fisk's crew. Or, at the very least, some kind of pirate. Since Fisk is the only pirate we know of to land in Tipolir and take to the road recently, it makes sense that it is his crewman. But we still cannot be sure this group is the one in which Fisk is traveling."

Skelaroth grumbled.

CHAPTER 9

Rivka could not fault Liam's logic, though she could wish he hadn't pointed out that their effort could be all in vain. She had the feeling they were on the right track, but Liam was right. They couldn't be absolutely certain, at this point.

"The messengers should have reached someone by now," Rivka told them all. "There will be more dragons and trackers on the other roads soon enough. This is still the most likely route, so we are probably on the right trail. We can't give up or give in to hopelessness. We have to keep going."

Liam looked taken aback by her words but seemed to use caution when he spoke. "I didn't mean to imply we should, milady," he told her. "I have just learned to be prudent in getting my hopes up where chasing Fisk is concerned. He's slipperier than a fish and twice as cunning as a fox. He has managed to evade me and all the men at my command for far too long for me to take anything for granted."

Rivka had to bow her head slightly, in acknowledgement of his past efforts, but this was a new day, and a new team. He'd never had two dragons searching with him before. "I take your point, Captain, but I think, this time, he will not escape."

"I pray you're right, milady. I truly do."

They took to the air again, a few minutes later, keeping close watch on the road below for more signs of the pirates' passage. Nothing showed obviously from the air, and it was getting toward midday, so Rivka headed for the ground once more after they had covered a few leagues distance.

The moment her feet touched the ground, Rivka could see the faint signs of hooves. Several horses had come this way, at speed, heading in the direction they'd been traveling all day. She was puzzled as to why she hadn't seen this from above.

As Skelaroth landed beside her, she turned to him. *"See the hoof marks?"* she asked, still in her dragon form.

"I do," the other dragon replied quickly. *"Though, I did not before,"* he added, puzzlement sounding in his tone.

"Me neither," Rivka agreed, feeling a prickling sensation at the back of her mind. There was something going on here. *"Let me just check something,"* she told Skelaroth. *"Stay here for a minute."*

She leapt into the air again, and flapped her wings to gain altitude. Then, she banked to turn and look at the road where Skelaroth stood, Liam now at his side. While she could see them both clearly, the hoof prints were gone, as if by…

"Magic!" she practically spat the word back at those on the road. *"They are hiding their trail so it cannot be seen from above by magical means."*

"Surely not," Skelaroth objected. *"They would have to know they are being chased from above to take such precautions."*

"My lord, we are in the land of dragons," she reminded him gently. *"If I were a criminal intent on hiding my trail, I would take pursuit by air into account. The knights and dragons of this land are well versed in tracking wrongdoers and have all the power of their station to bring villains to justice. It is their sworn duty."*

She circled and landed again, neatly beside the other dragon. Liam was a few yards distant, with Ella hovering at his side. It looked like he was examining the hoof prints in some detail.

"I will go aloft and see what you have discovered," Skelaroth said quietly before he took off in the opposite direction from

where Liam was standing.

Rivka watched them both for a moment before deciding to shift into her human shape and see if she could discern anything more from the marks on the road. She walked up to Liam's side on two feet and tried to see if there was anything more they could learn.

Almost immediately, she noticed the different hoof sizes and patterns. At least one of the horses was in need of new shoes, and the others looked to have been shod by completely different farriers, each with their own style.

"I count five distinct hoof patterns," she said as she bent to look more closely at the dirt road.

"I came up with five, as well," Liam concurred.

"From the depth of the prints, I'd say all were carrying a burden equal to the weight of a man," she told him, trying to be as cautious about drawing conclusions as he had been earlier.

"So, either four men and a heavily laden pack horse, or at least five men on horseback," he said, almost absently as he strode forward to examine more of the roadway. "No less than five, at any rate," he said a moment later. "There could be more that we're just not seeing in this mess." He took a few more strides then stopped. "The road gets harder from here. This is a soft spot in the dirt and holds prints better than what I can see ahead."

"And we can't see it at all from above," she added angrily.

"We should pause here, eat something, then go on cautiously—stopping every few minutes to check the road—until we find a town or farm or something. Someplace we can get horses of our own. I think the wisest move would be to go over land from here, since we wouldn't be able to see these prints from above."

She hated to agree, but she had to. In this instance, flying wasn't the best solution.

"We're not going to be able to catch up as quickly," she told him. "Perhaps not at all, if they can get fresh horses."

"I know, but if we get close enough, we can leave the

horses somewhere and attack from the air," he said.

"If we can see them from the air," she reminded him. "I'm not certain how this magic works. I don't know if he's just hiding his trail or if he can actually make himself, and his men, invisible from above."

"I have to think that, if we can at least spot them from down here, we will be able to remember the place and fly to it. Once we're on the ground, we should be able to see them, again, right? Even if we can't see them from above?"

"I'm just not sure," she admitted, biting her lip. "But I know we can't track from up there, right now." She pointed to Skelaroth, who was circling lower and lower, his neck craning this way and that as he surveyed the land below.

"All right, then." Liam walked back toward where Skelaroth was coming in for a landing. "Lunch first, then we find a place to get provisions and horses. We're almost completely out of food, so we would have had to stop somewhere today, anyway."

Rivka couldn't argue with that. She followed Liam to a convenient fallen log they could sit on while they ate. There was a brook running alongside the road, so they were all able to drink the fresh, clear water bubbling down from the mountains. Skelaroth seemed subdued but managed to find a few fish for his midday meal, and Ella fished with him, getting a small one for herself.

It was hard bread and the last of the cheese for the humans, but Rivka didn't mind. She had almost lost her appetite at the idea that her dragon side would be of little use in this hunt. She had always relied so heavily on her dragonish instincts, it was as if she had been forced to work with one hand tied behind her back if she had to remain human for the remainder of the chase. Not that she wasn't comfortable in her human guise, but when on the prowl, her dragon shape was usually the more useful one. Not so, now. Fisk had done something to make her unique skills superfluous. He had effectively neutralized her dragon, and that made her mad.

Angry and sort of lost. She'd never felt this powerless

before.

A few hours later, after meticulously stopping to examine the roadway every so often, Rivka spotted a small town in the distance. They'd be able to resupply there and perhaps learn something about the travelers who had come through before them. For, if her instincts were correct, the party of pirates wasn't too far ahead of them, now. Their quarry had maybe a half-day lead on them, which could be made up with not too much work, even over land.

She signaled to Lord Skelaroth and made for a clearing just outside the town, in the woods, where she could shift shape and the humans could walk in on foot. Whether or not to have Skelaroth reveal his presence would depend entirely on the reception they got from the townsfolk.

"I saw the town," Liam said, as he dismounted from Skelaroth's back.

Rivka realized with a start of surprise that the sea captain's skills at aerial surveillance were improving right along with the sea dragon's. That was something she hadn't contemplated. More and more, Skelaroth and Liam were beginning to operate as a team—just like a dragon and his knight.

Liam was checking his gear as he approached her. Rivka shifted into her human form and did the same. They didn't know what they would be walking into. It was best to be prepared for all contingencies. She looked him over and he looked to her like a rather successful warrior. Perhaps a mercenary?

He was clothed in dark leather with stretches of harder armor-quality leather in strategic places, as well as thin metal plate sewn into the garment on his chest and back. There were even small sections of chain maille work along his arms—especially in the joints. It was a unique garment she had never seen the like of in Draconia, but she knew such things were common in other parts of the world.

Foreign mercenary, then? Though, he talked with a pure

Draconian accent. So, local boy gone off to make his fortune as a sell-sword then returned. She nodded at her own surmise. If anyone asked, that would be their explanation. They were hunting a bounty on the troupe of pirates that had just gone through the town. If the townsfolk thought there might be some reward for sharing information, they might be more likely to speak.

She knew she dressed like the warrior she was, so they would be a duo of sell-swords—perhaps mates? The idea was tempting, but she would not suggest it to Liam unless a deeper cover story became necessary. Even if merely the thought of posing as his wife sent a little tingle down her spine. She knew he would not meet the idea as easily. No, Liam was a one-trick pony. He was still wrapped up in his dead wife and his need for vengeance. To even think of another woman in the sainted Olivia's place was not possible.

Rivka understood, even as it saddened her. To have such devotion, Olivia must have truly been a special woman. From all accounts, her daughter was just as lovely and took after her mother. Rivka had met Livia O'Dare on the fateful night the page had been taken from Gryffid's book. She remembered the girl as stunningly lovely with a bright spirit and cunning mind.

The thrill for adventure, Livia had, no doubt, inherited from her father. Her mother was said to be a lady of the first order. Livia was also a lady, but she had a daring warrior spirit and little fear. She had been at the forefront of the search for the book, and she and her mates had actually found it and returned it to Gryphon Isle. Only later was the discovery made, by the wizard himself, of the missing page, and a new quest had been born.

Liam had already been on the trail, chasing after Fisk. He'd had a head start on everyone else and knew the pirate well from the many years of chasing him. Rivka had chosen to ally herself with Liam, since she truly believed he had the best chance of catching up with Fisk and his crew before real damage could be done.

"We make for the town?" Liam asked, coming up beside her.

"Verily," she replied, her thoughts still troubling her. The virkin caught her eye, hovering near Liam's shoulder. "Should Ella not stay here with Skelaroth?"

"I have asked her to do so, but she insists on coming with us." Liam looked a bit chagrinned at not being able to control the small creature.

Rivka thought about it then nodded. "Well, since you already look like a foreign mercenary, Ella will only make you seem more exotic. Perhaps she can enchant the children of the town and win over their parents."

Liam's eyes flashed with amusement. Oh, he was a handsome brute when he wasn't scowling. Rivka counseled her insides to stop fluttering. He was not for her. He'd made that abundantly clear by his behavior since their kiss. His every move said he thought the momentary loss of control had been an utter mistake. Never to be repeated. Much to her disappointment.

"Shall we set off?" Rivka prodded him, not wanting to think about her embarrassment any longer. She'd had enough time to do that while flying all morning.

Liam walked at her side, not too close, but within a good distance to aid in their defense should they somehow be set upon by ruffians or the like. Ella fluttered along at his side, her long neck stretching and swiveling side to side in interest as she took in their surroundings. Rivka realized this land must be strange to the small creature.

Elderland had very different terrain. Different animals and plants, and a totally different feel. Ella had probably never been too far inland when Liam made port. Perhaps, she'd never been off the ship at all since joining it. Everything here must be interesting to her, and Rivka could understand why Ella had not wanted to be left behind.

As they approached the town, Rivka got a bad feeling in her bones. "Something's wrong," she whispered.

"I feel it," Liam replied. "It's too quiet."

Rivka's steps slowed. "Ambush?" she asked in the barest whisper.

"I think not," Liam answered, his eyes squinting ahead as if that might help him see what was going on in the village.

"There's no one on the streets," Rivka told him. She, after all, had keener sight than most humans, owing to her dragon half. "There isn't much sound at all."

They walked cautiously closer. "It's as if— Sweet Mother of All!" Liam swore as he spotted the dead horses lining the perimeter of the fenced field that bordered one side of the road.

Rivka took a closer look. The horses had not died of their own accord. "Someone has butchered them," she said, the grave feeling in the pit of her stomach coming through in her low tone.

"Fisk." Liam said the pirate's name like a curse. "He would slaughter innocent animals to discourage pursuit."

"Do you think he knows we're following him?" Rivka asked.

"He has to believe that somebody is checking the trails he left from Tipolir. Otherwise, he would not have taken steps to send a party out on every major road leading out from the city. He is a cautious brigand, is our Captain Fisk."

"But to kill all the horses..." Rivka couldn't even finish her thought. That Fisk had done this was beyond disgusting. These horses were vital to the town. Without their beasts, they could neither ride for help nor plow their fields or take their harvest anywhere. A town's livestock was their livelihood, no matter the season.

"Seeing this, my real concern is for the people," Liam intoned in a somber voice. "What did he do to them?"

"Stars!" Rivka was appalled at the idea that Fisk and his men could have easily decimated a small town like this with only farm folk and villagers to defend it. She turned toward the town, again. "We have to help them, if we can."

Liam looked grim. "Indeed, we do." They set off walking, again. "In any case, those horses were killed a day or two ago.

The trail is not fresh. We will not meet up with Fisk this day." He could not keep the disappointment out of his tone, but Rivka understood. Liam had been waiting a long time for justice.

As they walked into the town, Liam's worst fears were confirmed. Dark brown dried bloodstains marred the dirt of the street, and nobody was stirring. If anyone still lived, they were either busy elsewhere or hiding. He didn't blame them. They had likely been traumatized by Fisk and his men, and their evil deeds.

Liam heard the slight ring of steel on steel at his side. Rivka had drawn her swords. He did the same, just in case anybody took exception to their presence and came out swinging. It was just possible that Fisk had left some of his crew behind to waylay any pursuit.

But, as they walked together through the empty village, no one erupted from the shadows. Only a few chickens could be seen pecking in the dust at the side of one house. Nothing bigger than a cat came out to greet them. When they got closer to the center of town, there was some activity. A cart was pulled up in front of the largest structure they had yet seen. It had to be an inn of some kind, but there wasn't much sound to indicate what should have been a bustling meal service.

Instead, that one lonely cart lay, with its back propped toward the main door of the inn, as if someone had been loading or unloading it. The horse or donkey—whatever had pulled the cart—was long gone. Probably dead, judging by what they had seen on the way into town.

As Liam studied it, a woman suddenly appeared at the doorway of the inn. She stopped short when she saw them, and fear crossed her features. She put one hand on the door frame and was turning to go back inside as Liam spoke.

"We mean you no harm, Mistress," he called out in as gentle a voice as he could manage. "Pray, what happened here?"

The woman hesitated. She eyed their weapons with suspicion. "The village was attacked," she said after a moment. "What does it look like?"

"We saw the horses slain," Rivka put in. "That's why I drew steel. In case the ones who did this are still around."

The woman deflated and leaned against the doorjamb. "No, they're long gone," she said. "After the raid, I gathered all the injured here in the inn. Those that could be saved. I've been treating them for the past two days."

"Treating them?" Rivka queried as she put one of her swords away, sheathing it at her back. Liam was glad she hadn't put them both up yet. Just in case this woman was leading them astray.

"I am Jalina, journeyman healer of the Temple of Our Lady of Light. This village—Waymeet—is on my circuit. I arrived here just before the raid and ran to hide in the forest while the men were killing everyone and everything. I'm not a fighter," she explained. "They got Horatio, my horse. Loaded him up with supplies and took him with them, the bastards."

"They killed all the other village horses?" Liam asked.

"Killed their own nags, though they already looked as if the poor beasts had been run into the ground," the healer replied. "Then, they went raiding the livestock and killed anything fast enough to catch up with the horses they stole from the villagers. My poor Horatio is a youngster, full of life and pep. I suppose that is what saved him from being murdered, as well. The few able-bodied folk left helped me drag my cart up here so I could get to my supplies more easily. They're all helping me feed and tend the injured."

"This is grave news, Mistress Jalina. We have been on the trail of a band of pirates. We started our journey in Tiploir, and we will keep going until we have brought them to justice for *all* of their crimes," Rivka promised the healer. "We have crown authority, and when we meet up with someone who can take a message to the nearest Lair, I'm sure they will send help."

"The villagers sent out a lanky lad of about fourteen on

foot soon after the dust settled. He's walking overland to the nearest town, which is to the west. They expect him to get there in a day or two," Jalina told them.

Ella, who had been conspicuous by her absence since they entered the town, suddenly flew up to land on Liam's shoulder. Jalina's eyes widened.

"You have a virkin companion," she marveled, clearly fascinated by the creature who preened under the healer's scrutiny.

"You know about them?" Rivka asked, one eyebrow raised.

"I have heard tales of their healing abilities." Jalina surprised them with her answer.

Liam frowned. "Ella is very young. She's only just started talking, and I've never known her to heal anything." He didn't want the healer having any expectations where Ella was concerned. Liam would protect his small friend, whatever it took.

"We also have a sea dragon friend traveling with us," Rivka put in quietly. "We left him on the outskirts, just in case he would not be welcome. Tell me," she went on, running right over any questions the healer might have had. "Did the brigands do anything to the horses before they slew them? Poison or magic of any kind that could make the meat dangerous to consume?"

"No, not that I saw. They just hacked at them with their curved swords." The healer shuddered as she recounted the tale.

"Cutlasses," Liam muttered. "I should like to talk to any survivors you can spare. We need to know as much as we can about the men who attacked this village," he went on, speaking to the healer in a tone he hoped would gain her cooperation.

Jalina nodded slowly. "It can be done, but as you'll see, there aren't many folk left unharmed. But most of those abed will be able to speak with you, if it'll help you catch the raiders."

"Then, we must talk to them," Liam said. "First, I will alert our dragon friend that he may enter the town. He may assist with the disposal of some of the carcasses. It has been a while since he had fed well."

Jalina looked relieved. "That's good. I was wondering how we were going to deal with so many. They've already begun attracting scavengers. If your dragon friend could remove those closest to the village, that would be a help. The butcher's apprentice has already put up as much as he could handle. He's got a small smokehouse working, but there's just too much. What's left in the fields and on the streets on the outskirts of town will spoil rapidly."

Rivka nodded gravely. "Our big friend can definitely help with that. I'll just ask him."

While Rivka contacted Skelaroth mentally, Liam went into the inn with Jalina. Ella fluttered off his shoulder and went to perch on the side of a rough cot containing a young child with an obvious slash across one side of his face. Liam was pained just looking at the oozing cut and could only guess at the injuries that lay below the simple homespun blanket that practically swallowed the little boy. He was shaking with fever, and his cheeks were flushed bright red on a face that was otherwise all too pale. He had probably lost a lot of blood before the fever set in.

Ella walked daintily to the top of the cot and curved one tiny wing over the top of the boy's head, laying her cheek against his and closing her eyes. Jalina came up beside Liam as he took stock of the room. At least twenty people were in cots or lying on tables around the room. Others sat at their sides or bustled around, seeing to their comfort. There were more injured than well.

"Most of the villagers were either killed outright or badly injured. Only the old and young were mostly spared," Jalina murmured, so that only Liam could hear.

"A slimy tactic," he replied, hearing the anger in his own voice, though he tried to suppress it. "About what I'd expect from him."

"You know the villains who came here?" Jalina asked, her brows arching in surprise.

"I have hunted their leader for a long time. Which is why I need to know more about the group that came through. I need to find their leader. Cut off the head of the snake, and the rest will wither and die."

Jalina nodded, her jaw clenched. "Just so." She nodded toward the room. "I'm sure they will provide what help they can. As will I."

Liam stepped into the light, and the villagers became aware of his presence. Those who had the energy seemed afraid, at first, but Jalina's presence at his side seemed to calm them.

"Mama?" A little voice from the bed against the wall made Jalina and Liam spin around. It was the boy, and his eyes were open. He'd stopped shaking, and it looked to Liam as if his fever had broken.

"How are you feeling, poppet?" Jalina asked, going to the boy's side and putting her hand against his forehead. The boy's mother wasn't around, but the healer gave him what nurturing and reassurance she could provide. Ella had hopped up to perch on the back of a chair near the boy's cot.

Liam looked from the boy and his remarkable recovery to Ella. She met his gaze and flew over to land on his shoulder.

"Did you heal the boy, Ella?" Liam murmured to his virkin friend.

"Helped," she confirmed, nodding her head as she nestled her cheek against his jaw.

"Are you all right?" Liam asked, a bit alarmed, as well as amazed. He hadn't known the virkin had such powers.

"Fine. He is, too." She pointed her chin toward the boy who was looking at her with wide eyes.

"Magic," Liam concluded. That's all it could be. "Do you have magic, little one?"

"Of course," Ella replied. *"Am virkin. Have much magic."*

CHAPTER 10

Rivka joined Liam inside the inn's common room that had become an infirmary. He was standing a few feet from a cot where the little boy was being fussed over by a tearful woman, who was likely his mother.

"Skelaroth is already working on clearing the town," she told him. "At least we can do that much for these people before we have to go."

Liam seemed a bit distracted but turned to her and nodded. "That's good." Ella left his shoulder and flew to the bedside of an elderly woman who lay utterly still.

"Are they all right with her doing that?" Rivka asked as Ella stood above the woman's head and placed both of her wings at the elder's temples.

"Did you know that virkin had magic? Ella just healed that boy of a fever, and he woke up asking for his mother." Liam sounded as stunned as his words made her feel.

Rivka turned to look at the boy and his mother again. The child looked healthy, if a bit pale. Yet, everyone else occupying a bed in this makeshift hospital was in much worse shape.

"She did?" Rivka looked again at the virkin and her peaceful pose at the old lady's head. Was the woman regaining some of her color? "I had no idea virkin had magic like that."

Liam was eyeing her with suspicion when she met his gaze again. "Your words imply that you had some idea virkin were magical."

"Well, yes. I mean, there is a belief among the Jinn who have traveled to her homeland that virkin choose their companions and use magic to do it. The fact that Ella chose to accompany you and your ship indicated to me that she had magically derived some concept of your inner nature. Virkin are said to be excellent judges of character, and they will not stay with someone of the evil intent. They are good, through and through. At least, that's what the legends about them say."

Liam's eyebrows rose. "All that?" His surprise was evident in the way he followed Ella's progress as she left the old woman and moved to another bed to take a similar pose over a thickset man. "I had no idea she had magic at all. I didn't even know she could speak until a couple of days ago. You believe she chose me because she could... What? See into my soul?"

Rivka nodded. "So it is said," she murmured, splitting her attention between Ella and Liam. "Why are you so surprised? You are a good man, Liam. Apparently, Ella thinks so, too."

"But... I'm not. I have imagined killing Fisk in so many gruesome ways over the years. Those are not the thoughts of a pure soul," he admitted in a low, pain-filled voice.

Clearly, he was at war within himself over his thirst for revenge and his sense of honor. The way that Fisk was brought to justice was going to be essential in Liam's future ability to live with himself. If he gave in to the vengeance and did something awful, Liam would probably not be able to forgive himself. Rivka only then started to realize the depth of the captain's integrity. This quest—and the unforgivable things done to his family by the pirate Fisk—had already cost him dearly. Even imagining taking his revenge in some unspeakable way, tortured his soul.

Rivka was deeply moved. If it was within her power, she

swore to herself, that she would be the one to strike Fisk down, if at all possible. She would give Liam his justice but would try to help him limit the guilt he would feel personally. For, she had just discovered, Liam was a man who took things to heart.

"Your virkin is doing wonders," Jalina said happily in a soft voice as she approached. She was smiling—probably for the first time since the raid. "I had grave doubts about young Sammy's fever, but it is gone, and he should recover now, with the resilience of youth. Granny Doris is looking better, too, and I thought for certain she would leave us this afternoon. And look..." Jalina pointed to the big man Ella had just left. His eyes were blinking open. "That's the village blacksmith. He is also the headman. A good fellow named Larson. His wounds were grave, and infection was taking its toll. Thank the Lady you stopped here!" Jalina clapped her palms together gently and raised her eyes skyward briefly, toward her goddess. "I will go to Larson and examine him, but your virkin deserves praise and thanks. Please tell her for me, if I do not get a chance."

"We will," Rivka assured the woman as she walked away on quiet feet. Liam was watching Ella move around the room, seeking her next patient. She chose a man with a large belly, currently swathed in bandages.

Rivka knew that gut wounds could be deadly. It was surprising this man had lived long enough to receive Jalina's care, but he appeared to be hanging on to life by a tenacious thread. Ella landed at his side and placed her wing over his bandages. Then, the virkin closed her eyes and stretched out her long neck to rest her head on the man's arm.

"Sir?" The boy's mother approached Liam. Rivka watched with interest to see how he would handle her.

"Yes, ma'am," he replied politely, turning toward the woman.

"Healer Jalina says your pet helped my Sammy, and I just wanted to thank you," the woman said in a shy voice that was filled with emotion.

"I wouldn't call her a pet, exactly," Liam said with an inviting grin that seemed to put the woman more at ease. "Mistress Ella does as she wishes. I'm just glad she was able to help your son."

"Is there some way I can thank her, then?" the woman insisted. "Is there anything I can get for her? I've been running the kitchen here to feed everyone. It's not fancy food, but it's filling. The raiders left most of our stores intact. They just took what they could carry off with them but left the rest alone."

"That is good news," Liam replied, and Rivka was glad to hear that at least nobody in town would starve while they were getting over this tragedy. "We originally stopped here to see if we could resupply. Would that be possible?"

"Oh, aye," the woman replied easily. "There's plenty of food to be had. We went through everyone's cupboards that first day and gathered everything edible here in this kitchen. We've been using the perishables first, but there's plenty of cured meat laid by and other items that would last for your journey." The woman looked over where Ella was flitting to another patient. "What sorts of things does your small friend eat?"

Liam also watched Ella fly, though Rivka noted the portly man was stirring and seemed to look a lot better. Was Ella healing everyone? Rivka didn't realize virkin had *that* much magic.

"Ella will eat just about anything. She's a born hunter and picks off the vermin on the ship that come aboard every time we make port. When they're gone, she dines with me, and I feed her off my plate. She eats mostly meat but also likes sweet grains and bread. She also enjoys small fruits and nuts. Really, she'll eat just about anything we would eat," Liam told the woman.

"I was about to go get soup for my boy," she told them. "Now that his fever is gone, he's hungry, of course, blessed be the Mother of All." Her smile was one of relief and gratefulness. "My name is Meg, by the way. I'd be happy to get a proper meal started for you, if you're hungry."

Rivka saw an opportunity to help, and she stepped forward. "My name is Rivka, Meg. I'd be happy to help you in the kitchen. I assume it's near feeding time for those who are able to eat, is it not?"

"Aye, that it is," Meg agreed. "I'd be grateful for the help. Come with me."

'I'll question her about the raiders while we cook," Rivka sent to Liam silently. He turned to her and nodded, then strode forward to offer his help to the healer.

Rivka followed Meg into the inn's large kitchen. The townswoman hadn't been kidding when she'd claimed they'd gathered all the supplies and taken them to the inn. The counters were almost overflowing with foodstuffs. Baked goods that were probably a day or two old by now, but still quite edible, were on one counter, in baskets and on platters. There were bags full of beans and grains, as well as canisters of different kinds of flour and other ground substances. Dried herbs hung from the rafters in neat rows. In all, it was a model kitchen to Rivka's mind. The inn must have been quite nice before Fisk's men came through.

"There's a kitchen garden out back that the raiders missed," Meg told Rivka. "You're welcome to go out there and see what's ripe that you might like. By the way, same goes for anything you see growing in the village. Everyone who's left is pooling resources, and we've agreed that everything is communal for the time being. Chances are, if you see ripe fruit somewhere, nobody's left to pick it, so you might as well take some."

"That's very kind," Rivka replied, not mentioning how sad it also was. The fact that so many had been killed by the pirates was something that was going to take this town a long time to get over. "Let me help you clear away the dirty pots first, though." Rivka dug right into the wash tub full of pots and dishes. She wanted to stay with Meg for a bit and hopefully get her to talk about the raid.

They worked side by side for a while. Meg took the

promised bowl of soup out to her son but returned after a bit. Rivka was still working away on the dirty dishes when Meg joined her.

"Thank you for your help with this," Meg said shyly. "I know I shouldn't have let things pile up, but…"

"You had other priorities," Rivka completed the woman's thoughts. "I understand. I've been through this sort of thing before. How is your boy doing?"

"Jalina says he's out of the woods and will make a full recovery, thanks to that little dragon in there," Meg said, a fond smile on her face.

"Ella is a virkin from Elderland," Rivka told her gently.

"She is?" Meg seemed truly interested.

"I've only heard stories about them myself. Ella is the first I've ever encountered, but she is a very good huntress. Neither Liam nor myself knew of her healing abilities until today," Rivka admitted.

"I figured with the wings and the magic," Meg said. "Well, I've never seen a baby dragon before. I just assumed she was one."

"Baby dragons are huge," Rivka told the woman. "I've seen them. They are as big as a man or even larger. I think virkin stay about the size of a large housecat. Ella is young for her kind, but she is about as big as she's going to get, I believe."

"Amazing," Meg said as they finished up the dishes. "I had no idea there were such creatures in other lands."

"The world holds many wonders," Rivka agreed kindly as they both dried their hands.

"I bet you've traveled a lot," Meg probed gently, but Rivka didn't mind humoring her curiosity.

"I am Jinn. I traveled a great deal when I was younger, but we've come home, finally, to Draconia, and I hope to make my home somewhere along the coast, once this job is done," she answered honestly. She hadn't quite decided where she would settle yet, but she liked the sea air and the beach. She knew that she wanted to live in a coastal community, she just hadn't decided which one to make her home base.

"Your job is to track those men that did this to our village?" Meg's voice turned hard.

Rivka didn't blame her. She nodded. "If you can tell me about them. Anything you saw or heard. It could be helpful. We are trying to determine if the leader of these pirates is in this group or if he went along one of the other roads out of Tipolir."

"There was a man the others called *Captain* when they thought nobody was left alive to notice," Meg told her. "I was hiding with my boy, who'd run out into the street when the raiders first came through and got slashed. I grabbed him and took him with me down into the second cellar, right under here, that most folks don't know about and walk right past. Praise the Mother of All, so did the raiders. I could see up through the cracks in the flooring as they came through here and took what they wanted. They tore the place up and killed just about everybody they saw. I kept Sammy quiet with me, and we hid until they were gone." Meg was shivering a bit as she told her tale. "That's when Jalina came and started organizing whoever was left. When I saw her, I knew it was safe to come out."

"Did you see the men? How many were there?" Rivka asked, trying not to put too much pressure on the still-traumatized woman, but she really needed to know what Meg had seen.

"Half a dozen came in here. Those are the ones I saw, including the one they looked to for leadership."

"The captain, right?" Rivka tried to keep her talking, even as she sent an urgent call to Liam, mind to mind. *"Join us in the kitchen as soon as you can. I think you need to hear this."*

Meg nodded, unaware of Rivka's silent communication with Liam. "They were all big brutes with curved blades. Swarthy. And they talked funny. Used some words I just plain didn't know and the ones I understood were heavily accented. Only one seemed to be from Draconia—at least, he spoke like a native of this area. He was young, with a shock of red hair. He had a map, of sorts, that they consulted before they left. The captain seemed to look to the redhead as a guide."

"What did the captain look like?" Liam's voice came from the doorway. He'd entered without a sound but had not come all the way into the room. Still, he had to have heard the last part of the conversation.

"He was a tall man. Strong, but lean. His words were more cultured and not as heavily accented. He sounded like a learned man—or, at least, more so than his fellows. He had black hair, blue eyes, and a scar down the side of his face, from temple to chin." Meg drew the path of the scar on her own face as Rivka watched Liam's jaw clench. "His coat had a double row of golden buttons, and he wore tall boots. He also had a long sword, etched and chased in gold, it looked like. I could see it flash in the light, under the dripping blood." Her gaze turned inward at the horror she had witnessed, and Rivka remained silent. This woman—this whole village—had been through enough pain to last several lifetimes.

Liam came over and put one hand on Meg's shoulder, compassion in his every move. Rivka watched as Meg's eyes met Liam's. There were silent tears running down her face.

"Thank you for telling us all this. I'm sorry to have made you relive that memory, but your information is more important than you know," he told her gently. "The man you saw, the one they called the captain, murdered my wife in cold blood. I have been chasing his trail ever since. He and his men will not get away, this time. Justice we'll be brought to them. For the crimes they have done against me, and others, and especially what they have done here, to your people. You have my word."

Meg's tears dried, and a cold sort of strength showed on her face. "Thank you for telling me that, sir. We of Waymeet will all rest easier knowing that someone is looking to stop these men from visiting this pain on anyone else."

Liam squeezed Meg's shoulder, holding her gaze. Rivka was touched by the way he paused to reassure the woman.

No more words were needed to express his sympathy and resolve. He let Meg go and turned to go out the kitchen door.

Rivka took her leave of Meg and followed Liam. She found him leaning on a low stone wall in the vegetable garden, looking out into the small orchard beyond. His expression was grim.

"You recognized her description, didn't you?" she asked gently.

Liam hung his head, for a moment, then straightened and took a deep breath before answering. "I gave Fisk that scar. And the golden buttons? Few realize they are actually solid gold. It's how he has always carried his fortune. Portable and hidden in plain sight."

"Then, it really was Fisk? We're on the right track?" Rivka's heart raced at the notion. Finally, they had confirmation.

"I doubt even Fisk could conjure such a convincing decoy. It had to be him," Liam agreed, then pounded the wall once with his hand. "Finally!"

Rivka knew exactly how he felt. It was a relief to know that they were finally getting close to their goal. It was also exasperating that they had not caught up with him in time to stop the massacre in Waymeet.

Rivka caught sight of Skelaroth walking down the street heading in their direction. Liam seemed to spot him, as well, then took a look around. They were standing in the garden and fresh fruits and vegetables abounded. Rivka spotted a few items she'd like to take with them and resolved to make up a bag of goodies to take on the road. Now that they knew they were on the right trail, she felt eager to get back to the chase.

Skelaroth seemed to spot them and walked over. *"I have gathered the dead livestock into the field before the town,"* he reported. *"The people here must have already buried their dead. I saw evidence of fresh graves all over."*

"The healer probably made that a priority for the able-bodied," Liam reported. "But moving the horses without other horses to pull their weight was much more difficult.

You have done them a good service, my lord."

Skelaroth bowed his head modestly. *"It was the least I could do."* He looked around at the trees in the orchard. *"Are the reddish fruits edible?"* he asked at last.

"Aye," Liam answered, a faint grin touching his face for the first time since entering the village. "They are peaches. Sweet and tangy." Liam hopped over the wall and walked toward the closest tree, selecting a few of the fruits and picking them. He tossed one in Skelaroth's direction, and the sea dragon snatched it out of the air with his massive jaws.

One bite, and the peach was eaten. Skelaroth tilted his head. *"Those are delicious,"* he told them both.

"Meg said we could pick whatever we wanted to take with us from anywhere in the town. There are few people left and a great deal of ripening fruits and vegetables. They have a surplus at the moment and are glad to share."

"Bring more peaches," Skelaroth said with just a hint of eagerness in his tone.

CHAPTER 11

They left Waymeet an hour later with extra saddlebags, which Skelaroth carried easily, filled with as much fresh produce as they could reasonably expect to eat before it spoiled. They also had a new supply of grains and cured meats that would last even longer. The generosity of the town touched Liam deeply. They had lost so much. So many newly-dug graves marred the village's burial grounds. Yet, they were doing the best they could to go on and had been both kind and gracious to Liam and his party.

Thanks in no small part to Ella. She had healed the village's headman and the baker, as well as several others who had been in grave peril. Jalina had confirmed that Ella had taken on the most serious of her patients and done wonders. Everyone left would heal on their own, given time. Even those that Ella had healed would require plenty of rest to recoup the energies they had lost, but they were out of danger, thanks to the virkin's efforts on their behalf.

Ella slept peacefully after a full meal prepared especially for her by Meg. The woman had been so grateful, she'd prepared a tray with a bit of everything the village had to offer and presented it to Ella when she had completed her work. Ella ate greedily and surprised even Liam when she'd eaten every scrap off that tray. The virkin had consumed easily twice her own weight. Her tummy was a bit distended, but she seemed happy and content. She had curled up in Liam's improvised nest for her almost immediately after she'd finished eating and fallen fast asleep.

Since there were no horses to be had, and they now knew they were on the right trail, they took to the air again. Rivka continued to signal a stop every hour or more often if the terrain below warranted. They could see no tracks from above, but plenty whenever they landed. It was both maddening and encouraging. They knew they were on the right path, but they continued to be behind their quarry, though they were catching up, little by little.

They flew for the rest of the day, but it became apparent that they would not catch up with Fisk and his men that night. Skelaroth spotted a likely campsite, and they took to the ground once more.

"It looked like rain was heading this way," Rivka observed once she was in human form again. She had gone to collect firewood and dumped a small pile of it in the space Liam had cleared for that purpose.

"Could you tell how severe?" Liam asked, inexperienced with what storms looked like from the skyward vantage point, though he had noted the dark clouds on the horizon.

Rivka shook her head. "It looked bad, but I'm not sure how fast it'll get here. Could be tonight. Could be tomorrow. But, if it slows us down, it will also slow Fisk."

"There is that," Liam agreed with a grimace. Catching up with Fisk was an all-consuming need. He had been close before, and each time the slimy character slipped away. Liam vowed that this time would be different. This time, he would have his revenge.

"How are you set for sleeping if the rain comes in the night?" Rivka asked, startling him from his dark thoughts. That she would ask such a thing made him feel sort of warm inside. Nobody had cared for his comfort in a very long time.

"My cloak is waterproof," he reminded her. "I'll be all right."

She looked skeptical as she began to set up the tent he had given her, but didn't say anything. Liam set up the firewood in the circle he had dug for it, but when he went to light it, Rivka stopped him. She merely held out a finger and touched a piece of the wood. Within seconds, a little flame formed near where she touched. She removed her undamaged hand and smiled as the fire caught and spread throughout the little pile of sticks and broken tree branches.

Well, that confirmed what he'd already surmised. Rivka's dragon form breathed fire, and she retained some of that magic, even in her human form. She was something. A beauty and a warrior with an intensity he had never before encountered in a female. She was enchanting, in every sense of the word.

Of course, he could never get into that enchantment. His heart was long gone. Buried with his poor wife. Whatever was left was a shriveled-up stone in his chest, unable to care that deeply again. Or so he truly believed. He also believed that a special woman like Rivka deserved more than that. So much more. She deserved a man who could be totally devoted to her. Not just a roll in the hay. That would only make things awkward between them, and they still had many miles to travel together.

Liam realized it would be the next thing to impossible to try to catch up with Fisk by land. His only advantage was the dragons—both of them. For all his speed and power, Skelaroth was not familiar enough yet, with tracking over land to do this alone. Rivka's skill was needed here. By the same token, though Liam did not doubt her courage or bravery, he would not like to put her comparatively small dragon form up against a half-dozen—at least—of Fisk's cutthroats.

If they were going to be successful in their quest, this would take all of them. Even Ella had played a part in their success to this point. She had done more than he had ever expected of her to help the people of Waymeet. Her insistence on traveling with them began to make sense. She had known she could help, even if Liam had not fully understood her abilities. For that matter, he still didn't know the full extent of her magic. Perhaps she had more tricks up her sleeve. He'd be very intrigued to see whatever she revealed next.

They ate, washed up in the nearby spring-fed pool that had prompted Skelaroth to choose this site, then said goodnight after a short discussion of their plans for the next day. They didn't have to say much. Tomorrow would likely be a repeat of today. Hopefully, without that decimated village to deal with, and perhaps a bit of rain. Still, their primary task has not changed. They would fly and land to check the trail, then fly again, for as long as it took to run their quarry to ground.

Liam slept until the rumble of distant thunder and an increase in the winds woke him sometime after midnight. He scented rain in the air and checked that his gear was safely under the small tarp he'd found in one of the saddlebags from Waymeet. Their food and possessions would be safe from the rain thanks to whichever thoughtful person had packed that bag and given it to them.

Unfortunately, Liam himself would not be as well protected. He huddled in his waterproof cloak, but no matter how he spread the fabric, some part of him was exposed to the whipping wind. Then, the rain started in earnest.

It wasn't just rain. It was a torrential downpour that just kept on and on, without any discernible let up.

"I would put my wing over you," Skelaroth said into his mind, surprising Liam, *"but in this wind, it would be hard to keep in place."*

"Thank you for the thought, my lord. I'll be all right," Liam replied loud enough so that the dragon could hear him. He hadn't realized the dragon was awake, but Skelaroth had claimed to be a very light sleeper, and that was enough for them to leave any potential guard duty to him. A giant dragon was a formidable sentry that few brigands would dare to bother.

The flap of the tent tore out of Rivka's hand as she

opened it. "Come inside," she shouted against the rain. "You can't stay out there in this."

Liam thought about it for only a moment before a gust of wind sent him crawling to the other side of the campsite where the tent had been pitched in the shelter of two large trees with bushes all around. It was the most protected spot from the wind, though the trees might pose some danger should lightning start. So far, though, it was just wind and rain in their area. The lightning and thunder were farther north and heading eastward, away from their position. If it kept going that way, the front that held the worst of the lightning would steer well clear of them.

Clutching the leather satchel in which Ella still slept, Liam made his way over to the tent and lunged inside. He brought all the water that had been on his cloak with him into the tiny space, unfortunately.

"I'm sorry," he said at once. "I'm making everything wet."

Rivka shocked herself with her own lecherous thoughts. He surely *hadn't* meant his innocent words as a double entendre, but she couldn't help but snicker inwardly. He certainly was making things wet…and not just the tent.

"Allow me," she said softly, reaching out one finger and using just a trifle of her magical fire to dissipate the water. It turned to steam, which filtered through the breathable fabric of the tent, thankfully.

"Useful trick," Liam commented, sitting opposite her in the small space of the tent. "Thanks."

While the tent could fit two people comfortably side-by-side for sleep, it wasn't especially roomy. They could not stand, for example, and the winds did shake the fabric.

"Are you sure this thing is going to hold up to that wind?" Rivka asked, eyeing the sides of the tent, which alternately bowed inward, then outward with the wind.

"It should be fine. The people who make these live in the very high mountains on the Elderland border with the Northlands. It's a harsh climate, and their very lives depend on the dependability of their gear. This isn't one of those cheap versions of their work made for the trade market. This is the real thing. It will hold up to ice and snow, so a little rain won't bother it. As for the wind, the weakest point is where the stakes hold it into the ground."

"I put them all in as firmly as I could. The ground here was good," Rivka reported.

"Then, we should be fine."

His gaze met hers in the light of the small lantern she'd picked up in Waymeet. The fire outside the tent had long since gone out in the rain, and the only light to be had was from the lantern she'd hung in the rear corner of the tent.

"Thank you for offering to share your shelter," he said in a low, intimate tone that sent shivers down her spine.

"It was the least I could do," she answered back, hearing the breathiness of her own voice, but unable to do anything about her reaction to having Liam so close. She moved her bedroll to the one side of the narrow space, making room for him. "You might as well make yourself comfortable."

He nodded, removing his cloak and the satchel that held Ella. He peeked inside, and the hint of a smile touched his lips. "She's still asleep," he reported.

"I think, after the work she did in Waymeet, she could sleep through just about anything," Rivka told him, feeling her heart warm at his gentle concern for the virkin.

Rivka lay on her bedroll, leaning up on one side to watch him. She'd arranged herself with her feet toward the flap of the tent, which he'd closed tightly behind him. She's put her boots down there, so they'd be ready when she woke, but also to limit their movement within the tent. After all, they'd been walking the dusty streets of Waymeet all day, and though she'd tried to brush them off before entering the tent, they were still dirty.

Liam removed his boots, as well, following her example and keeping them near the entrance to the tent. The smell of wet leather dominated the enclosed space, and though it wasn't altogether unpleasant, Rivka pointed at the boots, using a bit more of her inner magical fire to dry what she could.

Liam looked at her as the steam rose from his wet boots, one eyebrow raised. "Thank you, once again, milady."

He spread his cloak so that he could have half beneath him and half to tuck over himself. She noted that he kept the open side of his cloak toward the middle of the tent...and her. She told herself not to read anything into that. He only had two choices, so maybe he'd chosen to face her side of the tent randomly. Why that thought depressed her, she refused to acknowledge.

Liam put the bag containing Ella above his head, in the far corner of the tent. The space was narrow, but plenty long enough for his tall frame. He made sure Ella was safe and comfortable, putting the bag on its side and opening the flap so she could get out easily if she wanted to. He was so thoughtful with the virkin. He would have been a thoughtful father, if fate hadn't intervened.

Rivka knew how Liam's only child, Livia, had been raised. He'd been at sea almost constantly while she was growing up, leaving her to the care of nannies and housekeepers. He'd visited, but that was no substitute for being there, Rivka believed. His search for vengeance had cheated both his daughter and himself out of those years. His now famous objections to Livia's mating with two knights only proved, in Rivka's mind, how out of touch he was with who his daughter was...though, he seemed to be learning. He may not like the mating situation, but he'd come to accept it. At least, she thought he had.

Liam began to lay down but paused. "Should I douse the light?" he asked politely.

"Sure," she replied, "I can always relight it if we need it." Being alone, in the dark, in the small tent with the storm raging around them suddenly seemed very intimate.

He blew out the flame in the camping lantern, and it was just as Rivka had feared. The small tent seemed to shrink even more. She stayed where she was, but she could sense

Liam's movements as he settled into his cloak, pillowing his head on one raised arm as he faced her across the short expanse. There was maybe a foot or two between them.

The silk of the tent muffled the sound of the storm, which seemed to have abated a bit since she'd invited him in. The thunder had moved farther away, and the rain came down in a steady beat against the fabric roof just a few feet above their heads.

"The winds seem to have died down a bit," she observed, her voice loud in the darkness.

Liam made a sound of agreement. While Rivka had good night vision due to her dragon half, she could only just make out the general shape of Liam's form beside her. She doubted he could see her at all, so soon after blowing out the lantern.

"I'm sorry to have to impose on you like this," he said finally, regret flavoring his words.

"It's little imposition. It's your tent, after all. Had you not been so thoughtful as to pack it, we would both be out there in the rain, right now," she reminded him.

Rivka didn't mention the fact that she probably would have shifted into her dragon form to wait out the storm. Dragon scale didn't get soaked the way hair and clothing did. She saw no need to point out their differences, yet again. She'd already done that by steaming the water away from his cloak and boots. She cringed. She just wasn't used to dealing with purely human men she found attractive, who already knew her secret.

Being a black dragon meant living in the shadows. Only her family and Clan knew of her abilities. Others might know that black dragons existed in the world, but no one but her Clan knew which of them carried the gift. Not all of the Clan were so blessed. In fact, she had a younger brother who was purely human. The Clan regarded them both equally, thank goodness. Rivka had merely inherited the legacy of Dranneth the Wise while her little brother had not. He was still shaping up to be an excellent swordsman. He'd be a great warrior for the Clan once he was finished growing. As had their father been before him.

In fact, Rivka was the first black dragon born to her family in generations. It had been a surprise all around when she had started shifting at the age of ten. While everyone in the Clan was familiar with dragon shifters, nobody in her immediate family knew exactly what to do with her. She'd been sent to the nearest black dragon for training in her gift, though she'd been allowed to visit her parents for holidays, and they would often travel to see her.

Rivka's upbringing hadn't been precisely like poor Livia O'Dare's. Rivka had always known her parents loved her, cared about how she was doing, and would be there for her in an instant if called. Rivka had lived with a kindly older lady who understood her gift and was able to open the world of flight to her and teach her the ways of her dragon side. She'd been like a second mother—or more like a grandmother, actually. It had been a good childhood, if a bit unorthodox.

"I'm just as glad to sleep in the dry," Liam said, breaking into Rivka's thoughts of the past. "I confess, all the years of being aboard ship with my own quarters have made me softer than I care to admit."

"You?" Soft was not a word that equated in Rivka's mind with anything at all about Liam. He chuckled, and the warm sound out of the dark sent delightful shivers down her spine.

"I'm not as young and adventurous as I once was," he said, his voice coming to her from very near in the darkness.

"You're not old, either, Liam." His name just slipped out without her thinking about it, but it was too late to call it back, and the darkness somehow invited such intimacies…and more. The question was, would he—or, could they—take this any further than just whispering in the dark?

"You're very kind, but I feel ancient next to a youngster like you."

"Just how old do you think I am?" she asked him, feeling suddenly playful.

He remained silent, for a moment, before finally speaking.

"The wisdom of years has taught me never to speculate aloud about a woman's age. Invariably, it gets one into trouble."

She giggled. It had been a long time since such a lighthearted sound came out of her mouth. She liked the way she felt when she was with him. He certainly kept her on her toes. And this midnight conversation was something else—something new between them. She liked it.

"Let's just say I'm a lot older than I look. Remember, Liam, I'm half dragon. We don't age the way regular people do. In fact, I'd hazard a guess that I'm just a bit older than you."

"That's not possible," he told her immediately. "For I am aged in a way that you can never know. Grief has changed me forever."

She couldn't help herself. She reached out in the darkness and put her hand on his shoulder. He tensed under her touch for a brief moment before giving in to the compassion in her gesture.

"I do understand grief," she told him quietly. The rain had died down to a muffled hum on the fabric above their heads. "I have lost those I loved most. Not a mate, but…family." She found it hard to speak the words. Her Clan knew what had happened to her family, but she had never spoken of it to anyone else. "It is a wound that never quite heals."

He sighed. "You do understand," he said finally, placing his hand over hers on his shoulder and squeezing gently. "I'm sorry you had to experience it. Life should be happy, I always thought. Instead, it can become day after day of pain and sorrow."

"It doesn't always have to be like that," she told him gently.

He took her hand in his and brought her palm to his lips, shocking her with the gentle kiss he placed there. Her whole body responded to his touch. If she had been standing, her knees would have wobbled.

CHAPTER 12

Liam didn't know what was driving him. He had resolved to avoid women, but Rivka... She wasn't like any woman he'd ever known. He was powerfully drawn to her. Had been from the first. He'd tried to deny her sensual allure, but given the situation they were in at the moment, it was nearly impossible. Her understanding and compassion were his undoing. He found himself kissing her hand, and it felt so...right.

It shouldn't feel right to touch another woman so intimately. It should be the worst blasphemy. The harshest betrayal of Olivia's memory.

But it didn't feel that way.

On the contrary, touching Rivka felt healing. Like her magic was reaching out to soothe the rough places in his soul. She just made him feel better whenever he was around her. And being here—in the privacy of the dark tent with her while the rain made their dry oasis a secret hideaway—felt more right than anything had in a very long time.

Liam knew she was responding to him, as well. He could hear the slight quaver in her voice, feel the trembling of her fingers in his. He heard the way her breath caught in her throat as he kissed her palm, and he could almost feel the yearning in her soul as her body involuntarily moved closer to his. There was so little space between them to begin with. It wouldn't take much to align his legs with hers, to press against her and feel the length of her fit form against his.

"I must be crazy," he whispered as he drew closer to her, his lips seeking hers. He moved slowly, giving her a chance to slide away, but she didn't. Then, he heard her breathless words.

"Me, too." And then, she reached across the space between them and kissed him.

Sweet Mother of All! She was kissing him and moving into his embrace the way he hadn't even dared to dream about. She was all softness and curves against his body, the clothing she wore to sleep in more delicate than he'd expected.

Liam had noted her swords placed at the side of the tent within easy reach. Her light leather armor was at the head of the tent. What remained was soft against his hands. Loose pants and blouse in dark colors that she habitually wore under her armor and cloak. It slid aside under his questing touch, and then, he felt the tingle as his fingers touched her skin. A little sparkle of what felt like magic tickled his senses for a quick moment, then he felt the heat and softness of her creamy skin, and he was lost. Completely lost.

All thought ceased. Only sensation was left. Feeling and hunger. Passion and need.

Rivka couldn't believe the fire racing through her veins. It had little to do with the familiar magical dragon fire. No, this was a flame of desire conjured by only one man. Liam's touch started something undeniable. Unquenchable. Unimaginable.

Whatever this was, it was pure and…good. Dangerous, too, she knew. But, oh, so tempting. Rivka could not resist. She'd been so fascinated with Liam since the moment they first met. Traveling with him these past days had brought her new knowledge of the man behind the reputation. He was everything they said of him…and more. He was kind and gentle when the spirit moved him. He was patient with Ella and the children of Waymeet. He was sympathetic and strong. Clever and incredibly attractive in every way that mattered to Rivka.

She had wanted him in passion but had never thought it would be possible. His devotion to his dead wife was legendary. That he should unbend enough to make a move on Rivka spoke volumes about need and attraction. She didn't mind. She felt the same. She knew going into this encounter that it probably wouldn't last past the dawn.

Liam's heart was already taken. Possessed by a dead woman who could not give it back. If Liam wanted to reclaim his heart to give to another, it would have to be up to him. Rivka knew deep down that he wasn't there yet. That place of peace, justice and forgiveness hadn't arrived for him. Maybe someday. But not this day.

Still, she would not deny him—or herself—the momentary passion that had sprung up between them. Rivka was no foolish girl to build daydreams around a man who could never be hers. She would take what she wanted—and what he could give—and be content. She had to. There was no other choice.

Rivka helped him rid her of her clothes and then pushed at his. He helped in return until their pants lay in a tangle near their feet and their tops lay in a similar pile, over her armor at the head of the long, narrow tent. His cloak and her bedroll made a soft, warm pad beneath them as they came together, skin to skin, body to body, heart to... Well, not heart to heart. Maybe person to person was a better thought to have at this moment, Rivka realized.

They were both needy. Both feeling the same wild attraction. That much was clear.

When he touched her with such fierce tenderness, she knew she was lost. His lips roamed down her throat to her breasts, licking, sucking and even gently nipping her skin in a way that drove her wild. He paused there, spending time enticing her, exciting her senses and ensuring that she was ready for more.

Rivka was impatient by the time his hands drifted lower to

cup her butt. She didn't want to waste time, but she was learning that Liam was a thorough lover. He stroked her legs with his hands and lifted her top knee over his thigh as she faced him. They were both laying on their sides in the dark space meant only for them. Rain thumped on the fabric over their heads, but nothing else mattered but the two of them, together, sharing these precious moments of passion.

His fingers sought and found the evidence of her desire. He traced little circles around the nub at the apex of her thighs, and she couldn't help the moan that escaped her lips as he caressed that sensitive spot. Then, his seeking fingers swept lower and found their target wet and ready.

Liam thrust one digit gently within her, as if testing her readiness. Then, he added another finger, stretching her, driving her need higher. She liked what he was doing, but what she wanted was something more substantial than his hand. She wanted him. His cock. His possession. His passion.

And she wanted it now. All of it. Everything he could give her. Even if she knew the one thing she wanted most was off limits. His bruised and battered heart would be forever out of her reach.

But it didn't matter. Nothing mattered at this moment but the satisfaction that was just out of reach.

"Don't make me wait," she whispered, need getting the better of her. She'd never begged a man for anything in her life, but Liam was coming damned close to making her do just that.

"Are you sure?" He paused long enough to ask, surprising her. One part of her mind didn't want him to say anything, lest the mood disintegrate and he pull away. But he was cognizant enough to make sure she was on board with his plans, and he wasn't stopping. Maybe he was a bit more aware of what they were doing here than she'd thought.

Maybe it wasn't all mindless need and hunger denied too long. Maybe she wasn't just any warm body in the dark night. Maybe Liam was more present here, making love to Rivka—not just some random female form. The thought touched something deep inside, stirring the forbidden hope that she'd thought she'd already dealt with.

Silly girl. Liam wasn't for keeps. Not as long as Olivia held his heart.

Rivka would just take what she could get of him and be content. Right?

"I'm sure," she replied.

He had no idea of the thoughts in her mind, and she'd keep it that way. This was a complicated thing, but it didn't have to be that way. It could be just sex. Great, hard, sweaty sex. She would do her best to keep it to that and let them both return to normal—or as near as they could get—in the morning.

She rolled to her back and opened her thighs. She couldn't be any more welcoming if she'd drawn up a sign. Liam's face was clearly visible to her night vision. She doubted he could see as much, but he definitely seemed to understand the invitation before him. Liam came to her and took his place between her legs.

Then, there was no more time for words, or even thought. Liam joined with her in a long, slow glide that filled every dark space within her soul she'd never known was empty. He paused, pumping gently, making sure of her comfort before he seated himself to the hilt. Then, he waited.

"All right?" he asked, his whisper gentle, though a bit strained.

"Fine. Keep going," she urged him, earning a dark chuckle from him as he began to move.

The friction of him made her gasp as delicious sensations coursed down her spine, tingling all the way through her body. He was the focus of all that pent-up power. If she didn't know better, she would call it the magic. The magic of two bodies coming together in passion.

He began a steady rhythm, designed, it seemed, completely for her pleasure. Oh, she got the impression that he was enjoying it too, but he was focused on her. She could see it in the gleam of his eyes. Feel it in the thrust of his hips. Sense it with everything that made her both dragon and woman.

This man above her was concentrating hard on making sure that the woman he was pleasuring walked away from the experience with a smile on her face. Make that a big, sappy grin. She'd never had a man so totally involved in making sure she got the best from him that she possibly could.

The experience, like the man, was incredibly special. He made her feel like a queen. Like a femme fatale. Like…he cared. Just the tiniest bit. And that thought was what broke her.

Rivka came with a groan as she clutched at his shoulders. She shook with spasms of delight as he held her, pulsing deep. And, when she started to come down from the climax, he started it, all over again, pushing her higher.

She hadn't thought she had anything left after that first orgasm, but he proved her wrong. Again. And again.

The pleasurable peaks began to blur together as he increased the power and frequency of his thrusts. He was like a man possessed as he drove them to the pinnacle of desire. The highest peak she had ever reached.

She shattered around him, and this time, he came with her. Groaning deep in his chest, he held himself tight within her, his hips grinding the last bit of pleasure out of them both. At length, when they were still both breathing hard and the planet seemed to begin rotating again beneath them, he drew back. He didn't go far. Liam bent to place a tender kiss on her forehead, the gesture bringing tears to her eyes.

He disengaged and lay down beside her, tucking her into his arms. He draped his own cloak over them both, considerate to the last. That was all she remembered before she fell fast asleep.

If she woke in the night, Liam was always there. Twice more, he joined with her body, taking her from behind and once on their sides. He was an inventive lover, with what she took to be vast experience. He knew just how to touch her to make her fly to the heavens, and just what to do to keep her there as long as he wished.

Rivka had never known another night like it. Intimate and full of pleasure the likes of which she had never experienced before. They barely spoke, and that seemed appropriate. The night was dark, and in this one small private space, it held no terrors. Only passion and acceptance. Desire and fulfillment.

And, when the dawn came, the rain had stopped, and Rivka wasn't surprised to find herself alone. Liam was gone from the tent, leaving no trace of himself behind, except one very satisfied woman and a memory that would linger for the rest of her life.

When Rivka emerged from the tent a bit after sunrise, Liam almost dreaded what might come next. He'd forgotten himself last night. He'd forgotten all the vows he had made and the quest he had yet to fulfill. For a few stolen hours, he had been just a man. A man, in the gloomy night, with a beautiful woman.

Nature had taken its course, in a way he had not allowed in far, far too long. He felt a bit of guilt this morning, but not as much as he had expected. The specter of his lost wife didn't haunt him with regret. No, it was as if something had shaken loose last night. Something that had been closed off within his own soul. He didn't know what it was. He hadn't even known it existed. But something had definitely changed in the darkest hours of the night.

Liam didn't yet know if these changes would be good or bad. He was confused, to say the least.

He feared he had hurt Rivka last night. Not physically—he'd been careful with her—but emotionally. He would hate to see pain in her eyes that he had put there. It would hurt him, as well.

But he needn't have feared she would face him with recriminations. When Rivka finally got up, she was nonchalant. He was surprised by the reaction, but grateful for it. Perhaps their encounter hadn't meant much to her. Perhaps she was one of those females who took her pleasure wherever and whenever they found it and didn't think about the future.

Liam had little experience with such women, but he knew they existed. Olivia hadn't been like that at all. She'd been a virgin when they married and had never been with a man other than Liam. He'd been true to her since their marriage... Until last night.

Liam shook his head. No use dwelling on the guilt he didn't feel, right now. Not when Rivka was packing up the tent and starting her day.

"You were up early," she commented, her tone light as she joined him by the small fire he'd lit using some dry sticks he had found, the folded tent in her hands. Thankfully, the Elderland silk had not picked up much moisture from the storm and still fit easily within its little carrying pouch.

"Ella woke just at dawn and wanted to go out," he told her, trying to match her casual tone. "I made breakfast," he told her, offering her the small pot they'd picked up in Waymeet that held cooked grains.

Although they had to get back on the trail as quickly as possible, Liam had reasoned that, after the night they'd just spent together, the least he could do was make a hot breakfast for Rivka. Her gaze lit up when she saw the cooked oats to which he had added the last of the berries. She took the warm pot from his hands with a greedy grin and grabbed the polished wooden spoon he'd used to stir the concoction while it cooked.

She took her treasure over to the sea dragon-sized dry spot on the ground, her brows rising as she looked around. "He didn't budge all night, did he?" she commented.

"That's where I got the dry sticks for this fire," Liam told her. "He was already gone when I woke, but he hadn't been gone long."

"He's probably hunting up breakfast for himself, though he had a really good feed in Waymeet," Rivka said pensively, between bites of her hot cereal.

"Is that him?" Liam asked, pointing into the distance. The sea dragon—if that speck in the sky really was him—was coming out of the sun, making it difficult to see. At least for Liam. For all he knew, Rivka had dragon vision even in her human form and could probably see a lot better than he could.

"It is," Rivka said, licking the spoon of the last remnants of her breakfast. "And he's got company. Another dragon. One of ours," she reported. "With a knight on top." She scraped the pot before stowing it and smiled up at Liam. "Looks like the cavalry has arrived. Or at least a small part of it."

Liam and Rivka continued working to pack their gear while the dragons came in for a landing. There was just enough room in the clearing to accommodate both large dragons, and the man on the back of the newcomer hopped down easily while Skelaroth made the introductions.

"I went out to scout ahead and crossed paths with Findlror and Stevan," Skelaroth said to all of them. *"This is Lady Rivka, Captain Liam O'Dare and Mistress Ella,"* Skelaroth concluded, introducing them each in turn.

"I'm Stevan, in case that wasn't completely obvious," said the young man, striding forward and holding out his hand to shake hands with Liam, since he was closest, then doing the same for Rivka. Liam had instinctively put himself between her and the newcomers, even though he knew she was half-dragon. Old habits died hard.

"I'm Liam," he told the other man. Rivka gave her name, as well. Then, Liam pointed to the low-hanging tree branch where Ella had perched. "That is Ella," Liam added helpfully, noting the knight's surprise.

Stevan was game, though. He went over to Ella and smiled at her. "Pleased to make your acquaintance, Misstress Ella," he said to the virkin.

Ella stopped preening long enough to look at the young man, then said, very deliberately in all their minds. *"Nice to meet you, too."*

The periwinkle blue colored dragon seemed shocked by Ella's words. He craned his neck closer. *"Greetings. I am*

Findlror," the strange dragon said to the little virkin, ignoring the people for now.

Ella blinked up at the giant dragon. *"Hi,"* she said, sounding a bit shy. *"You're a pretty color."*

The dragon chuckled at that, sending smoke rings skyward with his mirth. *"Thank you, my lady. You have a beautiful mix of colors yourself."*

"Lord Findlror, if you are heading anywhere near the capital, we have urgent news," Rivka broke into the mutual admiration, and the blue dragon refocused its gaze on her. Liam caught the way the dragon's eyes widened when he got a good look at Rivka.

"What is it you wish of us, my lady?" The dragon was very respectful of Rivka, bowing its head in her direction.

CHAPTER 13

"The crown needs to know what has happened in Waymeet and about our current quest. We don't have much time, so both of you—" Rivka motioned to the knight and his dragon "—had better listen carefully." She then launched into an account of the pirate Fisk and his group and what they had done to the village of Waymeet. Liam put in a few details when warranted but otherwise let her make the report.

Stevan and Findlror both listened with grave intent, speaking only to ask pertinent questions. They were as serious as Liam could wish and seemed to know what to do without being told. Liam had never interacted with knights or dragons much before recent times, but he was starting to understand that the men who were chosen as knights were not just fighters, they were thinkers, as well. Which, he supposed, was a good thing, considering they were agents of the crown authorized to mete out justice when warranted. They had great authority and near-autonomy to act in the king's stead. It was important to have an intelligent man in such a position.

Liam had never thought much about it before, but now that his daughter had married into the Southern Lair, Liam supposed he would have to learn to live with it. And with the men who now held his daughter's future happiness in their hands. Both of them. Liam shook his head, preferring not to think about that aspect too closely.

"We probably flew right over them," Stevan said, disgust clear in his tone. "We thought we saw a large party of men on horseback, making haste to the north, but only from a distance. When we neared, they seemed to have vanished. I assumed they had gone off the road while they were momentarily obscured by a hilltop."

"More likely, it was magic," Rivka told the knight. "We know Fisk has some ability to hide his trail by magical means. We don't know how he does it, but we have it on good authority that he does."

"I didn't know such things were possible," Stevan replied, shock evident on his young face. Liam thought the knight was no older than his daughter—if that. He was quite a young person to have such responsibility, but he seemed to be handling it well.

"Fisk has traveled widely," Liam put in. "He has the knowledge of many lands, and the men with him are from all over. No doubt, they know of many things that are foreign to this land."

Stevan nodded, as did his dragon, who had seemed to be in conversation with Skelaroth until this point. Both dragons were now watching the trio of humans talking.

"We should make haste to the north where Sirs Findlror and Stevan saw the party of pirates," Skelaroth declared.

"While we go to the capital with all possible haste to carry your message," Findlror added.

Stevan turned to his fighting partner, his mouth open in clear surprise. "I thought we would help them with the fight," the knight objected.

Findlror shook his head. *"The news is too important. And I pity any party of pirates with two dragons and a man-o-war on their trail. We will send help, but we cannot delay getting this news to the king."*

"Two dragons?" Stevan looked confused. "But I thought you said we were going to the capital."

"We are," Findlror replied, his gaze moving to Rivka.

She sighed. "He means me," she said. "I am of the Black Dragon Clan."

Stevan's eyes widened, and he seemed to regard Rivka in a new light. From his reaction, Liam supposed that the knights had been let in on the secrets of the Jinn black dragons, though they seemed unable to recognize them in their human form. Not so, the dragon. Findlror had clearly understood what Rivka was the moment they met.

Whether or not the knight understood Rivka's claim of being part of the Black Dragon Clan actually meant that she could turn into a dragon or not, Liam wasn't sure. Still, the young knight seemed content with her words and quickly took his leave, promising to deliver their news to the king.

Stevan climbed onto the handy knee the dragon bent for him to use as a step. Findlror walked a bit away for some room to take off. A running start and a few flaps of his enormous wings, and they were in the air, winging straight for the capital.

"How long do you suppose it will take them to get word to the king?" Skelaroth asked as they watched the other dragon fly away.

"By nightfall, I should think," Rivka replied, also watching the knight and dragon fade away into the sunny sky. When they were out of sight, she turned to Skelaroth and Liam. "Now, my friends, we have a clear target. With what Stevan and Findlror told us, we should be able to locate Fisk and his men within an hour or two. The question is, how do we approach?"

"Head on," Skelaroth said immediately. *"They will not expect attack from the sky."*

Rivka looked like she wanted to object but held her peace. Finally, she shrugged. "I don't know of a better way to make our attempt at stopping them, so I guess that'll be the plan." She held up one hand as Skelaroth nodded his head in approval of her words. "I will hang back, though. Just in case. I think you should make the first run over their heads, once we locate them, and see what happens."

Skelaroth's large eyes narrowed, and he nodded more slowly this time. *"That is, perhaps, wise. However, you, Liam, will be on my back unless I stop to let you off first. I don't think that would be wise, though. I'd have to stop well away from Fisk in order not to be seen, and you would probably not be able to catch up on foot."*

"If it's all the same," Liam said at once, "I'd prefer to stay with you, Lord Skelaroth, no matter the danger. I've been chasing Fisk a long time, and I'm the only one of us three who knows what the man actually looks like. We need to know for certain that we have *him*, and not some imposter decoy."

"A good point," Rivka allowed.

"You are a fine and brave man, Captain O'Dare," Skelaroth complimented him. *"It would be my honor to carry you into battle with me."*

"The honor is mine, I assure you," Liam replied with formality. Dragons were big on tradition and courtesy, and while he was dealing with Lord Skelaroth, he would do everything he could to be as gracious as possible under these extraordinary circumstances.

"Good," Rivka cut in, her tone eager. "Now that's settled, we should be on our way without delay."

"Agreed." Skelaroth's tone was laced with a grim sort of finality. They all knew their quest might soon be at an end. How it would end, exactly, they couldn't be quite sure, but they all hoped for the best.

Liam mounted up, using the knee Skelaroth bent for him to use as a sort of ladder after having seen the knight and his partner do the same. Liam had to admit it was much easier to get aboard with the small movement. He'd been climbing onto Skelaroth's back in a very haphazard way until now. It just goes to show, Liam thought, you can take the swabbie off his boat and stick him on a dragon's back, but that doesn't necessarily make him a knight.

They flew cautiously for the first hour and even more carefully the second. They stopped frequently to scout from the ground, growing ever closer to their quarry. Rivka and Skelaroth flew low to the treetops, doing their best to skim the ground. It was dangerous flying, but Skelaroth surprised Rivka at his agility. After all, she knew, he hadn't been flying over land much in his life. He was more at home under the waves, which was why he was so much more muscular than land dragons.

Oh, they were all strong and lithely muscled, but the sea dragons had greater resistance in the water than their counterparts who only flew in air. As a result, they were a bit bulkier in the shoulder area, not that most regular people would notice. Lair folk might. And other dragons, of course, but Rivka was a dragon herself, as well as human. She appreciated the subtle color patterns on the sea dragons' hides that she'd seen. They weren't colored the same as land dragons, but the differences weren't just skin deep. There were other subtle differences that set them apart from their land cousins.

They flew and landed several more times before Rivka realized they were very close, indeed, to their prey. So close, in fact, that she could hear their horses' hooves in the distance.

"*You hear that?*" she asked, not bothering to shift from her dragon form. "*That is the sound of hooves pounding along this dirt road,*" she said, mainly for Skelaroth's benefit. The sea dragon was a fast learner, but there were many things he had yet to encounter on land. "*We are very close. But they'll have to slow to a walk to make it over that rocky pass on the next hill. We can confront them there.*"

"*Even if we cannot see them?*" Skelaroth asked. The fact that Fisk and his party were using some sort of magic to hide them from being seen from the air had been a problem all along, but especially now that they were closing in on their prey.

"I would bet that once we're close enough, whatever magic they're using will fail," Liam put in. "I have seen much in my travels, including a great deal of magic that is unknown to this land. Most of it falls apart once uncovered. I'd bet this is something of that sort."

"*I hope you are correct,*" Skelaroth said, shaking his head. "*For you will be with me as we swoop down on our prey. Say so now if you wish me to leave you here.*"

"I haven't changed my mind, but thanks for the offer," Liam assured the sea dragon.

"*Good, then.*" Rivka backed up to get a running start. "*Hear the change in the hoofbeats? They're slowing down to crest the hill. Let's fly.*"

As they flew closer to their target, Rivka dropped back to observe, as they have agreed. She was much smaller than the sea dragon. If Skelaroth was ineffective against the pirate group, Rivka wouldn't be able to do much better. The only difference between herself and Skelaroth was that she had flame. If he ran into trouble, she could at least try to run interference, so he could get away.

They flew closer, low to the treetops to give them the stealthiest possible approach. As they'd hoped, once they got close enough, the men on horseback were all too easy to see. Skelaroth winged upward so as to perform a swooping dive. Rivka hung back, watching from a reasonably safe distance.

Skelaroth's skydance was a thing of beauty. He rose and then dove, feet first, roaring defiance. The horses screamed and scattered, some dumping their riders before racing off, others taking their hapless riders with them into a frenzied flight as they saw a dragon descending on them, claws out for the kill.

It was an awesome sight, except for the tickle of magic that came from one of the riders who had not moved too far. His horse stood beneath him, as if nothing in particular was happening. That was odd enough. No horse, no matter how well trained, wouldn't show at least some kind of reaction to Skelaroth's display. The beast had to be under some kind of spell. One of control or compulsion. If such a thing existed.

Then, the rider started waving his hands in the air. This didn't look good. No, it didn't look good, at all. The rider drew back both hands, and an evil-looking red fireball formed between his palms. Dark red fire. Not healthy orange or yellow, or even blue, but deep blood red.

"*Skelaroth! Beware!*" Rivka shouted a mental warning, but it was too late. Even as she moved in and gathered her own flame, she knew she would be too late.

The mage—for that was what the man on the horse must be—loosed the evil fire at Skelaroth, hitting him squarely in the center of his right wing. The sea dragon screamed and plummeted like a comet toward the east, smoke leaving a trail in the sky behind him.

Rivka roared and prevented the sorcerer from loosing another shot. She breathed flame on the man and his horse from above, but much to her dismay, it flowed around him and his beast, as if there was a bubble of protection surrounding him. She could not touch him with her fire, but she knew, from what had just happened to Skelaroth, that she was in danger from the mage's evil red flame.

She winged away as fast as she could, heading east, following Skelaroth's trail. She spared a look behind her to see the pirates regrouping and speeding off to the northwest as fast as their terrified mounts would take them. Last in the line of fleeing pirates was the sorcerer. He was acting as their rear guard, and the expression on his pugnacious face told Rivka that he felt triumphant at bringing down the mighty sea dragon.

Enjoy it while you can, she thought. *Your victory will not last long. This, I vow.*

*

Liam had watched carefully over the ridge of Skelaroth's neck, hoping to spot Fisk as the sea dragon had made a majestic dive toward their quarry. It had been unlike anything Liam had ever experienced. Even being on the ocean during the wildest gale could not compare with swooping down out of the clouds on a dragon's back. For one brief shining moment, Liam met Fisk's gaze and then…

Havoc. Chaos. Tumbling and the smell of scorched dragon scales. Liam held tight as Skelaroth was hit by…something…and plunged like a meteor across the sky, leaving a smoke trail behind him.

"Skelaroth!" he shouted, to no avail. The dragon's wings were out, but it was clear from a single glance that one of them had been badly damaged. Skelaroth was out of control, gliding all too quickly to an uncontrolled landing. This was going to hurt.

Ella was peering out of her nest, and Liam opened the flap, reaching down for her with one hand. "Get yourself clear if you can, sweetheart," he told her, tossing her as far as he could from the dragon. He watched for a moment to make sure she got her wings under her and she was away safely. At least she wouldn't get hurt by what was about to happen. The ground was rushing up at him too fast. Too close.

Trying his best to mitigate the damage, Liam jumped off the dragon's back when he judged he was about fifteen feet off the ground. With a bit of luck, he thought he might tumble clear of Skelaroth's untidy collapse. Many years spent at sea had given Liam a nimbleness that most men never learned, and he was able to roll with the landing, jumping up unhurt, if a bit sore in the places that had come into hard contact with the ground.

Skelaroth was not so fortunate. The dragon was down. Smoke rising from his wing, which was tattered in places. Raw and bleeding. And, worst of all, Skelaroth looked unconscious. Liam ran to the dragon's head and called to him, looking for signs of life. He was alive, but he had been knocked for a loop by something.

Ella landed on top of one of the horns adorning Skelaroth's scaled head. She looked concerned, and Liam worried that she might expend too much of her own energy if she tried to heal the giant dragon. He was about to say something to the virkin when Rivka landed with a gust of wind from her shiny black wings.

She shifted shape as she moved, walking up beside him on two human legs. She knelt at Skelaroth's side, next to Liam.

"Has he roused at all?" she asked, sounding worried.

"No," Liam had to report. "What should we do?" If anyone knew how to deal with an injured dragon, it would be Rivka.

She seemed to take stock for a moment before deciding on a course of action. "Right." Rivka nodded. "The first thing is to straighten out his wings and make him as comfortable as possible. It'll be easier to do that before he wakes up."

Liam stood as she did, and they set to work together, untangling the untidy heap of the most injured wing first. Skelaroth had come down in a large clearing, thankfully, where there was enough room to stretch him out. Rivka shifted back to her dragon form when they started working on Skelaroth's other side, needing the greater strength of that shape to roll Skelaroth's bulk off the wing so they could stretch it out.

The left wing was mostly unharmed. It was the right one that had a hole punched through the delicate membrane of skin and scales. Liam looked at it and wondered if the mighty sea dragon would ever fly right again.

"It looks worse than it is," Rivka said quietly, into his mind. *"Once he wakes up, we'll be able to do something about it."*

"What can I do to help?" he asked.

"Make camp. He's not going anywhere tonight, and we're far from the pirates. Let's get us all as comfortable as we can possibly get, and then, we'll go from there."

He liked the sound of her plan and quickly set about following her very sensible suggestion. Rivka lay down next to Skelaroth's head, keeping watch over him. Ella perched on one of the horns on his head. That left Liam to set up the tent and make a fire pit. He had the bags with most of their provisions on him, so it wasn't hard to get things set up.

"Do you want dinner?" Liam asked of Rivka, who hadn't moved from Skelaroth's side or changed to her human form.

"No, thanks. I'm going to stay like this until he wakes up. There's

something that will help that I can only show him in this form."

"Aren't you hungry?" Liam insisted. "I could hunt for something for you."

"You're very kind, but dragons can go several days without eating. When I'm in this form, I'm a lot less fragile than when I wear my human skin." She moved a little, resettling her head on her foreleg. *"In fact, you take the tent tonight. I'll be fine here, with the big guy."*

"Any idea when he might wake?" Liam asked, trying not to worry, though Skelaroth didn't look good at all.

"I'm not sure, but I'm hoping it's soon," Rivka replied.

"Soon," Ella echoed. *"Be soon."*

Both Liam and Rivka looked at the little virkin, perched on one of the horns on Skelaroth's head. Liam went over to her.

"Do you know something, sweetheart?" he asked the virkin gently.

She fluttered her wings and gave him what looked a bit like a smile. *"Know lots of things!"* she said happily. *"But know most that Skel will wake soon. Big headache. Big ouch."*

Sure enough, a few minutes later, Skelaroth stirred. He opened first one eye, then the other, but did not move. Rivka was right there, at his side, and Liam was on the other.

"How do you feel?" Liam asked gently.

"Awful," Skelaroth replied.

CHAPTER 14

"Do you know how to summon the dragon's breath?" Rivka asked Skelaroth in a quiet tone. She deliberately included Liam and Ella in her thoughts. She wanted them to know what was about to happen, if she could get Skelaroth to participate in his own healing, because it would affect everyone around him.

"I have heard tales, only," Skelaroth replied. *"It is not something we use under the waves."*

"I suppose that makes sense," she had to allow. *"It's not hard. I will show you the way, and if you can manifest your own magic, it should go a long way toward healing the damage to your wing."*

"You think so?" he asked, sounding very tired and not very confident.

"I know so," she told him, wanting to imbue him with certainty. He had to believe he would fly again, or it might never happen. Skelaroth simply had to participate in his own restoration. *"Can you feel the magic gathering around me?"* she asked, beginning to call the magic that was every dragon's right.

"I sense it," Skelaroth said, a tiny spark of interest in his tone. Good.

"Can you do the same?"

"I..." Skelaroth seemed to struggle for a moment, then

she felt his magic rise—and it was mighty. This could work even better than she'd hoped. *"I think I have it,"* he said, speaking more easily as a fog rose all around them.

If she'd been in her human form, Rivka would have smiled. *"I believe you do,"* she said softly, so as not to interrupt the large dragon. *"Now, focus that energy on the things that hurt most. Let the fog envelope you and make you whole."*

Rivka sent a private word to Liam, who had rather sensibly retreated to the tent area. *"This will go on for some time, and it may affect you and Ella, as well. Don't be alarmed. This is pure, strong and good magic. It cannot harm you, though it may cause unexpected reactions."*

"That sounds ominous," Liam said quietly, his words just reaching her dragonish ears. She had to chuckle, sending smoke rings up through the fog that was growing dense and potent around the sea dragon and their camp.

"Never fear. It will be fine. You'll see," she reassured him before turning her attention back to Skelaroth.

Having summoned the dragon's breath, Skelaroth had begun directing it as she had suggested. His right wing had taken the most damage, so she moved closer to it to keep an eye on his progress. The dragon's breath manifested as a grayish fog that billowed and wove mystical patterns around the dragon's wing and through the air. Into this healing smoke, the virkin flew.

Rivka's first impulse was to chase the small creature away, but she stopped herself from doing so, remembering Ella's amazing healing ability in the town of Waymeet. Ella's magic was many-colored and sparkling against the grayish fog. She flew into the patterns of healing and wove her own magic into them, making them stronger and much more potent. Rivka had never seen anything like it. The virkin continued to surprise her with its instinctive abilities and incredibly generous heart.

With Ella's help, the healing was progressing at a record pace. What Rivka had assumed would take several days of treatment was occurring in just minutes as Ella seemed to weave the missing flesh into being, out of the magical fog. It didn't seem possible, yet it was happening right before her eyes.

The magical fog was having an effect on Rivka, as well. It renewed her. Reenergized her. It made her a little horny, too. Rivka tried to be philosophical about it. The effect of the dragon's breath was often arousing to those who were not badly injured. Perhaps Liam was feeling some of its effects, as well. If so, maybe they could ease each other's bodies as they had the night before. Even with the magical healing, Skelaroth would not be flying this night. He would be weary after expending so much of his magic. He would require sleep, possibly well into the next day, or even days. There was just no way to predict how long it would take him to sleep it off.

Deciding to limit her own exposure, Rivka changed back into her smaller human form. It was Skelaroth who needed the healing vapors the most. She would not interfere with his getting the most benefit he could by staying in her larger guise. Ella dipped and dove, winding her own magics in among the gray mist that was Skelaroth's. At length, she began a more circuitous dance, flying the length of the sea dragon's long body, pausing for an aerial pirouette around his head before coming to a landing again, on one of his horns, which seemed to have become her favorite perch.

"You can let the mist dissipate now," Rivka crooned to Skelaroth, standing close to his head. "The majority of the work is done. You can rest easy, my friend. You've done well."

Skelaroth gave her a sleepy eye-blink before his head lolled slightly and he was asleep. Rivka stepped closer to look at Ella.

"Are you all right?" she asked the virkin. "You did very well, too, Mistress. You are full of surprises, aren't you?" Rivka reached out her hand, and Ella leaned into it, accepting a scratch behind her ears with a weary virkinish smile.

"*Skel needed help,*" Ella said quietly. "*I help.*"

"Yes, you did. You helped him very well. Thank you," Rivka praised the small creature. "Can I get you anything? Are you hungry? Thirsty?"

"Need sleep," Ella said, shaking her head slowly.

"Do you want me to carry you to the satchel where Liam made your nest?"

Ella shook her head. *"Sleep here. Near Skel."*

Rivka nodded slowly. "If that is your wish. Do you want a scarf or something to keep you warm?"

"Am warm," she claimed, her eyes blinking sleepily. *"Night."* And then, the little virkin joined Skelaroth in slumber, still perched on one of the horns on his head.

With both non-humans asleep, that just left Rivka and the captain…and a growing, aching need inside her. Would he welcome her into his bed again, or had that just been a one-time thing? She turned to find him watching her with half-lidded eyes. His expression spoke of intimacies. Of sex.

Hallelujah!

Liam felt strange. Energized. Vigorous. Horny.

He'd never experienced the kind of fog that had quickly risen to envelop their camp. He knew it was magical in nature. Something benevolent and emanating from the dragons, but he wasn't sure exactly what it was. Only that it made him yearn for more of the physical intimacy he'd shared with Rivka the night before.

While last night had been incredible, it was also something he hadn't thought would ever be repeated. He'd come to terms with the idea that he had been alone a long time. Giving in to the attraction between himself and Rivka had almost been inevitable. When he'd had time to think about it today, he'd forgiven himself for being human.

That forgiveness had come a lot easier than he had expected. In years past, when he had even *looked* at another woman, he'd felt guilty for days. Even weeks. Perhaps the easy acceptance of his own human frailty meant something deeper. Either time was finally healing the soul-deep hurts he had suffered when he lost Olivia or he was becoming more accepting of his own situation. Probably, a bit of both.

A third possibility occurred to him, but it was almost too much to comprehend. That was the very tricky proposition that somehow, his involvement with Rivka was meant to be. Preordained. Destiny.

He didn't really see that as a major cause for his transgressions in the dark of the night, but it was a possibility that had flickered through his mind. Some of the cultures he had visited in the east believed greatly in fate. Ella came from such a place, where magic still existed and the hand of the divine was expected to be found regularly interfering in the affairs of men.

As Rivka walked toward him, out of the wispy fog, she immediately captured every bit of his attention. She was a woman warrior who would not be trifled with. She was a delectable female who had once shared her bed with him, and if the heavens were smiling on him, she would do so again…right now.

He didn't bother thinking about right or wrong. Any thought of his deceased wife was wiped right out of his mind by the magic and the desirable woman stalking closer. He knew she was his prey, but he was a willing sacrifice to whatever she had in mind. He was hers to command.

So much different than the way he'd been with Olivia, his interactions with Rivka were in a class by themselves. She made him feel able to put down the mantle of protector. Not to give it up completely, but to share it with a woman for the first time he could ever remember.

She was just so capable. So fierce. So magical. She inspired confidence, and desire, with every step she took.

"I hope you don't mind," she said in a sexy, soft voice, the healing fog blanketing them in their own mysterious world as she walked up to him. "I think I mentioned that the dragon's breath could have…um…side effects."

She stepped close and aligned her hips with his. He was already hard. Wanting. She smiled.

"There are all sorts of lascivious rumors about what knights get up to in their Lairs. Is this why?" Liam firmly refused to think of his only daughter and her two knight mates, but the rumors about Lair life were widespread and had been as long as he'd been alive.

Rivka's head tilted to one side as if considering. "I'm not a Lair dragon, so I can't say for sure. What I can confirm is that we dragons have a powerful drive, and when that drive is triggered, there is little that will keep us from seeking pleasure. Fortunately, the desire isn't triggered all that often. For Lair dragons, only the presence of the dragon's true mate will bring on the urge and then, only if the knights are aligned and have found their own mate. It is widely believed that the Mother of All takes a hand in bringing the right parties together, but," she shrugged, "I've never spent much time among dragons in this land, so I don't know that for certain."

Liam tucked all that new information away in his mind for later consideration. Right now, he had a woman rubbing up against him, and his body was feeling those urges she'd described. He put his arms around her waist and drew her closer against him. She cooperated by looping her hands around his neck and pulling him down into a tempestuous kiss.

She strained against him, and he against her, while their tongues dueled in the most delicious way. She was fire in his arms. The smoky fog that he'd just learned both healed and aroused—Rivka was part of it, and it was part of her. Resistance would have been futile if he'd even thought to resist.

He took her in his arms and carried her to the tent. There was little time to waste. His body was ready, and hers was, as well, if he was any judge of her reactions. After last night, he'd learned pretty thoroughly what aroused her. He would put that new knowledge to good use, but first, he wanted her comfortable. Once he got inside her, he didn't plan to leave in a hurry. In fact, if he stayed within her welcoming depths for the rest of the night, he would be a very happy man, indeed.

Liam picked her up and carried her the short distance to the tent opening. So few men had ever treated Rivka as if she was delicate and feminine. Liam did it without thought, and it made her feel incredibly special. She eagerly entered the tent, and he closed the flap securely behind them. He had already laid out the bedroll and his cloak, similar to how things had been arranged the night before, but separate. He'd made preparations for sleeping. Not seduction.

She smiled. She liked that he hadn't taken anything for granted.

Last night had been his show. Liam had decided when and how and in what position to take her. Rivka had played along, fearing that he could change his mind, at any moment, if he started thinking about his dead wife. Rivka had been reticent to do anything to spoil the mood.

Tonight, all bets were off. They were both under the influence of the dragon's breath, and they had already made love several times the night before. They knew each other, now. They knew each other's bodies and what brought pleasure. There was more to learn, to be sure, but they'd gotten off to a great start last night, and tonight... Well...tonight, if Rivka had her way, she would learn a great deal more about what the good captain liked in bed.

Just the thought made her want to roar, but she held it in. It wouldn't do to scare the poor man off by reminding him he was bedding not only a woman but a woman who was half dragon. She was confident in his desire and the passion that was between them, but she knew it was a lot to take in for a human man to bed a dragon. Tales abounded within her own Clan of men who couldn't handle dragon women long term.

Not that Rivka expected this relationship to last beyond their shared quest. She wouldn't be that foolish, no matter how attached she was becoming to the man. She knew better than to risk her heart on something that could never be.

Rivka pushed Liam down on her bedroll and took charge.

It was time he learned what the dragon lady liked. With the dragon's breath fueling her desire—which was already off the charts where Liam was concerned—Rivka was even bolder than she might normally have been as she undressed him. Straddling his body, she slowed to enjoy the moment when she removed her blouse.

He didn't disappoint. As soon as they were freed, he cupped her breasts in his warm palms, shaping them and tweaking her nipples with a hard, perfect touch that she loved. She lifted herself higher and balanced on first one foot, then the other as she stripped off her pants and under-things until she was bare.

Savoring her task, she slid down his body until she could work the buttons on his pants with her fingers and teeth. She took a moment to run her teeth down the length of his erection through the leather covering, liking the way he jumped a bit under her unexpected touch. She smiled as she drew back, meeting his eyes as she revealed his hard cock, taking it in her hands and squeezing gently.

He growled. The dragon in her liked that. Desire flared in her body, which felt as ready to take him inside as his hardness proved he was to be there. She rose on her knees, moving upward until her pussy spread open just above the tip of his cock. She used her hands to guide him into the right spot as his hands went to her hips, urging, guiding...savoring.

She pressed downward, and he slid into her a little at a time. Delicious.

Unable to hold back the torrent of her desire, she began to move almost immediately. What happened then, became a bit of a blur as she rode him hard and long, taking herself to peak after peak before he joined her in bliss. Then, he flipped their positions and started again.

Her thirsty lover drank, again and again, of the wine of desire, giving her pleasure after pleasure and taking his own whenever she thought she could take no more. He always proved her wrong. They lay together throughout the long night in a tangle of limbs and the honest sweat of passion.

She dozed for a bit, only to wake and want him, all over again. The dragon's breath took its time dissipating, and while it lasted, it fed both their desire and their personal energies. Rivka felt no guilt at indulging herself, knowing that tomorrow they would pay no penalty for this night of athletic lovemaking. They would be rested and ready to go due to the magic of the healing fog.

Skelaroth's first attempt to summon the dragon's breath had been a masterful effort. Rivka would be sure to tell him so when he woke, but seldom had she seen a more potent display of the healing fog than that which Skelaroth had called forth. She wouldn't be surprised if—along with Ella's help—if his wing wasn't almost completely repaired after the fog did its work.

The important thing was that he would be able to fly again, and soon. They still had to neutralize Fisk and that mage he had traveling with him. Rivka had a special reason to want that evil magic worker dead. He'd hurt her friends. He'd caused her great worry. And he'd undoubtedly aided and abetted Fisk's evil work in obtaining the page from Gryffid's book and taking it Northward. There was no way the mage could be on the right side of this conflict.

Therefore, he was the enemy. Rivka knew just what to do with an enemy. Annihilate him.

That thought came straight from her dragon soul, and her human side knew it to be the right course in this situation. Such a creature as that evil mage could not be allowed to go any farther into the homeland of dragons and knights. Her homeland, now. She and all the Jinn would protect Draconia as certainly as the dragons and knights who had lived here all along would. They'd been fighting on the same side, but the Jinn had done so from the shadows.

That time was over. The Jinn had finally stopped traveling and hiding. They might still work from the shadows, but their presence in the land of their ancestors was no secret. They were back, and they had been welcomed at the highest levels. The Jinn Brotherhood was here to stay.

And, as soon as Rivka made love to her sea captain again, she would take what sleep she could get this night and be fresh to battle anew in the morning. She turned to Liam and tackled him to the ground, kissing him playfully. He was ready and willing. She liked that about him. As she liked so much about her dashing sea captain. A man she could so easily come to love…

CHAPTER 15

Liam woke the next morning to discover the cavalry had arrived. So to speak. He had left the tent to check on Skelaroth and Ella, and the hastily made camp, in general. He started out to gather some fresh water to make tea for Rivka and himself when a shadow passed over the sun. More than one shadow, actually.

He looked up to find dragons circling above. Dragons with knights on their backs. And one very familiar sight—a black dragon in among the others. He'd left Rivka sleeping in the tent, so this had to be someone else. One of her relatives, perhaps? Or, maybe, they were about to receive a royal visit.

The dragons were circling and flying lower with each spiral, so Liam reasoned they were coming down to land. He noted that the dragons with knights atop were coming down first, the smaller black dragon somewhere in the middle of the group. Liam assumed that meant the others were protecting the black, which meant it was likely a member of the royal family. Now that he knew their secret, it seemed so obvious. He wondered why he hadn't put two and two together before meeting Rivka.

The clearing Skelaroth had landed in was large enough to accommodate a few more dragons—just barely. Two landed first and, immediately, walked closer to where Liam waited next to Skelaroth. Ella had opened her eyes and looked interested in the proceedings as the two mounted knights took up positions on either side of the fallen sea dragon.

"Greetings," one of them called out. "I am Trevor, and that is my partner, Boros," he nodded toward the other man. "Our dragon partners are Wyndimira and Klathenor."

"I am Liam O'Dare," Liam replied. "The sea dragon before you is Lord Skelaroth, and this," Liam ducked a bit as Ella picked that moment to fly from her perch on Skelaroth's head to land on Liam's shoulder, "is Mistress Ella, my friend and companion."

"Is there not also a woman traveling with you?" Boros asked, his eyes narrowing.

"Aye," Liam nodded. "She is in the tent. Lady Rivka." He didn't say more about her, opting to leave that up to her. Only Rivka knew how much she wanted to reveal of her background to these people. Liam would not presume.

"I'll be out in a minute!" They all heard Rivka's raised voice from within the tent as the sides of the fabric construction started to billow with her movements.

While they spoke, Liam noticed that two more dragons and knights had landed behind the first set. The new pair went to the sea dragon's tail, which was stretched out to the edge of the clearing, and took up guard positions.

"What happened to your dragon companion?" Sir Boros asked, looking at Skelaroth with a practiced glance. This man knew dragons. He also seemed to know what it took to knock one out of the sky.

"I assume the king got our message about the band of pirates heading North along the road to our West." Liam thought it wise not to be too specific about the page from Gryffid's book, just in case these knights didn't know the full story.

Boros nodded his agreement with Liam's statement. "The king received a messenger, and we were dispatched almost immediately."

"Well, we finally caught up to them yesterday afternoon,"

The Captain's Dragon

Liam told the knights and dragons. "Lord Skelaroth dove at the party and scattered most of their horses, but there was one man on a horse that did not move. And the man was able to call some sort of malevolent blood red fireball and launch it at Skelaroth. It hit his wing and made a smoking hole clear through." Liam nodded to the right wing, which was still stretched out as they had left Skelaroth the night before. He had not moved at all, to Liam's knowledge, since passing out after the dragon's breath did its thing.

Sir Trevor whistled through his teeth and frowned in concern at the unconscious sea dragon. The other dragons craned their long necks to see what they could of the damage to Skelaroth's wing.

"He crashed?" Boros asked in a grave tone.

"*We* crashed," Liam corrected him gently. "I threw Ella clear, and she was able to fly to safety on her own. I jumped off about fifteen feet above the ground and rolled clear. Skelaroth..." Liam paused, remembering those moments after they'd made contact with the ground. "He was out for a time, but Rivka helped him summon something she called the dragon's breath, and then, Ella wove her own magic around him. When I went to sleep last night, he was as you see him, now. Unconscious and healing, from all accounts."

"May I?" Boros asked as he climbed down from his dragon partner's back. He made a gesture toward Skelaroth's wing, and Liam nodded, walking with the other knight to inspect the progress of Skelaroth's wound.

"The wing looks mended," Trevor said, surprising Liam. He hadn't known the other knight had descended from his seat atop his dragon. The two dragons had come up behind the men and were also looking closely at Skelaroth's wing.

"There was a great deal of fog, and Ella helped." Liam reached up to scratch Ella's head as she snuggled into his neck.

"You said that before," Trevor squinted at him and looked hard at Ella. "Is she... Is that a real virkin?"

Liam was so startled, he chuckled. "Yes, indeed. Ella is a

virkin from Elderland. She was newly hatched when she chose to join me and my crew on my ship. We have sailed together for nearly a year, and when I put ashore to follow this quest, she chose to join me."

"Does she speak to you?" Boros wanted to know.

"She does." Liam saw no point in denying it. "Though that is a recent development. She has only just started talking."

"And you say she helped in the healing?" Trevor asked, clearly puzzled.

"I, myself, did not know that virkin had any sort of healing ability until the disaster at Waymeet. She helped heal half the town, according to the journeyman healer who was also there. Ella was able to stabilize and bring several people back from the brink," Liam said, proud of his little friend's accomplishments.

"Whatever you did for your big friend," Boros said, looking directly at Ella, "it was well done. Thank you on behalf of all dragonkind for your assistance, Mistress Ella."

Ella ducked her head and blinked prettily. *'Happy help Skel,'* she said so that everyone could hear her silent words. She then turned to butt her head against Liam's cheek. *'I go hunt, now. Long ear mouse in bushes.'*

"We call them rabbits, sweetheart," Liam told her indulgently as she lifted off his shoulder, using her delicate wings to flitter away.

All three men were smiling at her departure. Especially when she dove like an arrow into the nearby bushes. The shriek of a rabbit was heard a split second later and then silence.

"I would say Mistress Ella caught her rabbit," Boros surmised, turning back to matter at hand. "Is there anything we can do for your larger friend here?"

Rivka chose that moment to appear. Clad in her leather armor with her swords crossed in their sheathes behind her back, she looked formidable, even if she was the shortest thing on two legs in the area. That was not to say she was a petite woman. Just that she was a bit shorter than Liam and the knights. Yet, somehow, she had more stature than any of them.

"I think he'll come around soon," Rivka said, joining them. She held out her hand for a brisk shake. "I am Rivka of the Black Dragon Clan."

Trevor had taken her hand as she said those words, and he started a bit before shaking her hand and letting go. "Are you one of *those* Black Dragon Clan members?" he asked, somewhat indiscreetly. His dragon hissed behind him.

"Pay no attention to my bumbling partner," Boros said, shaking her hand in turn. "It is an honor to meet you, Lady Rivka. If all is well here, the prince will descend. He wanted to get a bit more reconnaissance done from above before he joined us."

"By all means, have him descend. It's probably safer for him down here than up there where the mage might see him and lob fireballs at him," Rivka said with a slight grin on her face.

"I am Klathenor, and this is my mate, Wyndimira," a new voice boomed through Liam's head. He looked up at the male dragon who was speaking to Rivka, apparently. *"It is an honor to meet you, Lady Rivka."*

Rivka smiled and bowed her head. "Likewise," she said directly to the male dragon. "I am honored to meet both of you, Lord Klathenor and Lady Wyndamira. Thank you for coming to our aid."

"It is our pleasure." What must have been Wyndamira's voice came to him. It was lighter than her mate's. More feminine, somehow.

Rivka surprised Liam by putting one hand on his shoulder. "Captain O'Dare can also hear you," she advised the dragons. Liam noted that both the dragons and their knights eyed him with surprise at Rivka's news. "He has been flying with Lord Skelaroth on this quest, and his daughter is newly mated into the Southern Lair."

Liam's eyebrows rose as Rivka shared what felt to him like

gossip about his daughter, but the dragons and knights seemed impressed by the news. Suddenly, he felt like they were regarding him with more indulgence than their previous suspicion.

"He allows you to ride on his back? Are you a knight, sir?" Trevor asked, proving, once again, that he was the nosier and less subtle of the pair of knights.

Liam shook his head. "I am a sea captain with a fleet of ships under my command. Lord Skelaroth is the leader of the sea dragons in the South. We are travel companions, right now, and we share a common quest. I'm no knight," he protested, feeling for the first time a small pang of envy for the young men before him who would share their lives with the magnificent creatures behind them.

It was a striking thought. For so long, Liam had thought nothing of the knights who protected his homeland. He'd believed the gossip about sexual deviance and hadn't really thought much about the men and dragons who did the job of keeping the peace in the land. Then, when his daughter had taken up with her two men, he'd lost all sense of reason. The thought that his little girl would get involved in such things as were rumored to take place in the Lairs… Well, it had driven him around the bend.

But, Liam had to admit, the dragons and knights he'd encountered so far on this journey had really opened his eyes. Perhaps he'd been too hasty to listen to idle gossip. To be sure, there was a three-way marriage happening with his daughter and those two scoundrels who called themselves knights, but maybe it wasn't as bad as he'd feared.

"Here comes Trent," Boros said, looking skyward, precluding any further conversation as they all watched a compact black dragon land with grace and style. He was bigger than Rivka's dragon form, Liam noticed immediately, but not by much.

Liam suspected the knights or their dragon friends had been communicating with the black dragon before he ever landed because he didn't hesitate to shift form from dragon to man while walking directly toward Liam and those gathered around him. Trent went directly to Rivka first, offering his hand and then pulling her in for a hug that made Liam bristle a bit.

"Well met, cousin," Trent said to Rivka, surprising Liam with the title. Then again, he supposed, going by what Rivka had revealed to him about the black dragons' lineage, they were cousins of a sort...many times removed.

"You are Prince Trent?" Rivka asked, a hint of uncertainty in her tone, though her smile was wide.

"Just Trent. I don't stand on formality. I'm only sixth in line for the throne, and it might as well be six millionth. I don't ever want the job. Not if it means the loss of five of my brothers. I'm better working in the background, anyway."

Trent winked at Rivka, and Liam tried not to bristle at the younger man's easy manner. He was related to Rivka, after all. Her head wouldn't be turned by the young pup. She had more class than that. Or, maybe, Liam just hoped she wouldn't go straight from his bed to the prince's.

"I saw a small group of riderless horses not too far away," Trent told them all. "It looked like there were a few men on foot, trying to round them up. They didn't look like farmers. Some of their dress was foreign, and several of them were injured."

"Villains who fell off their mounts when Skelaroth scared them into panic?" Liam mused.

"It's likely," Trent said, holding out his hand for a businesslike shake. "Pleased to meet you, Captain O'Dare. I've heard good things about the help you've been to the kingdom in the south."

Liam did his best not to let his eyebrows rise in surprise, returning the strong grasp of the prince. "I'm glad to be of service to my homeland and the crown," he replied politely.

"I'm going to send the others out after the straggler pirates," Trent said. "Might as well stop them while we can."

"That would be wise," Rivka agreed. "I only saw the one mage. Such creatures are rare, even in foreign lands. He is likely far ahead with Fisk and the artifact. If we can cut off the stragglers from rejoining the main group, it could help us in the long run."

Trent looked upward at the three dragons and knights still circling and sent them off with a thought. Liam realized all of them could speak silently with each other and their dragons. One of the mysteries of knighthood became apparent. It was said that only men who could communicate with dragons were considered for the job. There were other qualities, as well. They had to be good fighters or able to train to become good fighters. They had to be clever enough to dispense the king's justice and act as judge whenever the need arose.

Liam had not thought much about it before now, having spent most of his life on the sea. He admitted inwardly that he'd probably been short-sighted not to at least consider the qualifications and character of the men who had seduced his daughter into becoming their mate. Perhaps he'd have to rethink the whole situation. When there was time, of course. Right now, there were more urgent matters to focus on.

Prince Trent refocused his attention on the prone dragon. "There was a hole in his wing?" Trent asked of Liam, who drew closer to the prince's side when the royal beckoned.

"Yes, just there. You can see the faint outline of the new skin," Liam pointed out the spot, and Trent looked pained.

"A grievous wound. No wonder he continues to sleep." Trent looked down the length of Skelaroth's neck to his head. "But we need him to rouse so he can continue his quest. It would be a shame to come so far, only to miss the final resolution." Trent walked purposefully toward Skelaroth's head, and everyone, it seemed, followed.

"I was going to try to wake him when I got up but your party arrived before I'd even gotten out of my bedroll," Rivka said with a smile that took the sting out of her words.

"Your pardon, milady," Trent said, grinning back at her. "We flew through the night to get here and didn't consider the fact that saner folk would be sleeping in."

They both chuckled at his words but grew serious as they

took up positions on either side of Skelaroth's head. Liam would have followed, but Rivka shot a look at him that he interpreted as a request to stand back. Trent wasn't so subtle. He waved his hands at the knights and motioned the dragons to come up behind him. Liam noted that they left room for Trent to shift into his dragon form, which he did with a nod toward Rivka as she did the same. Liam stood a short distance behind her, backing her up as the bigger dragons were backing up the prince.

What could he could do if Skelaroth woke violently, Liam had no idea. But he felt it was important to stand ready. Perhaps, if Skelaroth saw friendly faces rather than those of strangers, it would help him wake more peacefully. It was worth a try.

The smaller black dragons stood on either side of the sea dragon's massive head. Each laid a clawed forehand on one of the horns on Skelaroth's head. Then, the black dragons closed their eyes, and a rumbling hum sounded from deep within their chests. The sound was soon echoed by the dragons behind the prince. Liam noticed that the two knights had taken up guard positions some distance from the dragon gathering. Only Liam, it seemed, was fool enough to stand close to whatever was happening around Skelaroth.

Smoke rose from the nostrils of all four dragons as the humming increased. The sensations were so thick, Liam could feel them vibrating through his chest. A bass thrum that shook the very earth beneath his feet.

And then, a delicate descant pierced the bass rumble as Ella appeared, her little tummy swollen from her recent kill. She fluttered above Skelaroth's head, apparently feeling no fear of the black dragons as she flew right between them. She sang against the rumble of the much larger dragons, and Liam could see little swirls of sparkling color where her wings traced through the air. He had no doubt that she was adding her own—not inconsiderable—magic to the effort.

The moment Ella flew past Skelaroth's nose, the dragon sneezed, propelling her into a bit of a tumble that ended when Liam caught her in his arms. Everybody stilled as Skelaroth's eyes opened. His mighty sneeze had made all the dragons back off a bit.

"Excuse me," Skelaroth said in his silent way, speaking to Ella so everyone could hear. *"My apologies for disturbing your flight, Mistress Ella."*

"Was fun!" Ella replied in her playful way. *"Glad you're back, Skel."*

"I am grateful to be back," the mighty sea dragon agreed with the little virkin. His eyelids opened farther, and he looked around, seemingly surprised to see the new dragons on his right side, while Rivka, Liam and Ella stood on his left. *"What happened? Did Fisk get away?"*

"Fisk got away for now, but not for long," Liam said, stepping closer. "May I introduce Prince Trent," Liam said formally, knowing how dragons, in general, felt about manners. "And his companions, Lord Klathenor and his mate, Lady Wyndimira, and their knights, Trevor and Boros. They are newly arrived. You've been asleep for a single night since our attempt to stop Fisk and his men."

"My wing?" Skelaroth asked, sounding a bit afraid of the answer.

"Healing nicely," Liam told him immediately, wanting to calm any fears the sea dragon might have about his future infirmity. "Lady Rivka and yourself did some kind of magic last night, and Ella did her part, too. There is new skin where the hole was, and though I'm no expert, it looks good as new to me."

Rivka shifted back to her human form. "The real test will be flying, but it looks very promising," she told the sea dragon. "Prince Trent brought reinforcements, and some of them are rounding up stragglers from Fisk's crew right this minute. You succeeded in removing a portion of his men from the equation, but none of us counted on that mage."

"Is that what it was?" Skelaroth asked, clearly still tired from his ordeal.

"I flew in after you got hit and hit him with a blast of

flame. He had some sort of shield around himself and those with him. My fire hit it, and went around it," she told Skelaroth and the others together. "I couldn't hit him. He had to be a mage."

"Was that Fisk?" Trent asked, having also shifted back to his human form.

Liam stepped closer, standing right next to Rivka. "No. Fisk is the leader of the group, but he's no mage. I've been chasing him for a long time, and if he had that kind of power or skills, I would have known about it a long time ago. It was always said he hired mages who would sell their services to the highest bidder. Fisk has been successful at his chosen trade of piracy for many years, and it's not inconceivable to me that a mage with low morals and a desire for a share of the booty would sell his services to a man such as Fisk."

"But what about the book?" Trent asked, then corrected himself. "The page from the book? Would the pirate captain entrust that to his pet mage? Or would he still have it on his own person?"

"Knowing Fisk, he would never entrust an underling with it. Fisk wants the glory and the credit if they manage to evade us and awaken the wizards imprisoned in the Citadel. He would not chance letting the page of Gryffid's book out of his sight," Liam said, knowing in his heart he was speaking no less than the truth.

Liam noticed the two knights shifting uncomfortably on their feet at mention of the Citadel. Had they not known the stakes for which they fought? Perhaps not. Perhaps it had been enough that their king had asked them to risk their lives and safety to protect someone they didn't know. Perhaps Liam had misjudged the entire knight breed.

CHAPTER 16

Rivka was so relieved that Skelaroth had woken up with no obvious problems. She was even more grateful that their message had gotten through to the king, and he'd taken them seriously enough to send not only a contingent of knights and dragons, but one of his brothers, as well. That was a sign of respect and concern that Rivka appreciated.

Trent was a handsome young man, but she found herself comparing him to Liam and finding him wanting. She shouldn't. Trent was a dragon, after all, like herself, but Liam was... Well... Liam was something special.

"We must find a way to deal with this mage," Prince Trent said to Rivka and Liam.

Surprisingly, it was Ella who piped up, flitting from Liam's shoulder to land on Skelaroth's horn. *"Can help,"* she said to them all. *"Can break bubble."*

"Do you mean to say that you can break through the shield that the mage uses to protect himself and the others with him?" Trent asked in a gentle voice, leaning closer to the virkin.

Ella nodded. *"Silly mage from home. All virkin know their tricks."*

"The man was dressed in the style of Elderland, from what little I saw," Liam confirmed. "I got a good look at him when he was lobbing that fireball toward Skelaroth."

"*I break bubble. You toast him good. Teach lesson,*" Ella added, looking lovingly at Rivka. Ella coughed up a little wisp of smoke as if she was trying to summon the fire that Rivka had breathed so easily. Rivka was charmed, all over again, by the pretty virkin.

"We can do that," Rivka told Ella. "But I want to be sure you won't be in too much danger. Are you sure about this plan, Ella?"

Ella nodded her little head up and down. "*Am too small. Too fast. Won't get caught. Fun game.*"

Rivka felt her stomach clench. How could she explain to the small creature that this wasn't a game? Ella's life and the lives of all those who were now gathered in aid of this quest were on the line. Rivka wouldn't want to see Ella harmed for all the world.

"This is serious, sweetheart," Liam stepped in, talking to the virkin that he had traveled with for longer than any of them. "You could get hurt."

"*Won't. Got bubble. See?*" Ella assured him and rose in the air a foot or two above Skelaroth's head. A shimmering transparent globe surrounded the virkin, and Rivka thought she recognized Ella's version of magical protection.

"She's got her own shield," Trent breathed, clearly as surprised as Rivka.

"That's pretty amazing, El," Liam said. "But are you certain it will protect you?"

Ella chuckled in her own way, her little body jerking in the air as her eyes squinted shut and tiny wisps of colorful smoke rose from her nostrils. She flew to Liam and settled on his shoulder, the shell still around her, and now reaching down around Liam's chest. He raised his other hand to try to touch Ella through the bubble, as she called it, and he couldn't get past the transparent shell.

Liam's eyes widened as he looked up at Rivka. "I can't get through."

"And I bet that where she's extended her bubble of

protection over you, nothing could get through to harm you either," Rivka said, walking closer. "Liam, she's on your left shoulder. She's protecting your heart." Tears rose to Rivka's eyes, but she refused to let them fall as she looked at Ella. "You've been looking out for him all along, haven't you, little one?"

"*Leem special,*" Ella said, nodding and rubbing her head against Liam's hair.

"*Yes, he is, isn't he?*" Rivka sent to the virkin alone, silently. "*He's very special.*"

*

Skelaroth flew steadier the farther he went. Liam had struck camp, and they had been back on the hunt more quickly than he'd expected. They made a quick stop to check in with the knights and dragons who had rounded up the stray pirates and their horses. They'd already questioned the men and were able to pass along surprisingly little information. The pirates weren't talking, and it wasn't the way of Draconians to torture anyone. They were able to confirm that there was only the one mage with Fisk's party—if his henchmen could be believed.

Liam would still operate with the utmost caution. He'd learned to take nothing for granted when dealing with Fisk and his agents. Still, Fisk's men seemed to hold the mage in disdain and mentioned how he would watch from a safe distance while the rest of them did the real work during any fighting that took place. That sounded viable to Liam, though the mage had been the one fighting during their last encounter.

Skelaroth was feeling almost as good as new, which amazed Liam every time he thought about it. Ella was nestled safely in her carry bag, securely around Liam's chest, sleeping as Skelaroth flew. Rivka was in the lead, flying next to Prince Trent. They paused to land every few miles and examine the road.

The trail was very obvious from the place where the battle had been fought the day before. Scorched earth and bloodshed had stained the packed dirt of the road, and those who had escaped hadn't bothered to even try to hide evidence of their passage for quite some distance. They were running their horses into the ground.

What had started as panicked flight on the part of the horses—as well as the men—had turned into an ordeal for the animals who were being driven as hard as possible with kicks and whips. Occasionally, flecks of blood and horse hide would be found on the road, which made Liam grimace at the thought of how Fisk and his people were torturing the poor beasts, but it also made it handy for tracking. They could judge how close they were getting by how fresh the blood was, sad as it was to do so.

In addition to Prince Trent, their party also now included the pair of knights and their dragons who had interacted with them the most. The others were either seeing to the prisoners or had been sent off on various missions of their own.

They were making good progress catching up with Fisk by later in the day. They stopped so the dragons could rest and have a drink from a stream and eat as many fish as they could catch. Ella came out of her satchel nest to go fishing, as well. She was recovered from her healing work and had fun chasing the smaller fish around in a little pool that formed off to one side of the larger stream where the dragons were trying their luck.

Liam went over to Rivka, who had reclaimed her human form, and offered her an apple from the provision bag, which was markedly lighter and would need refilling sooner rather than later. She took it gladly and bit into it before starting a conversation.

"The prince says we're coming close to the City of Oler. I keep thinking about Waymeet, but I don't think Fisk would dare try anything like that, again. He's lost a good third of his men, and Oler would have been too big to take on, even if he had doubled the number of men he'd started out with," Rivka said.

Liam nodded. "Makes sense. But he could get lost in such a large place and confuse the trail," Liam pointed out, unhappily.

Rivka frowned. "There is that." She finished crunching on her apple as the knights joined them. Trevor and Boros had been talking with the prince, but Trent had shifted back to his dragon form and was fishing with the others.

"Do you have any insight, Captain, into what the man we're chasing might do?" Trevor asked Liam politely.

"If I were a betting man, I'd wager on Fisk splitting what's left of his group into several smaller ones and sending them out in different directions at the same time. That might've been his intention from the beginning, and why he took so many of his crew with him when he rode North. Perhaps Skelaroth's intervention helped narrow the field some," Liam said, his brow rising in speculation.

"At least his injury wasn't for nothing," Rivka said quietly, looking hard at the big sea dragon teaching the land dragons a thing or two about how to stalk fish.

After the larger members of their party had eaten a light repast of wriggling fish, and the human contingent had depleted a good portion of their supplies in anticipation of restocking in Oler, they were flying again. Ella was nestled in her satchel, but she had opened the flap with her nose and was watching where they were going with eager eyes.

Liam hadn't forgotten what Rivka had said about Ella protecting his heart. Truth be told, he'd been so touched by the idea, in that moment, he hadn't known what to say. He'd enjoyed the virkin's company when they were at sea, but in the last few days, he'd really come to appreciate her companionship—not just for the amazing feats of healing she had performed, but because she was a kind spirit, and it made him feel good to have her around. Ella had called him special, but he truly felt it was Ella that was the special one.

"Do you like flying with the big dragon, Ella?" he asked her.

"*Yes!*" she replied at once. "*Fly so fast!*"

"I just wanted to thank you for before," he said, hoping she could hear him over the rushing wind. "I think you're special too, Ella, and I'm honored you chose to come with me on my ship, and on this quest."

She turned her head and looked up at him. Her eyes were so wide, then she blinked. "*Honor is mine,*" she said, mysteriously, and left it at that. She returned to watching where they were headed and said no more, leaving Liam to puzzle over her response for the next little while.

Rivka and Trent took turns landing and examining the trail, leading them ever faster down the road toward the city of Oler. They had hoped to catch up with Fisk's party before entering the city, but it looked like they were going to be out of luck.

Still, cities had their advantages, and Liam suspected Rivka could use her Jinn contacts to learn of their quarry. Maybe they'd be able to get to Fisk before he split his men—which Liam thought for certain Fisk would do on his way out of town, to confuse the trail.

When they could finally see the outskirts of the city in the distance, Liam judged it to be more a fortified town than what he would call a city, but no one had consulted him when they were naming the place. There were several roads approaching the city, and the one they were on was actually one of the smaller of them. The city had gates on each roadway that led in through a tall wall made of timber and stone that looked like it ringed the whole place.

As they drew closer, Liam could see that each entry was wide open. Probably, the gates were only closed and the entrances manned at night. The dense woods all around the city, which crowned a tall hill, probably held all sorts of wildlife that might pose a danger during nighttime hunting hours. There were farms lower down the hill in what appeared to be very fertile valleys with winding roads that allowed the farmers to drive their produce up to the city.

Liam wondered why the town had been built on top of the

hill rather than in one of the valleys but he didn't really know how such things were decided. Perhaps there had been some kind of hostility that made the people want to live on top of the hill, behind walls. Or, perhaps there was some seasonal weather that made the valleys unattractive for large numbers of people. Whatever the case, the city of Oler had been there a very long time, judging by the condition of the wall, the trees around it and the structures within.

"Liam." Rivka's voice came into his mind like a warm caress. *"The prince and I will land on the road in the trees and shift. We'll walk in together. You go with the knights and the other dragons. They'll land inside the walls. We'll catch up with you."*

She had dropped back to fly beside Skelaroth to deliver her message, and Liam gave her a hand signal to let her know he had heard and would comply. He wished he could tell her to be careful. He also wished she wasn't going anywhere alone with the handsome prince, but really, he couldn't be greedy. She had lain with him twice now, but he had no claim to her heart.

He couldn't. He didn't want it. Though, even as he had the thought, it rang false in his mind. Something had changed. Something was happening here that he didn't fully understand. He wasn't sure he even liked what was going on inside him, but he was powerless to stop it. Change was inevitable, he had learned through hard experience. It appeared something was changing inside him, and he would have to brazen it out and see where it led him.

Rivka and Prince Trent landed behind the shelter of the trees, just out of sight of the gate leading into the city. They shifted and walked together the relatively short distance to the gate, which was unmanned at this time of day, and into the city. Rivka looked for the subtle signs that would be familiar to all Jinn, telling them which establishments were Jinn-owned.

"The dragons landed that way," Trent said, pointing toward the northwest, some distance into the collection of buildings called Oler.

"Good. I see signs pointing in that direction where we may find some of the Brotherhood. They will have information, if anyone will," she told the prince.

Trent shook his head and chuckled as they walked. "You know, even though Nico is my brother, I'll never get used to all the Jinn spy intrigue. It's only gotten worse since he married."

"You must know Arikia is our queen, which makes the Prince of Spies our King-Consort," Rivka explained. "It was all prophesied a long time ago. Your brother, Nico, was born to be what he is. Just like most Jinn are born into the tradition of keeping our ears to the ground to learn what we can and observe everything around us. It's one of our jobs. What we were bred for. Particularly those of my lineage who are descendants of Dranneth's younger son," she declared. "Just as he helped his eldest brother, we are here to help the descendants of the first king of Draconia. It's what we were made for, in a sense. So that evil may not triumph over good."

"It is a worthy goal, and one I understand as a younger brother to the king," Trent said quietly. "We share that common ground. I would never seek to rule, but I will do all in my power to support my brothers in keeping out land safe and free from evil."

Rivka smiled. She'd had a good feeling about Trent from the moment they'd met, but this conversation proved to her that her instincts were right about him. She could hear the ring of truth in his words, and her respect for him grew.

They rounded a corner, and the dragons came into view. They were in the large front yard of a lively inn. Rivka saw immediately by the scrollwork pattern on the sign above the door that this was a Jinn establishment. She smiled.

"Perfect," she murmured as they drew closer.

"What is?" Trent asked quietly.

"This is a Silver Serpent Clan inn. They are closely allied with the Black Dragon Clan and founding members of the

Jinn brotherhood," she told him.

"How do you know?" Trent sounded truly interested, and the members of the royal family should know some of the basic ways to identify Jinn, even though the secretive nature of the Brotherhood would continue among regular folk.

"See the scrollwork on the sign?" she said, not pointing or even looking at the distinctive sign, though she noted Trent's casual glance upward as they approached. That was well done, she thought. He might be better at the spy game than he thought.

"I see it," he replied.

"There are certain patterns in decorative work like that. Patterns we are taught to recognize so we can always find members of our Brotherhood in strange places. This is not something I would tell just anyone, but you are of the blood. You and your brothers should have this knowledge." She sighed, knowing there was no time to teach him, here and now, but at least she'd made him aware.

They entered the inn yard and saw that the dragons were being treated well. Each had access to water and food, and the inn children looked enchanted by the sight of real live dragons in their yard. Especially Skelaroth, who looked quite a bit different from the others.

Rivka spoke directly to Skelaroth's mind. *"Is everything satisfactory, milord?"* she asked, knowing she could ask for anything he might need and have a high probability of getting it here in a Jinn establishment.

"Very good, thank you," Skelaroth replied immediately. *"Liam and the knights have gone inside. Don't worry about us. The folk here seem familiar with dragons, though they may never have seen my variety before."* His dragonish chuckle came without the usual ringlets of smoke rising into the air. A stark reminder that Skelaroth was not a dragon of Draconia, but a stranger to these lands and its ways.

Still, he was fitting in rather well with the others. Rivka had nothing but the highest respect for Skelaroth, who had been nothing but stalwart and brave on this entire journey.

She wondered what the lord of the sea dragons thought about his distant cousins who flew over land and hoped this was the beginning of more cooperation and contact between the two varieties—as Skelaroth had put it—of dragons.

"I'll be just inside if you need anything," she told him as she went inside with Trent.

The inn was large and well kept. Large windows allowed a lot of natural light into the common room, where Rivka easily spotted the two knights and Liam seated near the hearth, enjoying bowls of what looked like some hearty stew. Trent went right up to his knight friends and sat down while Rivka held back.

She made a subtle signal to the man behind the long bar and he nodded once, putting down the mug he'd been cleaning. He went immediately into a room at the back, which she figured had to be the kitchen. A moment later, a woman came out and walked directly over to Rivka.

"Are you with those men?" the woman asked in a conversational tone that would not carry.

Rivka nodded, returning the hand signal the woman had just flashed casually, as if gesturing toward where the men were sitting. "Yes, ma'am. I am Rivka. My father mentioned this inn to me and suggested I stop by when we passed through Oler."

The carefully chosen words gave more information than face value, containing code phrases that would help one Jinn recognize another. The woman smiled and stepped a bit closer. "We are Silver Serpent Clan," she said, testing Rivka's knowledge.

"The Serpent is an Ice Dragon," Rivka replied to the challenge. "I am a black dragon."

The way she phrased it meant more than her Clan affiliation. It was an acknowledgment that she was one of the rare dragon shapeshifters known among the Jinn, and nowhere else...until they'd encountered the royal family of Draconia, that was.

The woman's eyes widened. "I am Leis," she said, bowing

her head respectfully. "My husband, Daan, tends bar, but he is a quiet man and prefers to leave the talking to me." She smiled fondly at the man who had retaken his place behind the long bar. "How can we help you?"

"I travel with those knights and another of my kind who is not of the Brotherhood," Rivka said urgently.

"Not of the…" Leis's eyes widened again as she looked at Trent. "Then, he is royal?"

Rivka nodded. "I tell you this to impress upon you the importance of our quest. We are following a band of cutthroats who entered this city several hours before us. It is likely they provisioned here and may have split up into smaller groups. They came in on abused and likely half-dead horses. They probably hired or bought new mounts. Their leader is pirate sea captain named Fisk, and he travels with a pet mage from Elderland. Do you know anything of this?"

"Not yet, but I will," Leis said, her eyes narrowing. "Sit and eat. I will send out my scouts, and we will know what can be known before you finish your meal. This, I swear."

Rivka took the woman at her word, sensing the depth of her honesty. Besides…with three dragons outside and two in here, even if Leis wanted to betray them, there was little chance that any attack might actually succeed.

All the men stood as Rivka approached the table and took her seat. She chose the empty spot next to Liam and was gratified by his smile of welcome. A bowl of stew was placed before her in short order by the young woman who looked after the common room, and Rivka ate with good appetite.

"I saw you talking with the landlady," Liam said quietly at her side. "Any news?"

"Not yet, but she's gathering it, now," Rivka replied casually. "This is a Jinn establishment. She didn't know anything of our quarry, but she is finding out. I'm confident we'll have news shortly."

Trent looked over and shook his head. "I envy your people their network. My brother does tend to go on and on, extolling the virtues of the Brotherhood's network, but I've never really seen it action before. I hope it's every bit as good as Nico claims."

Rivka shrugged. "It's probably even better."

All the men chuckled at her words, and a platter of sliced ham was laid before them as the bowls were removed and trenchers were handed out. They were getting a full meal, which probably meant Leis had taken matters into her own hands in the kitchen, as well as with the spy network, now that she knew she was entertaining royalty in her common room.

CHAPTER 17

Liam and all the men were duly impressed when, in less than an hour, Leis had eyewitness reports from all the city gates where Fisk's men had passed. Her people were also able to recreate the pirates' trail, to some extent, within the city. The bad news was that Fisk and all his men had already left, and as Liam had predicted, they had split up into multiple groups. Each group took a different route out of the city.

The pursuers would have to break up into groups, as well. Unfortunately, even though they had witnesses reporting what they had seen at each gate, none of the accounts sounded like Fisk and his pet mage. Perhaps the Elderland sorcerer had something to do with that, but there was no way to be sure.

All they knew, for certain, was that the same number of men had both arrived and left. The counts tallied. Their horses had been abandoned. They hadn't even taken the time to try to sell them to anyone. They'd procured new mounts and had bought provisions as quickly as possible, then set out, again.

It made sense. Fisk knew they were being pursued. The mage may have hit Skelaroth, but Fisk had to know that the black dragon would be hot on their trail. He didn't know about the others, which might give them some advantage.

"We have to split up," Liam said as the last of the witnesses finished his report.

The Jinn informant was a young city guardsman who was barely old enough to shave, but he had been wily enough to trail the strangers and alert others of the Brotherhood to help when the main group split into smaller ones. Liam fished a gold coin out of his purse and flipped it through the air to the young man with a nod of thanks. The youngster grinned and made the coin disappear into his pouch, like magic.

"I'll take the northwest road," Trent said immediately. "If nothing else, it leads directly to the capital. If I'm on the wrong track, I can at least summon more help to the cause."

Liam nodded his agreement. "I'd like to follow the north road. It is the most direct route toward the Citadel, which makes it the obvious choice for Fisk to have avoided, but I've never seen him throw caution to the wind as he has recently. He just might be foolish enough to go for the fastest route."

"I concur," Skelaroth backed Liam up as they all stood in the inn's wide front yard, where they had gathered after their meal *"The path we have followed, to this point, does not indicate subtlety. He's making a run for the Northern border. I will carry you North, Captain."*

"And I'll go with you two," Rivka put in. "No sense breaking up the team now."

"I go with Leem," Ella added from her perch on Liam's shoulder. He reached up to scratch her head, and she moved into his hand with gentle affection. He'd come to value Ella's presence at his side even more on this journey, though she continued to surprise him.

"Trevor and I will take the Northeast road," Lord Klathenor said in a booming voice in Liam's mind.

"While Boros and I go due east," Lady Wyndimira added.

"We have all four groups covered," Trent said, satisfaction in his voice, though his expression remained troubled.

"We really should leave as soon as possible," Rivka reminded them all. "Leis is having her people pack provisions for us all. I think we should depart as soon as we have them."

"Agreed," Trent said, shaking his head as if to clear it. "I can't say that I like splitting up our forces this way, but I see no alternative." He went around to the two-legged beings and shook everyone's hand, wishing them good fortune and adding last minute words of advice.

He was just finishing up when Leis's kitchen staff arrived with four parcels. Three were about the same size, but one was larger, and Liam realized that Rivka must have explained their needs in detail. The larger pack came to him, and would serve himself, Rivka and Ella, as well. The others went to the knights and Prince Trent, whose magic would take the provisions into his shifted form and allow them to reappear when he once again took his human shape. Liam did know how it worked, but he'd seen the way Rivka's belongings returned after every shift.

Once they were all packed and ready, one by one, they left the inn's yard. First, the knights mounted their dragons and took off, one at a time. Then, Liam got on Skelaroth's back and did the same. Trent and Rivka shifted, with only the other Jinn as witness, and took the sky a moment later. Each of the dragons wheeled around to their chosen direction and then...the hunt was on again.

Rivka was glad that Liam had not objected to their group being the largest of those sent out to track the pirates. The honest truth was that Skelaroth—impressive, though he was—was not particularly skilled in land operations. Rivka had been teaching him what she could over the past few days, and he was a quick study, but he lacked the experience and knowledge to act effectively.

Likewise, Rivka had little doubt that Liam was an accomplished fighter, but like Skelaroth, he didn't have the skills that knights trained years to acquire. He couldn't help Skelaroth spot things from the air the way each trained knight could. Liam and Skelaroth had partnered only a few days ago, and just for this expedition. They weren't a true fighting team. Not like the knights who had each taken a route to check on their own.

Trent was also a fighting man, and he had taken the Northern route where he would be likely to find help easily, if he happened to be the one to corner Fisk. The simple fact was, Rivka thought the road that Liam and Skelaroth would be following was the most likely route for Fisk to take. She wanted to back up Skelaroth and Liam, and it just made sense to put more people on the path that held the most promise.

Either sea dragon or sea captain could have taken offense, but they were both sensible beings, thank goodness. Neither dragon nor man had made any comment about her continued presence with them. Perhaps they thought they would be protecting her, but she knew her skills would be needed to fill in the gaps where theirs were lacking. Still, both could fight, and neither lacked courage. They were good companions to have along if combat became necessary.

In fact, she hoped it would. Rivka wanted nothing more than to be the one to find Fisk and stop him. Perhaps it would take their combined efforts to defeat the mage and get to Fisk. Whatever the case turned out to be, she felt in her bones that they were following the right group. They *had* to be the ones to confront the pirate captain who had caused so much pain to so many.

Rivka did all she could over the next hours to track the much smaller group that had left from Oler. They were very good at hiding their tracks, but Rivka wasn't Jinn for nothing. She'd been taught how to track the most difficult prey from the time she was a small girl, and her inner dragon's instincts for the hunt were unparalleled. She would find them. Already, she saw minute signs that others would likely miss.

"We're getting close," she told her companions after taking a moment to study the ground in human form. This was the fourth time she'd landed to check the road, and the most profitable, by far. "See the damage to these branches?" She pointed to a spindly bush at the side of the road. "One of them brushed too close and broke these stems. The damage is fresh. They passed this way within the hour."

"How can you be certain it is them?" Skelaroth asked.

"Well, we haven't seen any other traffic on this road so far. If there are others traveling along it, they are either far ahead or far behind. No other group that I know of would use magic to shield their presence from above, so we would be able to see others on the road as we fly along."

Skelaroth nodded. *"Good point. I see nothing in the far distance, and looking back, I see only one lonely farm cart that started out of Oler not long after we did."*

Ella flitted over to examine the broken stems on the bush. She had the ability to hover in one place that most dragons lacked. She seemed to sniff the air around the broken foliage then followed a scent trail a little way down the road before turning back to land on Liam's shoulder.

"Magic," she said quietly. *"Close, now."*

"Well, that clinches it," Liam observed. "I think we should prepare ourselves as best we can for confrontation. But how do we get to them if they cannot be seen from the air?"

"Can't hide from me," Ella announced, making all of them look at her in surprise.

"Are you sure, sweetheart?" Liam asked the virkin, tilting his head to look at her.

Ella nodded. *"Can see through all kinds of magic,"* she affirmed, sounding a tiny bit smug.

Liam let out a short laugh. "And just when were you going to tell us this?"

"Now. When close. No need before," she insisted, making Rivka shake her head. That little virkin was slyer than Rivka had expected.

"She's got you there," Rivka admitted, chuckling softly. "So, that problem is settled. We'll take short, slow hops, and with any luck, Mistress Ella will be able to spot them before they spot us."

"Not maybe," Ella insisted. *"For sure."*

After worrying this whole trip about how they would find the magically protected group of pirates, Ella's sudden disclosure was a relief to Rivka. They flew as stealthily as they could, keeping to either side of the roadway, flying low, just over the tops of the trees and gliding as much as possible, to limit noise.

About a half hour after the stop where Rivka had found the broken twigs, Ella called out to everyone in a surprisingly strong mental call. *"See them!"* she said. *"Going up."*

The road in this area rose and fell over gentle green hills, for the most part, but up ahead there was a higher point that was not covered in trees or greenery. The bare rock left the hilltop exposed more than any other around. It was a perfect spot for a battle, as far as Rivka was concerned. The only problem was that the enemy would see them coming.

"If we can catch them on the hilltop, we need to do it with speed," Skelaroth observed.

"A fast attack," Rivka agreed, thinking hard about how this could work.

"I go first," Ella surprised them by saying, hopping out of the satchel she had ridden in, to this point, and standing on Skelaroth's back, just in front of Liam. *"Get me close and drop me,"* she instructed.

"Are you sure about this, Ella?" Liam asked his companion, but Ella's attention was focused on the hilltop that was looming closer.

"I go at last tree," Ella insisted, drawing Rivka's attention to the thinning tree canopy, and the fact that, once past it, they would be very visible to anyone on the ground.

If this worked, Ella would pierce the veil of protection over the small group of pirates just after Rivka and Skelaroth broke cover. If everyone could see everyone else, at that point, Rivka would count it as a small victory. What came after Ella did her magic-busting thing was up to the dragons…and Liam.

All too quickly, they arrived at the spot where the last trees grew on their way up the rocky slope. Ella dove off of Skelaroth's back and folded her wings like a stooping falcon. She angled her flight a bit, and when she hit the invisible barrier of the mage's protection, it popped like the bubble Ella had called it.

The mage had a moment to scream in what sounded like terror and rage just before his protections fell. A split second later, the four horsemen were visible, riding hard on four sweat-streaked horses, up the rocky hill. At first, none of them seemed to realize they could be seen. Then, the one Rivka now recognized as the mage lifted his head in confusion and dawning alarm. Ella flew at him, her little claws raking the man's raised hand before she streaked off in another direction.

Time to act. Rivka saw the opening and began her own diving descent. But Skelaroth was before her. He landed on the peak of the hill, stopping the horses in their tracks. Two of the four reared and dumped their riders into the dust of the road before streaking off, back the way they'd come. The other two—the horses that carried the mage and one other man—kept their riders, though only the mage's horse didn't rear at the dragon's sudden appearance. The other pirate kept his seat, only because he was a better horseman than his companions.

But not for long. Rivka came up behind the two men still on horseback, and this time, the third pirate lost his mount. She allowed the terrified horse to get past her to gallop back down the road. If they had to, they could always catch up with the animals later. It was the men they had to deal with, right now.

Rivka wanted that mage dead for what he'd done to Skelaroth and for the allies he'd chosen. He wanted to bring evil back into the world, but there was no way she would let that happen. Not on her watch.

"Flame him!" Ella urged, flitting back toward the road and the imminent battle.

Rivka figured it was worth a try. She opened her mouth even as the mage lifted his hands to utter some dark spell. Ella had damaged him a little. One of his arms dripped blood. But he was by no means neutralized.

Rivka let loose with a stream of fire. Out of the corner of her eye, she saw Liam slide off Skelaroth's back, sword in hand, ready to do battle. She engaged the mage, who had managed to erect a much smaller bubble of protection around himself. Even if she only kept the mage busy while the others fought, it was something. This sorcerer would not be allowed to interfere. She would not let him use his evil magic to influence the outcome of the battle ahead. His meddling days would soon be over, if Rivka had anything to say about it.

Liam was ready for a fight. He saw Fisk. For the first time in years, he was face to face with his old nemesis. This time, he vowed, Fisk would die. Fire erupted behind Fisk. Liam spared a single glance to note that Rivka had engulfed the mage in her flame, effectively cutting off the two henchmen who were on foot. They'd have to go wide around the fireball if they wanted to help their leader.

"It's been a long time, Fisk," Liam said once the other man caught sight of him. Fisk's curved rapier was out and ready.

"Not long enough, O'Dare." The pirate captain spat on the ground between them. "I should've killed you long ago."

"I feel the same." Liam cursed as he lunged, and their swords rang against each other with the clamor of steel against steel.

They were well matched. Fisk hadn't let himself go in the years since they'd last met in mortal combat. The last time they fought was when Fisk had daringly tried to board Liam's own ship.

Liam had let Fisk get close enough, confident that his crew could hold their own against the pirates. Up to that point, Fisk had no knowledge of the fact that Liam had been quietly replacing his merchant crew with trained fighters. He had hoped for just such an encounter on the high seas, where he could put his crew up against Fisk's and his blade against the other captain's.

Liam had gotten his wish, but Fisk had over-crewed his

ship, and it was all Liam's people could do to repel the boarding party. Fisk had come over—overconfident as he always was—and Liam had wasted no time engaging the other captain, blade to blade. They had fought to a draw when Fisk had one of his henchmen pull alongside the ship with a longboat. Fisk had saluted Liam with his sword before dropping over the side to land in the longboat that was rowing away at top speed.

Liam had ordered his ship to follow, but they had been unable to find Fisk's ship in a sudden fog bank. A very mysterious appearance on an otherwise cloudless night. Liam had suspected magical interference, even back then, but he'd had no real proof. Now, he knew better.

Liam was aware of the wall of flame to one side. Fisk couldn't really move the fight in that direction without risk to himself. The road went downward on the other side, offering no protection. Across from him, there was a steep drop off where part of the hill had sheared away. From the air, there had looked to be no safe way down and quite a bit of danger if one ventured too close to the edge. Behind was a downward slope of rock and pebbles, which posed dangers of their own.

The fight moved around, testing the boundaries of their location, and Liam got pushed back to where his feet found the uncertain slope of loose rock. He slipped and fell to one knee, seeing stars for a moment as pain engulfed him. Not good. But he wouldn't let a sore knee hinder him. Not when he finally had Fisk in his sights. He regained his footing and pressed forward, rushing Fisk and taking the fight to the middle of the hard-packed road, then beyond.

Liam became aware of the two henchmen rounding the wall of flame that still poured from Rivka's dragonish mouth. They were coming to help their leader, but Skelaroth imposed himself between the ongoing sword battle and the wall of flame, clinging to the edge of the cliff with his back talons while gathering the two henchmen—one in each tightly fisted forehand, caged within sharp talons. The men struggled but couldn't move.

Fisk didn't let it distract him and neither did Liam when Skelaroth winged away, taking the two pirates with him. Liam trusted the sea dragon to take good care of those fiends. It was up to Liam to take care of their boss.

Rivka let loose with the flame that she had never turned on a human being before. She knew, one day, she might have to do so, and her dragon side had no problem with it, but her human half felt a bit of squeamishness about the whole thing. Unfortunately, the mage had reformed his shield of protection and was fighting back. He'd already managed to push her flame farther away from himself, though his robes were a little singed.

Rivka took a moment to regroup and draw breath. The mage studied her as she looked at him. He was waving his hands around, probably casting some sort of spell, but she needed a moment to gather air before she could flame, again. Producing a sustained stream of fire took a lot out of her both physically and magically.

Just as the sorcerer was about to unleash whatever spell he had been conjuring, Ella reappeared, screaming in from an oblique angle, claws outstretched in front of her as if to pierce the bubble of protection around the mage, once again. This time, however, she broadcast a message to the mage that Rivka could also hear.

"I am vengeance. I am justice," she said, sounding very un-Ella-like, using big words and complete sentences. Almost as if she had memorized these things to say upon this occasion. *"The virkin of Elderland trusted you, Ruloff, and you betrayed us."* Ella's claws struck the magical shield, and it popped once more, leaving the mage vulnerable to her sharp little talons, which she used to good effect, raking his uninjured arm. Now, he had matching red stains all along both of his forearms.

"Damn you, silly creature! Damn you and all your kind!" the mage screamed as Ella wheeled off, as if readying herself for another pass.

"For your crimes against virkin, you have been judged, and now, you will pay," Ella went on, hovering just behind Rivka's right wing. *"Am done. Flame now, please."*

That last bit sounded more like the Ella Rivka had come to know over the past days. She was recovered enough to let loose with another torrent of flame. This time, it found its mark on the unprotected sorcerer's person. His robes, in particular, went up with great fervor as the man twisted in agony and screamed.

Thankfully, he didn't scream for long. He was dead within moments, though it was still a little too long for Rivka's human half. The dragon side, however, felt great satisfaction as having ended a force for evil.

When all that was left of the mage was smoldering ash, Rivka turned her attention to the greater battle. Skelaroth was flying off somewhere with two squirming bundles in his claws. Pirates, she assumed. It was Liam who caught her attention as he battled with Fisk. They were deep into a sword fight, and both were bloody in places. Liam limped a bit, favoring one knee, and Fisk kept aiming for it, as if to exploit any weakness.

Before Rivka could even move, Fisk had pressed his advantage and driven Liam to the ground. Ella took off like a shot, rushing over to Liam, where he lay on the ground, and imposing her bubble of protection over him. Fisk would have landed a serious blow, if not for her shield, and it gave Liam a moment to regroup when Fisk rebounded off the invisible barrier and momentarily lost his balance.

Liam got up and chased after the pirate captain, slashing at Fisk as they danced closer and closer to the edge of the cliff. Rivka held her breath as the battle raged on. Either one of the men could easily fall to his death, but she didn't dare intervene, lest she distract Liam at a crucial moment.

She positioned herself so that, if Liam fell, she could try to swoop down and catch him. It would be hard, though she'd do her best to save him if the worst should happen, but even as she moved closer to the edge, the tide of battle turned. Liam pushed forward, again, making Fisk scramble. The pirate captain was quick on his feet, but he was definitely on the defensive as Liam pressed every advantage. She held her breath, the sword action a blur that was almost too fast to follow.

CHAPTER 18

Liam felt calm come over him as his focus narrowed to just the ring of steel on steel, the dance of feet playing near the edge of an abyss. When he'd imagined this confrontation in the past, he'd always imagined rage would power him, but it wasn't rage that fueled his fervor. It was justice.

Something inside him knew that he was confronting the face of evil and that he would be the instrument to end it, once and for all. Rivka had dealt with the mage. Skelaroth had taken away the henchmen. And Ella—sweet little Ella—had played a pivotal part he never could have anticipated. Now, this last bit was up to him.

Liam had thirsted for vengeance for the death of his wife. Somewhere along this journey, the revenge motive had dropped away, to be replaced by the fervent desire to do what was right and serve the side of good. Fisk had harmed more than just Liam. He'd run amok for decades, wreaking havoc. Even now, he planned to do something incredibly disruptive and dangerous to all the lands, by taking the page from Gryffid's magic book to a place it should never be allowed to go. Liam's driving need now, was not for vengeance, but to make things right for all those who sought peace and security in the world of men and dragons.

That revelation gave him the strength to push on when he

was on his last dregs of energy. It gave him the resolve to stretch his skills to their very breaking point...and beyond. He danced close to the edge, uncaring of his own safety. Some higher power was driving him, lifting him, assisting him. He must not fail. He could not fail.

With a final flourish, Liam pressed the tip of his sword against Fisk's unprotected chest and pushed gently for that split second of shock on Fisk's face. The pirate lost his battle for balance and slipped over the edge of the cliff...into oblivion.

"That was for Olivia," Liam said in a grave voice as he stepped to the edge and saw Fisk's crumpled body far below. It wasn't clear at a glance if the pirate who had caused so many, so much pain was finally dead, but he wasn't moving.

Liam sank to his knees, his energy momentarily deserting him. The battle had been fierce. He needed a moment to regroup. Ella came to him, even as Rivka slipped over the edge of the cliff in her dragon form, gliding downward to pick up Fisk's body and bring it back to the hilltop. As she set Fisk down in the middle of the road, Liam felt Ella's energy flowing into him, beginning to heal the worst of his hurts.

"Thank you, Ella," he told the virkin gently. "But don't tire yourself. You've already done so much. I want you to save some of your energy for yourself, my dear."

Ella snuggled into his shoulder and made a purring sound of happiness. *"You did good, Leem. Just like my mama said."*

He put Ella's surprising words away for later consideration as Rivka shifted into her human form. Liam got to his feet and joined her in the middle of the road. He bent down to check Fisk's pockets for the all-important page from Gryffid's book, when Fisk took a wheezing gasp and one hand came up to grab at Liam's arm.

Liam reared back, but it was clear Fisk had no real fight left in him. The pirate's eyes opened, even as blood trickled out of his nose and mouth.

"It's not over," Fisk rasped as he lost his grip on Liam's arm and fell back to the ground.

"It is for you," Liam said quietly, relieving Fisk of the packet of papers that had been in his breast pocket.

"*That's it!*" Ella put in from Liam's shoulder. "*Old magic paper.*"

Liam unfolded the packet and saw ancient writing on yellowed parchment. This had to be the page they were looking for, hadn't it? He held it up for Rivka to see.

"That looks like what we're after," she confirmed. "Though, only Gryffid can say for certain."

"You will never make it to…the wizard," Fisk rasped.

"That's where you're wrong," Rivka said.

Liam would have said more, but Fisk took one last rattling breath, and then, he slipped away. The bastard was finally dead.

And Liam felt a little empty.

*

Skelaroth returned not long after the pirate captain breathed his last. The two henchmen were no longer in his talons.

"What did you do with them?" Rivka asked, curious.

"*I ran into a set of dragon knights that Prince Trent had sent out from the capital. I gave the prisoners to them. Apparently, Prince Trent caught up to his group of cutthroats and easily captured them, then went directly to the capital, where the king and the Prince of Spies are questioning them,*" Skelaroth reported. "*He sent out sets of knights and dragons to meet up with the rest of us, to help, if possible. Looks like you took care of things while I was gone.*" Skelaroth looked around, nodding approval at what he saw. "*I assume that is Fisk. Where is the mage's body?*"

"See that smear of ash back there?" Rivka's dragon side made her want to grin in triumph, but her human sensibilities warred with those killer instincts.

"*Oh, well done, Lady Rivka. Well done,*" Skelaroth enthused. "*That almost makes me wish we sea dragons could flame like you land cousins. I bet it comes in handy for getting rid of trash.*"

"You could say that," Rivka agreed with a chuckle.

"*And you took care of the pirate captain?*" Skelaroth asked Liam directly.

Rivka thought Liam still looked a bit stunned. He hadn't said anything since Fisk died. He'd just sat there beside the body, holding the sheaf of parchment and staring out over the cliff. She thought she understood at least part of his response. He'd spent so many years chasing this one goal, and now that it was complete, he probably felt a little rudderless.

"*Is he all right?*" Skelaroth asked Rivka privately as his gaze narrowed in concern on Liam.

"*He will be,*" Rivka answered back silently, speaking only to the sea dragon. "*He just needs a little time.*"

"*I help Leem,*" Ella put in, surprising Rivka.

She'd thought she was only talking to Skelaroth, but perhaps, this was another bit of the virkin's magic, to be able to hear whenever someone spoke mind-to-mind. She'd have to ask Ella about it later. For now, she was concerned enough about Liam to let it slide.

Ella's tail wrapped loosely around Liam's neck as her head burrowed into his damp hair. She seemed to stroke his head a bit with her own as faint crooning sounds issued from her throat. She was healing him, Rivka realized. Even as he sat there, in the middle of the dusty road.

Liam felt...hollow.

He had won the battle. He'd finally killed Fisk and had his revenge, but it didn't feel like he'd thought it would. He'd had his justice, but nothing would ever bring Olivia back. So much had changed. So much had been lost. Time. So much *time* had been lost to this quest. Time when he should have been enjoying the childhood of his daughter. That time was forever gone, now.

So much had changed. Livia had essentially grown up without him. Liam had a lot of regrets about the choice he'd made so long ago to seek vengeance to the exclusion of almost everything else. Fisk was dead, but what did Liam have to show for it?

"Got page," Ella reminded him, making him wonder vaguely if she was listening to all his thoughts. *"Important to all."*

Yes, he'd retrieved what looked like the page from the wizard's book. That was important. But it had been secondary, in his mind, to getting Fisk. He'd done the right thing...possibly for the wrong reason. That didn't sit well.

In fact, looking back now, nothing he'd done in the past decades sat well with him. Sure, he'd amassed a fighting fleet never before seen in the waters of Draconia. They'd come in handy recently when Fisk's fleet attacked, but Liam hadn't done it to protect his homeland. He'd done it to hunt Fisk.

That bastard—dead bastard, now—had been the driving force behind all of Liam's work these past many years. Now that Fisk *was* dead, what would guide Liam's actions? He didn't know. He didn't know himself, anymore, either.

"Liam?" Rivka's voice came to him as if from a distance, though she was standing close by. He looked up at her, unable to speak. "Liam, I'm going to go through Fisk's possessions and put them aside. Then, Skelaroth advises turning him to ash so all possibility of magical intervention is put to an end."

Burn him? Liam blinked. "A wise precaution," he said, his voice sounding strange to his own ears. "Let's search him thoroughly, first."

And, in the blink of an eye, he was able to function again. Heavy thoughts followed him, of course, but they didn't incapacitate him any longer. He would think about everything later. At length, he was sure. One didn't just have his life's work come to fruition and think nothing more of it. For one thing, Liam had to figure out where to go from this point.

He knew his next few moves, but beyond that, all was a mystery...for the first time in many, many long years. He would clean up here then return the page to the wizard, but after that, Liam was free to choose his next steps as he hadn't been free since his wife's death. If he thought about that too hard, it made him apprehensive, so he pushed thoughts of the uncertain future away for the time being while he and Rivka went through Fisk's pockets.

Rivka removed Fisk's outer clothes, putting them in a pile to one side. When Liam sent her a questioning glance, she shrugged. "Men have been known to secret items in the hems of their clothing. I'd rather not burn everything, so we can go through it—or better yet, have an expert look at these things—down the road."

Liam nodded. "Good thought," he agreed, and helped her take off the dead man's boots. A quick glance at the heels told Liam there was probably some kind of small stash in them. That was a common place to hide valuables. He'd take a closer look later.

"It might have been useful to go through the mage's robes like this," Rivka observed as they finished removing all they would remove of Fisk's garments. "But there was just no way."

"Not good man," Ella said, fluttering over the pile of Fisk's clothes. *"Better mage burn secrets with him."*

"If you say so," Rivka said, giving the virkin a sidelong glance. "You know, you sounded a lot more verbal right before you helped me take out the mage. Where did those words come from?"

"Mama," Ella replied, blinking her big eyes. *"Made me remember when sent with Leem."*

"Your mother sent you to travel with me, sweetheart?" Liam asked, his interest piqued by the virkin's revelations.

Ella nodded, her long neck exaggerating the motion of her small head. *"Watched you. Saw I liked you. Said I could go but had to remember things. Mama knew this day would come."*

"Do you miss your mama, Ella?" Rivka asked gently.

Ella shrugged her small shoulders. *"Sometimes,"* she admitted, breaking his heart. *"But Leem best friend. Soul friend."*

The words staggered him. They felt right. Like Ella had just put in words the way he'd felt whenever he was with her. Like their souls belonged together. They just...fit. Best friends, forever.

Liam held out his arms and hugged Ella close to his chest when she came to him. "I love you, too, sweetheart. You are my family. My best friend."

"Of course," was Ella's only reply as she snuggled into Liam's embrace.

And, from those simple words, Liam knew that some things in life were just meant to be.

"Maybe, after we give the wizard back his paper, we can sail to Elderland and visit your mama," he said, hoping things would work out so that he could give that gift to his small companion.

"That's nice," Ella replied, flitting away as if it didn't really matter.

Perhaps it didn't. Perhaps the virkin had made her choice, and that was the way of her kind. He didn't know, but he had time. He'd ask her about her family, now that he knew he could, and he'd learn all she would tell him about virkin, so he could help her live the best life possible. He could do no less for her…his *soul friend*, as she put it.

"We can pack this for later examination," Rivka said, rolling Fisk's coat into a tight ball. She was about to say more when she caught sight of something in the sky over Liam's shoulder. Skelaroth looked up, as well, craning his neck around to examine what had to be a pair of dragons making their way closer to the hilltop. "Looks like the Prince may have sent more help out after us," she observed, pointing to the sky.

Liam turned to gaze at the pair of dragons who were closer with each passing moment. They were flying fast, knights stuck to their backs, just becoming visible as they appeared to grow larger in the sky.

"I guess we should wait to see what they have to say before we do anything else," Rivka said, her human side a little queasy at the idea of deliberately burning Fisk's body with her flame. The dragon side had no problem with the concept, but she wasn't *just* a dragon. She was a woman, too. With human sensibilities.

With any luck, the new dragons would take care of the task. Yes, that would be ideal. Rivka backed off, bundling Fisk's clothing into an empty pack. They would have to track down the horses and see what could be discovered in their saddlebags, as well, she reminded herself.

The new dragons landed partway down the hill and walked up to the battle site. Once there, their knights slid off their backs and strode forward while the dragons backed them up.

"Are you Lord Skelaroth, Lady Rivka and Captain O'Dare?" the elder of the two men asked politely, but in a firm, rough voice.

"We are," Rivka answered, stepping forward to meet the knights. Liam was still in shock, and Skelaroth was hanging back, observing the newly arrived dragons.

"I am Arkady, and this is Lewison," he said, introducing himself and the other knight first. "Our dragon partners are Githrunal and Beyowir," he indicated each dragon in turn. One was a shiny burnished dark gold and the other a deep emerald green. "We are from the Castle Lair, sent to help in whatever way we can. It looks like we have arrived too late to be of help in the battle."

"Perhaps," Rivka allowed, "but you can definitely help with the cleanup." She smiled to soften her words. "As you can see, Captain Fisk died of his injuries. As a known user of magic, we believe it would be best to burn his remains, but we have taken the precaution of searching his body and retaining some of his clothing for further study."

"Do you have the artifact that started your quest?" Lewison asked, speaking for the first time. He was younger than his fellow knight. Perhaps he was newly chosen and had been partnered with an older knight to show him the ropes, as it were.

"I believe we do," Rivka answered, steadfastly *not* looking at Liam. She would not give these knights the page from Gryffid's book. It was not their quest to return it. This was something Rivka and Liam—Skelaroth, too—had to do. No one else.

"Thanks be to the Mother of All," Lewison replied, sounding relieved. "The king and his brothers will be relieved to hear that news."

Sir Arkady spoke again. "King Roland wanted us to provide whatever assistance you might need to help you get on your way to return the artifact to its owner as soon as possible. What can we do to help?"

"Perhaps, if your dragon partners don't mind, they could flame the remains?" Rivka asked, looking not at the knights, but at their dragon partners.

"We would be honored to assist, milady," Lord Githrunal, who was Sir Arkady's partner, spoke into Rivka's mind.

"Thank you," she replied the same way, speaking only to the dragons. She thought they could probably hear the tone of relief in her words, but at this point, she didn't mind.

"Something else has been burned here, though," Beyowir put in, cocking her head in a puzzled tilt as she looked at the smear of ash on the road that had once been the Elderland mage.

"I did that," Rivka confessed. *"But my human side, I've just learned, is a bit squeamish about such things when not in the heat of battle."*

Both dragons seemed amused by her admission, sending a couple of smoke rings skyward as they chuckled in their dragonish way. *"Your secret is safe with us,"* Githrunal replied after a moment.

"We'll just get out of your way," Rivka said, already moving toward Liam and studiously avoiding the questioning looks from both knights who had not been privy to the words she'd just exchanged with their dragons.

She took Liam by the arm and moved him off to one side of the road, allowing plenty of room for the dragons to do their work. Rivka stood solemnly for a moment, at Liam's side, while Fisk's body burned. She said a prayer for his departed soul, that he would find the right path in the afterlife and forsake his evil and greedy ways.

At one point, Liam reached for her hand, holding tight while his most hated enemy was wiped from existence, once and for all. She was glad to be there for him and even happier that he had reached out to her, even in this small way.

When the dragons had finished and Fisk was no more than ash, Rivka and Liam moved back onto the road to speak with the two knights. They quickly arranged to help them track down the horses and get the saddlebags. Rivka wanted to bring everything with them to Gryphon Isle for the wizard Gryffid to examine.

Catching the horses wasn't as easy as it seemed, but with Ella's surprising help and Liam and the other men on the ground, the dragons were able to herd the scared creatures toward the men. All four horses were corralled within a short while, and their saddles and tack had been searched and found to contain no hidden compartments. Their saddlebags went to Skelaroth to carry as they left the horses for the knights to take care of and headed south again.

"We'll have to stop for the night somewhere," Rivka said to Liam when they paused a few hours later to eat something.

"We could try a town, but I'd prefer to stay out in the open, if you don't mind," he replied.

"No, I agree," she told him. "Less chance of pilfering when it's just us and the trees. Towns are always a risk." She tossed the bag containing their provisions back his way. "I think, now that we don't have to track anyone, we can make straight for the coast. We might even be able to make Dragonscove by tomorrow night."

CHAPTER 19

Rivka helped set up the tent and make camp just before nightfall. They had left the knights to deal with everything else and headed south again, as quickly as possible. The world wouldn't be truly safe until the page was back with Gryffid and the wizard had examined it to be certain all was well.

None of them had spoken much since turning around to head south. Rivka thought Liam was probably still in shock. He'd seemed stunned by the completion of his quest and the death of Fisk. She'd been on the pirate's trail of her since the Jinn had gotten involved, back when Livia and her two knights had been chasing the entire book in a coastal city. They'd retrieved the book, but that one page had gone missing.

By comparison, Liam had been hunting Fisk for over a decade. Rivka could only imagine what Liam was feeling at the moment. In addition to the fatigue plaguing them all after a long, hard chase, he was also experiencing the letdown of having achieved his goal. While a certain amount of triumph was involved, she knew from her own past experience that such events often left one feeling restless and unsure of their future path.

When so much concentration and effort had gone toward a specific goal for so long, it was sometimes difficult to realign your priorities and figure out what came next. Liam would have to adjust. It would take time for him to plan out a new direction for his life.

She was so tired—exhausted, really—that she hadn't said much to any of the beings she traveled with all afternoon. The others seemed to feel the same. They'd all been traveling hard for several days, but their journey was not yet complete. They had to reach the island, and the wizard. Only Gryffid could tell them if they had truly completed their mission.

All indications were that the page in Liam's possession was the one they had been seeking. Of course, none of them were all that well versed in magic. It would take the wizard's examination to be positive.

They made camp quietly, no one really speaking much, except as needed to set things up. Everybody was tired. Skelaroth curled up across from the tent and promptly fell asleep. Rivka helped Liam gather wood and make a fire pit. He refilled their water skins from the nearby stream and started heating some after Rivka used her inner flame to start the small campfire. He made tea to share with her while Ella went out hunting on her own.

The virkin came back with a distended belly and sleepy eyes. She joined Skelaroth in slumber not long after. It would be up to the two-legged members of the party to keep watch for the first part of the night. They dare not take chances with the page now in their possession. Someone would have to stay awake and be on guard.

"I'll take first watch," Liam offered as they sat by the fire, sipping their tea and nibbling on food from the provision sack. Neither of them was very hungry, but they ate, nonetheless.

"I'm just tired enough to take you up on that offer," Rivka replied. "I guess you have a lot of thinking to do." She wouldn't push, but if he wanted to talk about his situation, she wanted him to know she would listen.

He sighed heavily and stared into the fire. "The past years have been a constant struggle. A constant chase. I'm not sure what to do now that the search for Fisk is over."

"I figured as much. You know, my people have a saying. *What's meant to be will always find a way.* You don't have to figure it all out tonight. I'm willing to bet, in the days to come, a new path will present itself to you." She sipped her tea. "You're too resourceful a man to sit idle for long."

"I guess I'm just used to having a plan that reaches far into the future. Right now, I have no plans beyond getting the page to the wizard. After that, I really have no idea what comes next," he admitted.

"And maybe, that's all right," she assured him. "Maybe you don't have to have a long-range goal right this minute. You deserve a few minutes to rest after your long labor, Liam. Don't you? I'm certain a man of your ability will not be idle long. If the crown can't find something for you to do, I'm sure the Jinn can." She grinned at him and felt vindicated when he offered a small smile back.

She climbed into the tent not long after that and slept a few hours before taking her turn at watch. The night was peaceful, and when everyone was ready to go the next morning, the sun was just starting to peer over the horizon. They set out again, in the dawn light, heading straight for Dragonscove, which was the closest point in Draconia to Gryphon Isle.

They would stop for the night in the coastal town before heading out over the open ocean for the island. Rivka had never been to Gryphon Isle before, and she was looking forward to seeing it. Skelaroth would be their guide to reach the large island far offshore. He knew the seas and the terrain well, since it was in his domain as lord of the sea dragons.

Rivka was a little apprehensive about the potential of meeting the last of the great wizards of old. Gryffid was said to be a reasonable being, but she'd never encountered a being of such power before and she was a little frightened of what he would make of her. He would no doubt see her dual nature immediately.

While it was said he had some experience with the royal

family of Draconia, she wasn't sure if any of her Jinn brethren from her Clan, who had the dragon spirit within them, had yet encountered Gryffid. She would observe all and report back to her Clan, of course. She wondered if the wizard realized that was the obligation of all Jinn—to report what they learned and saw to their Clan leadership.

Sometimes, that caused friction in certain places. Which was why the Brotherhood was so secretive. She didn't usually advertise exactly who and what she was. Being so out in the open in Draconia was a new development, and something most Jinn hadn't gotten used to, just yet. She would revert to her old ways of watching, and playing her own cards close to her vest, when it came to visiting the wizard in his lair.

The group made Dragonscove by nightfall. Liam directed them to land on a wide dock, just below his house. Skelaroth managed it, let Liam off his back, and then promptly dove into the water, seeming happy to be back in his chosen element.

"Oh, that is much better," he said to them silently. *"It feels good to wash the dust off."*

"I bet," Rivka agreed, watching the sea dragon below the water line as best she could. He really did look at home in the water.

"We can do the same. My house is just above. Livia doesn't live there, anymore, of course, but the house is kept in readiness on my orders. There is a deep tub that can be filled with heated water, and while you soak, I'll send out for food from an inn I know. We can sleep in featherbeds tonight and really rest before the next leg of our journey tomorrow," he told her.

"Sounds like you've thought of everything," she observed with a raised eyebrow and the hint of a grin.

"I've thought of little else since we started out today. Flying and camping is fine for a while, but I'm not used to it. I'm not all that used to sleeping on a bed that doesn't roll with the tide, either, but it'll be better than another night on the ground." He laughed. "I've gotten soft in my old age."

She knew from firsthand experience that he was neither old nor soft, but she dared not say it quite that way. "Don't worry. I like my creature comforts too. A feather mattress sounds like heaven, right now. And a hot bath? Absolutely divine."

"Then, follow me, milady," he said with an exaggerated bow. "My humble abode awaits."

"After my swim, I would like to use your boathouse for my rest," Skelaroth informed them. *"Sir Hrardor used it, I understand, and I'd like to check out the advantages, as well as be nearby so we can continue our journey without much delay in the morning."*

"You're very welcome to the boathouse," Liam called behind him as he began moving toward the stairs that led up to the house. *"If you could fit through the door, you'd be welcome in the house above, as well."* Liam chuckled tiredly as he motioned for Rivka to precede him up the stairs.

"The spirit of your offer is well appreciated," Skelaroth replied, humor in his tone, *"but I will decline. I will fly up to the Lair and ask for guards in the night that you both may sleep. I'm sure they'd be happy to assist."*

"If you think that's wise," Liam said as he climbed the stairs behind Rivka. She could tell from his tone that he wasn't quite sure about asking the Lair for help.

"I think that's an excellent idea," Rivka put in. *"And, if I wasn't so tired myself, I'd like to think I would have thought of it."* She chuckled and trudged up the stairs. It had been a long day.

Skelaroth exploded out of the water of the harbor many yards distant in an awesome display of his power. He flew in the direction of the Lair, the water on his wings quickly dispersing to rain gently down on them as they reached the back door of Liam's house. He produced a small key from one of his pockets and opened it, shaking his head at the sea dragon's passage.

"Looks like we'll have both a shower and a bath this night," he said as he opened the door for her.

The house was dark, of course, but there was a lamp laid ready at the side of the door. Rivka took it in her hand and lit the wick with a touch of her inner fire. It wasn't quite full dark outside, but the shadows were already reaching to cloak the insides of the structure.

Liam led her through into the front area of the house, where there was a parlor and various other rooms where guests could be entertained, including a cozy library. He didn't bother much other than to point out the rooms as they passed, leading her, instead, upstairs to a bedroom with an attached bathing chamber. Quite a luxury compared to the way most people lived, but then again, the O'Dare shipping empire was vast, and Liam had told her he'd built this house for his daughter's comfort.

"I'll go light the fire under the cistern upstairs, and we should have hot water in a few minutes," he told her.

"That soon?" she asked, surprised.

"The bottom of the cistern is fast-heating copper, and except in the cold of winter, it warms up the inside of the barrel fairly quickly," he explained.

"Where does the water come from?" she asked, fascinated by the lengths he'd gone to in equipping this house for his daughter.

"It is rainwater captured from the roof that gets sifted through a screen, then a tub of charcoal, and finally a pot of sand, to remove any debris or impurities." He paused in the doorway. "I modeled it after a system I saw in Elderland. It's very efficient, and all we have to do is clear the screen occasionally, plus change out the charcoal and rinse the sand about twice a year."

"That's ingenious," she complimented him.

"Each bedroom on this floor has its own bathtub fed from the same system," he went on. "I'll go get the heat started, and I'll knock on your door as I pass on my way down, so you'll know when you can start checking the water temperature."

"Sounds good to me," she told him, already dreaming of the hot bath she was about to have.

"There should be a supply of soap and towels in the little

cabinet. If you need anything else, just call." He headed out the door and made for a staircase at the end of the hall that led upward.

"Where will you be?" she called after him.

"Next door down," he said tiredly, pointing to a door in the opposite direction from where he was headed. "My room. I plan to have a bath, too."

It was on the tip of her tongue to suggest they bathe together, but her practical side won out. The tub was likely too small, and she really was dirty. She'd rather save the fun and games for after she'd gotten herself fully clean for the first time in days.

The bath was everything Rivka had hoped. The water was nice and hot, and she discovered there was another tap with unheated water that she could use to achieve just the right temperature. She stayed in that bath for longer than she probably should have, then dressed in the last of the clean spare clothes she had in her pack and went in search of Liam.

He wasn't upstairs, but she thought she could hear him moving around downstairs. She descended the stairs, only realizing about halfway down that someone had brought food and there were voices in conversation coming from one of the rooms on the first floor. A dining room, as it turned out. Rivka found Liam there, also in fresh clothing, his hair slicked back, still a bit damp. He was sitting at the table with two other men. They all stood, politely, when she entered the room.

"Drake of the Five Lands?" The words came out of her mouth the moment she got a good look at the blond man now standing by the table. He grinned and shook his head in charming chagrin.

"I am forced to admit I went by that name for many years. You are Lady Rivka, I presume." He smiled at her, and even though her heart was firmly attached to Liam, she felt the impact of that handsome rogue's smile. His voice had a magical quality that some Jinn bards cultivated. Of course,

Drake of the Five Lands was a notorious bard who had been a master spy among the Brotherhood for many years before returning to his homeland and being claimed as a knight.

"Sir Drake," she amended her words, adding a small smile. "Your reputation precedes you." Let him make of that what he would. She turned her gaze on the other newcomer. "I am Rivka of the Black Dragon Clan." She held her hand out to the dark-haired man who had not spoken. He took it, shaking it politely.

"I'm Mace," he said, his voice as husky as his partner's was smooth.

"Sir Mace, a pleasure to meet you," she replied politely.

"They are the new leaders of the local Lair," Liam told her, pulling out a chair at his side for her to be seated. "I've just been speaking with them about security arrangements for tonight."

"Good. We'll need to rest if we are to make the journey to see the wizard tomorrow," she said, looking at the newcomers as everyone was seated again. "I expect Liam told you that we retrieved what we believe to be the page from Gryffid's book. Only he can tell us for sure, of course, which makes getting it to him for proper inspection as quickly as possible the highest priority."

"And its safety while in our possession critical," Liam added.

"The dragons have been talking. Lord Skelaroth delivered an account of your travels to Jenet and Nellin, our dragon partners, and they left the Lair at once, demanding we come along." Drake's words were tinged with humor. He really had a most persuasive voice and manner. No wonder he'd been such a successful bard. Such a successful spy, as well.

Liam and Rivka filled in the new leaders of the Lair about their quest and its outcome over dinner while the dragons kept watch outside. Liam hadn't had to send out for dinner. The knights took care of it, sending word through one of the local stable lads of what they wanted delivered to Captain O'Dare's house from one of the finest inns in the town.

Drake confided that the owner of the inn was currently trying to convince him to perform there on a regular basis, now that he was living up at the Lair.

"I probably will spend a few evenings there," Drake admitted later, as they consumed a delicious meal. "First, the food is awfully good." Drake's grin invited everyone to join in. He had a truly magnetic quality about him. "Second, I like performing. It's in my blood after all these years, and it's hard to give up. The folks in the Lair are getting sick of me, I think. A new audience would be welcome."

"And no better place to pick up information than in a busy tavern," Rivka said knowingly. She was Jinn, after all. She knew how the spy game was played.

"Exactly so, milady," Drake agreed.

They went on to talk about the Jinn innkeepers that deserved mention for their assistance on their quest and gave a detailed account of the different places they had stopped. Mace promised to send a flyer to Waymeet to check on progress there. He and Drake seemed to complement each other well. Mace was quieter, but while Drake shone bright, Mace supported his partner with his steady ways. With these two men in charge, Rivka thought the Lair was in good hands.

"I'm sorry our lady couldn't come this evening," Drake told Rivka as they were preparing to take their leave. "Our Krysta would have enjoyed meeting you. She is of the Wayfarer Clan." Rivka had wondered if they would get around to mentioning their Jinn bride.

"I have heard good things about her," Rivka told them. "Please pass along my greetings. Perhaps, when we return from the island, there will be time to meet."

They left not long after that, having arranged dragon and knight guards all around the house for the rest of the night. It was still somewhat early, but Rivka and Liam had traveled a long distance and were both ready for bed. As Liam locked up for the night, Ella suddenly reappeared. She had gone off with Skelaroth when he'd left earlier and hadn't indicated where she was going.

Liam had frowned when she took off, but she was her own creature. Liam shrugged and had said that he knew he could not hold her if she didn't wish to be held. Rivka had agreed, knowing his attitude was a wise one to adopt. Still, she could tell he was concerned about Ella. He'd kept looking out the windows during dinner, and when Ella came back, she knocked on the front window with her little talons while she hovered in mid-air on her fluttery wings.

Liam opened the window and let her in, clearly relieved that she had come back in one piece. She flew to him and landed on his shoulder in her preferred spot, while he closed and locked the window once more.

"Looks like you found something to eat," Rivka said, smiling at the virkin. Her belly was rounded with food.

"Skel showed me where little fish live in beach pools," Ella said proudly.

Her sentences were getting longer as she spoke more, Rivka realized. The virkin was evolving almost before their eyes.

Ella's gaze went to the overstuffed couch with its myriad soft cushions, and she launched herself off Liam's shoulder to land amid them. She took a few moments to rearrange the pillows into a sort of nest then lay her head down and almost immediately shut her eyes.

"Well, I guess she's going to sleep there," Liam murmured, watching his little friend for a moment before shaking his head ruefully. "Shall we go up?"

Rivka agreed and preceded him up the stairs. She wasn't sure how the next part of the evening would go, but she knew how she wanted it to end. With Liam and her in one of those big fluffy beds. Together. All night.

When he would have left her at her door, she took his hand and invited him in. He drew her close and kissed her, all without saying a word. At length, he lifted his head and looked down into her eyes. It was dark up here, except for the lamp he'd placed on the table beside her door, but she could see him clearly.

"Are you sure?" he asked simply. She nodded.

"I want this. I want *you*, Liam," she admitted.

His gaze seemed to sharpen, and a flare of some deep emotion showed in his gaze for a brief moment. Then, he lifted her in his arms and strode down the hall to the room he had indicated was his and kicked open the door, which had been slightly ajar.

The bed was bigger in here, she noticed at first glance. Good choice. She smiled up at him as his lips descended to hers once more.

CHAPTER 20

Liam lowered Rivka onto his bed with a gentleness that took her breath away. Then, he paused. He rose above her, leaning on his forearms, just staring down into her eyes, his own clouded with some kind of painful emotion.

"It's all right, whatever it is," she told him in a soft voice, stroking his shoulders, his hair, whatever she could reach.

At length, he spoke, and it was as if each word was pulled from his being. "I think I told you that built this house for Livia. For her to grow up in. Away from where we had lived and where Olivia had died. I wanted no sad memories for my daughter. I stayed here when I was on land, but it wasn't as often as it should have been," he admitted. "I just want you to know. I've never brought a woman here. In fact, there have been no other women... Until you, Rivka. You did something to me. You changed something profound."

He didn't sound as if he liked it, but at least he had admitted it. She felt that was a big step. A positive move forward, into the new future before him.

"Believe it or not, you changed something in me too, Liam. I don't usually go around falling for every handsome sea captain who crooks his finger at me." She chuckled to lighten her own admission, and thankfully, he joined in her amusement.

"So, you think I'm handsome?" he asked playfully, his mood lightening.

"Oh, come on, Liam. You know you are." She punched his shoulder lightly.

"Not like that blond popinjay with the silky voice and smooth manners who fawned all over you during dinner," he said, surprising her with the clear note of jealousy in his voice.

"He's married," she retorted immediately. "This girl doesn't go after married men. And besides..." She stroked her hands over Liam's broad shoulders. "He's not you. He's far too perfect. Too polished. A woman would have to be mad to want a man like that in her life on a permanent basis. I mean, he's so...decorative. I'm sure he can fight, too, but I, for one, don't want to be with a man who is prettier than I am."

"Well, thank the stars for that!" Liam joked. "The last thing I ever want to be described as is *pretty*." Both of them laughed at that.

"No, you're handsome as sin and twice as tough," she told him, the mood growing sultry again, as she stroked his muscular arms. "I've seen you fight. It got me excited," she admitted.

"Now, that's not something a woman's ever said to me before," he said, cocking his head to one side as if considering. "I think I like it." He grinned down at her before lowering his head to place nibbling kisses all over her lips. "I've seen you fight too, milady, and it made me *hard*," he whispered against her lips before taking them in an all-consuming kiss.

When he let her up for air, her breathing was ragged. She wanted their clothing off, and she struggled until he let her up, rolling to his side. She made short work of her clothes, stripping off as she knelt above him on the wide bed. She loved the way his eyes followed her movements and just before she bared her breasts, she slowed her motion, smiling at him in a coquettish way she'd never quite felt before. She'd never been playful with a lover. Liam brought all sorts of new feelings and experiences to her each time they were together.

Almost shyly, she raised her arms above her head, removing the last barrier between his gaze and her bare torso. When the fabric was gone and she met his gaze, she saw the heat reflected there. Heat she was feeling deep in her soul. Heat unlike the fire of her dragon's flame. No, this was the fire of desire. For Liam. *Only* for Liam.

"Come here, Rivka," he said, his voice both gentle and commanding.

She went to him, straddling his hips and lowering her lips to his as she hovered over him.

"For the record," he said against her lips, not allowing the deeper kiss she craved, just yet, "I have never once crooked my finger at you, though you would tempt a saint to do so."

She laughed. She couldn't help herself. He was teasing her, and she liked that, too.

"Stop talking, Captain, and kiss me," she ordered, her smile meeting his lips and dissolving into pure heat. Flame made flesh.

Their tongues dueled, and their bodies strained. She pushed at his shirt, and he helped her get it off his shoulders, eventually allowing her to toss the whole thing to the floor at the side of the bed. Then, she went to work on his trousers. She got them down just enough to free what she wanted most in that moment. And then...she was riding her way to glorious pleasure, taking him along with her.

She rode him hard and hot, fast and nimble. And, when she'd come to an orgasmic conclusion, he took over and drove her wild, all over again. They tangled in the sheets, rolling around on the big bed, luxuriating in the warmth and softness of their secure nest. It was different from the other times they'd been together, but just as delicious. Just as startlingly pure. Perfect. Right.

After the first round finished, he held her to his side as they both tried to catch their breath. She loved the feel of the soft featherbed beneath her, but she loved the man holding her even more.

Love. There it was. The thing she had been trying to avoid admitting, even to herself.

Even if Liam could get over the tragedies in his past, there were many obstacles between them. For one thing, Rivka was Jinn. She had a duty to her Clan and responsibilities Liam knew nothing about. He would have to be initiated into the Clan in order for her to be able to share certain things with him. Another potential problem was that Liam loved the sea. He had a fleet of ships at his command—a fleet he had built from the ground up. Or, perhaps, she should say the *waves* up.

He had responsibilities to his crew, and the crews of all those ships that he had working under his banner. He had people depending on him, both on land and on the sea. Those who depended on his import-export business for their livelihoods and continued existence. It was clear to her, based on the short time she had known him, that he was more comfortable on the ocean than on land. Could he be the partner she dreamed about, with one foot in Draconia and one on the high seas? She didn't know how that would work.

And then, there was his daughter. Livia might be married now, with mates of her own, but she was still Liam's only kin. Would Livia object to another woman in her father's life? Rivka had only met Livia once, very briefly. She didn't really know her, or how she would react.

But all these thoughts could wait. They *should* wait, because Rivka really wanted to enjoy the moment with Liam. The man she loved. Against all rational thought, she truly did love him.

Liam lay next to Rivka, his mind in chaos. He'd thought maybe the thrill of the quest had added to the amazing feelings Rivka had brought to their lovemaking, but he'd been wrong. The quest was all but finished, and here he was, feeling even more powerful emotions while making love to this remarkable, incredible, magical woman.

She brought something out in him that he had seldom encountered before. She made him lose control, and she seemed happy to do so. Liam had always been very careful to hold back his baser instincts when he'd been with Oliva. His late wife had been a delicate flower of womanhood. He hadn't wanted to frighten her with the needs that drove him, though the few times he'd come close, she'd seemed excited rather than scared. Still, he'd held himself in check out of respect and care. He'd loved taking care of Olivia, and she'd loved him for doing so.

Rivka was an altogether different story. This was a woman with the soul of a dragon. She didn't really need his protection, though she did respond well to his instinct to offer it. That was nice. She didn't ask him to change his innate nature—one of the protector—to suit her more rugged exterior.

He got the impression that few men had treated her with the simple care he had shown her. They probably assumed she was a dragon—tough stuff—and not needful of the simple, thoughtful gestures most women enjoyed. She'd been so happy that he'd thought to bring that tent for her along on their journey. Had no male ever been so considerate of her comfort? It boggled his mind to think so. She might be fierce, but she was also feminine. All women liked gentle treatment from time to time, in his experience. He was honored she had allowed him to show her kindness and she had been incredibly kind to him in return.

She hadn't pushed him to reveal his inner thoughts, though she seemed to know them without him talking about anything. She'd been intuitive and supportive. She'd offered him the comfort of friendship—and more. She'd been his anchor, at times, and he'd like to think he'd done the same for her, as well.

He regretted deeply that their journey together was almost at an end. If he could find some way to extend their mission, he would take it in a heartbeat. He...liked being around her, though that was a weak description for the deep feelings she evoked in his heart. He liked the man he was when she was with him and wanted to continue being that man, though he wasn't altogether certain he could do so without her steadying presence.

So much had happened. So much to get accustomed to, now. His former way of life was over. There was no more phantom to chase. He was at loose ends, and he wasn't sure where he would go now. All he knew for certain was that he had been set adrift...to sink or swim on his own.

"Liam?" Rivka's sleepy voice came to him as she rolled over to lean up on her elbow and look at him. She raised one hand and ran it through his hair, pushing it back off his forehead in a way that made him feel warm all over.

"Yes, princess?" She seemed to start at the pet name, but she was a princess, even if nobody else acknowledged it. By her dual nature, she was of wizard blood. Royal blood. She would forevermore, from this moment forward, be *his* princess, if no one else's.

A sly smile raised one side of her mouth and lit her eyes. "Are you mine to command, then?"

He smiled back at her. "Always," he promised, meaning it on more levels than she probably realized.

"Then...as your princess...I order you to make love to me again, Captain. I want to you to send me to the stars and hold me as we come back down. Do you think you can do that?"

Liam leaned up to bring his mouth very close to hers. "Oh, I can promise to do my best, my princess. And, if I don't get it right the first time, I can always try again. And again. As long as it takes to get it right."

She giggled. "Oh, I like the sound of that, very much, indeed."

He took her lips and pressed her down on the bed beneath him, rolling to cover her body with his. He took things slower this time, now that the edge was off. He brought her to many small climaxes before joining with her and riding them both to the stars, as requested.

Deep in the night, when they had dozed between sessions of unparalleled ecstasy, Liam woke suddenly. He'd been dreaming of the moment Fisk had died. Only, instead of empty threats, Fisk outlined an empty future rolling out forever, in front of Liam. It had been so realistic, the fathomless images in his mind, he was shaking in reaction when he woke.

Rivka was there. She woke alongside him, gathering him gently in her arms, holding him tight and crooning soothing words near his ear. Nobody had been so gentle with him since he'd been a small child.

Liam hadn't realized how comforting it was—even as an adult—to have someone simply hold him and tell him everything was going to be all right. He felt a moment of disorientation as the last of the dream left him, and he faced the reality of the dark night and the woman in his bed. Waking alongside someone wasn't something he was used to, anymore, and he had mixed feelings about how easily he'd come to accept Rivka's presence in his bed...and in his life.

"I'm sorry," he whispered in the dark.

"Don't be. You're a strong man, Liam, but everyone has weak moments. Even dragons." She kissed his cheek and held him tight.

"I dreamed of an empty future. Fisk showing me that I'd lost more than I'd bargained for by my endless vendetta," he confessed. "It felt so real."

"But it's not." Her tone was steadfast in the quite of the night. Something he could cling to. "Your future is up to you, Liam. You've fulfilled your quest, and it's time for a fresh start. Perhaps your unconscious mind was just worrying at the edges of that problem, helping you realize that you have to make some choices in the near future."

"Perhaps," he allowed, drawing back so he could look into her eyes. The moon shone in through the window, giving him just enough light to see her lovely face. "But, momentous decisions or not, I'm going to put off thinking about that until tomorrow. Or the day after. Right now, I just want to enjoy being here...with you."

Rivka smiled at him, and his heart skipped a beat. "I like that. I like that a lot, Liam. I want the same."

She reached up and kissed him, drawing him close, and this time, they were partners in a sweet, loving ecstasy unlike what had passed between them before. Each time was unique. Each time chipped away a little more at the wall he'd erected so long ago around his heart.

It wasn't just the sex, either. It was the little things. The way she took care of him without making it obvious that she was doing so. The way she was there for him—and had been there for him throughout their entire journey. She was dependable, but more than that, she...cared.

He could feel it. He wasn't stupid enough to ignore the signs. She cared for his welfare and his happiness. It had been so long since he'd let a woman get this close to him, he'd almost forgotten how great it felt to have someone else show that level of concern.

Liam had to admit that he cared for her, as well. At first, the level of his emotional involvement with Rivka had felt like a betrayal of his lost love for Olivia, but he'd come to realize over the past days that it wasn't. What he felt for Rivka was on an altogether different scale than what he'd felt for Olivia. Both feelings were strong and all-encompassing, but they had entirely different flavors.

Olivia had depended on him for just about everything. She'd been somewhat helpless to do much for herself in the way of everyday life. She'd been raised to be a lady, and not much else had been taught her. The simple act of arranging for the common needs of life often escaped her. It had been up to Liam to schedule deliveries for their home and make sure it kept running in all respects, other than dealing with the more *womanly* areas of food preparation, decorative furnishings and clothing. It had been up to Liam to arrange everything else that kept their lives rolling along steadily.

It hadn't really been Olivia's fault. She was a clever woman, but she'd been raised in a genteel setting where she had not been allowed to learn any other things that might be of use in a normal person's life. She'd been taught only those things which her parents and teachers had thought suitable for a high-bred lady.

Liam had encouraged her to learn other things once they were married, and she'd taken to bookkeeping and managing the household accounts with great interest. She had an eye for fine things and helped him select profitable items to import. She'd helped him in many ways, but her life had been cut short before she could blossom into the mature woman she had been becoming.

Rivka was already a mature being with a dragon in her soul. She saw the world not as a genteel lady, but as a winged predator with mysterious Jinn origins. She was magical and strong, but also delicate in her own way. She couldn't be any more different from Olivia if she'd tried, yet she had a tender vulnerability about her that she seldom showed. He knew it was there and felt privileged to have seen it. He suspected not many people had ever even guessed at that softer side to her nature.

He cared a great deal for her. He truly did. So much so that he thought he might even be in love with her. That thought both scared him to his very core and delighted him in a way he hadn't experienced in far too long.

Love. Dangerous, delicious, decadent love. Could he possibly take the chance on loving another woman? Could he possibly deny the feelings Rivka stirred in his soul by her very presence?

He felt soul-deep fear at the idea of allowing himself to love, again…and probably lose, again. For Rivka had obligations that stretched far beyond her own desires. She was a dragon, not just a woman. And she was Jinn, with all that implied. Long-standing vows of fealty to her Clan and her people, at the very least. Liam didn't know how, or even *if*, he could be part of her life, considering all that.

The crux of the problem, though, from his point of view, was courage. Did he have the courage to even try to love again? That was the biggest question he had at the moment…for which he had no easy answer.

They made love several times over the course of the night,

sleeping sporadically but soundly between. They were well matched. Somehow, they were able to get adequate rest through the night and awaken refreshed in the morning. Liam woke first, hearing someone moving around downstairs.

He was surprised by that, but he wasn't alarmed. The dragon silhouetted in his window assured him that the knights and dragons from the Lair had kept watch over the house all night. Nobody should have been able to get past them. Perhaps one of the knights came in to use the downstairs bathroom or deliver something. Whatever the case, Liam dressed and went down to see what was going on.

He left Rivka sleeping in his bed with a last lingering look. She looked like a well-loved angel, sunk deep into the lush featherbed. She was sound asleep, her hair wild on his pillows. It was an image he would keep with him for the rest of his life.

When Liam reached the staircase, he heard humming from below. Feminine humming. There was another woman in his house? Curiosity piqued, he went downstairs.

Liam stopped short, shocked to find his daughter, Livia, smiling at him from the kitchen doorway.

CHAPTER 21

"Good morning, Papa," she greeted him, her manner more reserved than he remembered her being.

Of course, they hadn't parted on the best of terms. Her marriage to the two knights still rankled him a bit. He'd wanted a gentler life for her, but Livia took too much after him and seemed to crave adventure more than was healthy for his peace of mind.

"Livia," he replied, unsure of how to proceed. So much had changed in such a short time. Frankly, he was still having trouble reconciling his thoughts.

"I brought breakfast for you. I thought, maybe, we could talk," she offered. "Krysta told me of your arrival here last night and that you'd planned to leave for Gryphon Isle early this morning. I wanted a chance to see you before you left."

"Krysta is the mate of Mace and Drake?" he asked, to gain a little time to think. How was he going to explain Rivka's presence in the house? In *his* bed?

Livia nodded. "I hope you don't mind, but I did want to talk to you."

"I don't mind at all. I've been wanting to set things right with you, too," he admitted. Now, he decided, was not the time to berate his little girl.

For one thing, she was no longer a little girl. He'd begun

to realize that over the past weeks. She was a grown woman who had been managing the on-shore side of his shipping empire pretty much on her own for the past few years. He hadn't quite realized how much his obsession with creating his fighting fleet had kept him away from the day-to-day running of his own business. He'd left it mostly up to land-based managers, but Livia had played an increasingly important part that he had been only peripherally aware of until she moved to the Lair.

Livia's smile touched something deep inside. She looked a lot like her mother, but Livia was definitely her own woman. She had a supply of courage and daring her mother had never tapped. Livia had grown into the kind of woman her mother could have become if given half a chance, and he was proud to be Livia's father. Even if he had been an absentee parent for a lot of years.

He only hoped she could forgive him.

"Livia..." This was going to be hard for him, but it had to be said. "I'm sorry."

She stilled, then looked up at him with wary eyes. "For what?"

"For getting so upset with the fact that you've grown up," he said at once. "Without me. Which was entirely my fault. You deserved better and I wasn't equipped to give it at the time. You suffered when it was my responsibility to make sure you didn't. I was a bad father, and I only hope you can forgive me someday."

She went to him, standing close enough that he could see the tears that gathered behind her eyes but didn't fall. "You did the best you could," she said with quiet dignity. "I know how hard you took it when Mama died."

"I lost a wife, but you lost your *mother*," he insisted. "I didn't see that I wasn't the only one hurting. I was so wrapped up in my own grief and later, my thirst for revenge." He shook his head, regret filling him again, as he thought about it. "I was a blind fool. I realize that now."

Livia took both of his hands in hers and squeezed. "Your

reaction was a testament to how deeply you loved."

He nodded after a long pause to regain his composure. It shouldn't be this easy. She shouldn't forgive him like this. He deserved her rage. Her anger. Why wasn't she screaming at him? Then, he realized something.

"You're more like your mother than you know, sweetheart." He reached out, and she came into his arms for a hug, and as he held his daughter, the last of his grief subsided a little more.

"I'm sorry I was so upset about your...mates. I still need a little time to come to terms with that, I think, but I'm learning about dragons and the people who live among them."

Livia stepped back, looking up into his eyes. "You were pretty awful to them," she admonished gently.

"I know," he admitted. "But I would have been just as awful to any man who dared touch my daughter. If you ever have daughters, I expect their papas will be just as difficult when they start bringing boys home."

She looked at him for a moment as if trying to figure out if he was joking or not, then burst into laughter. Liam felt as if, in time, everything would be all right between them, though he had a lot more apologizing to do. He also wanted to make up lost time with his daughter, if at all possible. He wanted to be part of her life in whatever way he could be now that she was grown. He'd let her set the pace, but he didn't want to let her down, ever again.

"I brought breakfast," she said, gesturing toward the table a moment later.

Liam sat down to eat with his daughter, and they talked...openly and honestly...for a good half hour. They couldn't settle everything between them in just one short talk, but they laid the groundwork for understanding, and future discussions. It was a good start.

They were much easier in each other's company when Rivka came down the stairs. Livia was startled but hid it well. She offered the other woman what remained of the breakfast she'd brought. Luckily, Livia had provided more than enough for Rivka to eat, as well.

"I'm sorry to intrude," Rivka told Livia, speaking more tentatively than he'd ever seen her. "We really have to get an early start."

Livia smiled. "I've been back and forth to Gryphon Isle a few times. It's a long journey, and I understand the need to set off early." She turned to her father. "Will you be taking your ship? I believe the crew is ready, if that's your plan."

"No, uh… We're flying, actually," Liam admitted, feeling a bit uncomfortable.

"Flying?" Livia frowned. "Truly?"

"I haven't been chosen as a knight or anything," Liam was quick to add. "Not at my age. But I've sort of made friends with Lord Skelaroth, and he's going to guide us in."

"You'll be flying on the back of a sea dragon?" Livia looked both impressed and amused. "You too, Rivka?"

"No," Rivka replied, smiling slyly. "I can fly myself."

"You can… What?" Livia did a double take. "Wait a minute. I thought I recognized you! We met in that inn when we were chasing the book. Your father was the Jinn minstrel we were sent to find."

Rivka bowed her head, smiling. "One and the same. I've stayed on the trail of the missing page from that book, ever since. Eventually, I crossed paths with your father, and the rest… Well, I suppose you will hear the full story at some point, but it's too much to go into in the short time we have this morning." Rivka ate a bite of breakfast. "Thank you for bringing the food. It's delicious."

"Just a basket from the Lair kitchen," Livia said. "They have really good cooks there."

The window had been opened to allow the fresh morning breeze into the room, and just at that moment, Ella decided to make an appearance. She flew immediately to Liam, taking her favorite perch on his left shoulder. Liam shifted uncomfortably aware of his daughter's wide eyes. She'd probably never seen a virkin before. Then again, she probably hadn't ever thought her stiff-necked father would grow so attached to a small creature like Ella, but he had to admit, he was attached. Hook, line and sinker. Ella had him wrapped right around her little talon.

"*Hi,*" Ella said in her silent way, talking to all of them.

"Hello," Livia said immediately, her expression delighted.

"I'm Livia."

"*M Ella,*" the virkin replied, looking at Livia quizzically. "*You feel like Leem inside.*"

"Leem?" Livia repeated aloud, looking around for guidance.

Rivka chuckled while Liam felt his face heat for the first time in years. "That's what Ella calls me. Her speech skills are coming along, but she's still very young." He reached up and stroked the virkin's head, scratching her long neck the way she liked. "Sweetheart, Livia is my daughter. That's probably why she feels similar to your senses."

"*Oh! Leem hatchling! Understand, now. Hi, Liva,*" Ella said, enchanting them all with her simple speech.

She really was still a baby, though Liam wasn't sure how quickly, exactly, virkin grew up, or how long they lived, for that matter. He was going to have to do some research, once he had a little free time. After he met the wizard and they were certain the page he was guarding was the right page from the wizard's blasted book.

"Ella is a virkin from Elderland. She decided to come along on the ship the last time we made port there and has been traveling with me ever since," Liam felt the need to explain to his daughter. "When Skelaroth made his presence known, and then Rivka...and then, they all wanted to follow Fisk with me over land... Well, Ella said she would come too, and she's been a great help to all our endeavors."

"I couldn't have pierced the mage's protective shell without her," Rivka said, smiling at Ella as she preened under their praise. "She was vital to the success of our quest."

"Yes, she was," Liam agreed.

"*Now, go see wizard,*" Ella said, reminding them all of the journey to come.

Livia straightened. "Well, if you're all flying, you should be able to make Gryphon Isle by nightfall. I'll get the food I had prepared for your journey, and you can be off as soon as you like. I just left it in the kitchen," Livia told them, as she went out of the room.

"I think that went well," Rivka said, amusement clear in her droll tone. "Your daughter is quite a woman. She was right in the thick of things in the search for the book, and she and her mates are very well suited to working together. Their dragon partners, too. I really like Genlitha, and Hrardorr is a hard case, but he's got a deep core of honor and ability."

Liam realized Rivka had seen them all in action. Something that gave Liam nightmares when he stopped to think of the danger his daughter had put herself in, confronting Fisk the way she had.

Liam didn't have any more time to speak to his daughter before they had to get going. Skelaroth was in front of the house, conversing with the other dragons when they went outside. He looked impatient to be on their way, and the others seemed to feel the same. Liam hugged Livia close while the dragons formed a wall of privacy for Rivka to shapeshift, not that anyone could really see much in the secluded setting of Liam's front court.

He'd built this house with privacy in mind, as well as easy access to the water. He'd built a small courtyard in front of the house for his daughter to play in when she was small, and it also acted as a buffer between his house and the rest of the town. Now, that same space served to accommodate dragons. Liam had never dreamed of such a thing when he'd designed the place.

Rivka took to the air with the two Lair dragons, leaving Liam and Livia...and Skelaroth. Livia had already met the sea dragon lord, and they exchanged greetings. Liam felt a bit self-conscious with Livia watching as he took on the role of the men who had stolen her away from him. Mounting Skelaroth's back and launching into the sky never got old, but this time, Livia's smiling face saw him off, which made it even more special.

The flight to Gryphon Isle was long. The Lair dragons went with them part of the way then turned back. Liam had Ella in her little carrying bag strapped across his chest, and Skelaroth flew even smoother than before. All the days of traveling this way had honed his skills...and Liam's. He knew more about sticking to the top of a dragon now, than any non-knight probably should.

It wasn't a skill he ever expected to be able to use after this journey was over, but he was enjoying the experience while he could. The ocean was calm, and Liam spotted only one trade ship slipping by far below. They were up among the sparse clouds, but his cloak protected him from the cold.

As the sky in the west began to turn orange with the brilliant sunset, Skelaroth told them they were close. Rivka spotted the island, with Skelaroth's guidance, well before Liam. Human eyesight was nothing compared to a dragon's. The sun was riding low in the sky when a flight of gryphons came out to meet them.

The challenge was spoken among the dragons and gryphons, with Liam listening in. When the gryphon defenders found out they had what they believed to be the missing page from Gryffid's book with them, the feathered cats formed an honor guard to guide them in safely to the wizard's courtyard.

Liam could see the beach and the cliffs that seemed to have caves in them. Gryphons were everywhere. Big gryphons and little gryphons who seemed unsteady on their feet and wings. He hadn't ever imagined there were so many gryphons, but the island was named for them, after all.

They were escorted over all that and directed to a stone keep on one side of the island. Gryffid's home. Liam had been there once before. He'd followed Fisk to the island when the pirate had attacked and stolen the wizard's magical book.

Liam had been too preoccupied at the time to really take

note of anything other than the fact that her daughter was there—against his wishes—with those two rascals she had later married, and that Fisk had escaped, yet again, with a priceless and dangerous artifact this time. Liam had set off in pursuit and had been on the trail ever since.

This time, he was arriving at the island by air and with considerably less stress on his nerves. Livia was married to the two knights, whether he liked it or not, and the artifact had been returned but for the single page he now had in his breast pocket. Once it was in Gryffid's hands and confirmed to be the missing artifact, Liam would be completely free for the first time in years. Free to pursue whatever direction he chose.

If only he could figure out what to choose.

Skelaroth landed smoothly in the wizard's courtyard. Rivka was duly impressed with everything she'd seen so far of Gryphon Isle. She landed next to Skelaroth and waited. She wasn't sure if she should change into her human form or wait, in case of unforeseen danger.

The doors to the keep opened, and a group of fair folk emerged, well-armed and warrior-like. Rivka stayed in dragon form. Then, a man in robes came out, a smile on his face that was at odds with the military honor guard.

"Welcome back, Lord Skelaroth and Captain O'Dare. I hear you have brought something for me to look at," the wizard said in a voice that carried through the courtyard. "And you might as well change, my dear. The keep is large enough for dragons to enter, but I'd rather talk to your human guise, if you don't mind."

Rivka felt chastised. The wizard had seen right through her, but she supposed that was to be expected. She shifted shape into her human form quickly, without fuss. She was still armed, even if her armor wasn't quite as good as her dragon hide for repelling projectiles, should the fair folk get rambunctious.

"Ah, that's better. Well met, milady. I am Gryffid." He

bowed his head slightly in acknowledgment.

"I'm Rivka of the Black Dragon Clan," she replied, introducing herself in return.

"Of course you are," he said, making her scowl.

"Don't mind him," Skelaroth said into her mind. *"He's just teasing you a bit."*

By the time they were seated in the great hall, enjoying the dinner they had apparently interrupted, Gryffid was nowhere to be seen. He'd asked Liam to hand over the page and had promptly gone back into the keep and disappeared. The fair folk had ushered them into the great hall and given them seats at one of the many tables laid there.

Rivka was hungry enough from the long flight to eat without much conversation. She noted that Liam was more talkative than she expected, conversing with a bard who was seated to his left. Everyone in the hall was one of the immortal fair folk. It was the first time Rivka had seen such a gathering in her life. Oh, she'd come across a minstrel once or twice that made her think maybe she was dealing with one of these folk in disguise, but she could never be sure. As long as they hid their pointy ears, they looked just like very attractive people in varying shades of blonde.

Perhaps the fact that they had seen her arrive as a dragon put them off, but the fair folk at their table seemed to leave her alone while plying Liam with questions. He talked of his travels and the things he had seen and learned in far off lands until, at some point, a hush descended over the room, and Rivka realized Gryffid had returned.

The wizard strode in through the massive doors to the great hall and walked right up to the table where Liam and Rivka were seated, Ella still in her satchel on the vacant seat next to Liam. The table was not full. Only a handful of fair folk sat at the long table and none too close to Rivka, which suited her at the moment. She was still feeling a little grumpy from the wizard's earlier teasing, and she was hungry enough to eat a horse.

Gryffid stopped across the table from Liam and smiled. "The page is authentic and now back where it belongs. I thank you, Captain O'Dare, for returning my property to me. I, and all the lands, though they know it not, owe you a great debt."

Rivka felt relief flood her being. She had believed they'd retrieved the page, but until Gryffid saw it, they couldn't be absolutely sure. Now, it seemed their efforts have been rewarded. All was right, once again, with the world. Gryffid's book was, once again, whole, and the dangerous secrets contained within could not be used by those of evil intent.

"Forgive me for asking this," Liam said, "but what if someone made a copy? Am I correct in thinking that they had to have had the original in order to use the information contained on it?"

"Yes," Gryffid drew out the word. "Sometimes, magic works that way. The spell itself is not strong enough on its own. It would need all the magic imbued over these many centuries into the page of the book itself in order to work. Therefore, even if they copied the page, sigil by sigil, it will be of little use to them."

"There was a mage from Elderland traveling with Fisk," Rivka put in. "If anyone made a copy, it would be him. Fortunately, he and all his possessions were lost to my flame."

Gryffid looked at her with respect. "That was well done of you, Lady Rivka. While there are no true wizards left in the world but myself, there are those who have learned certain secrets, and if they use that knowledge for evil, they must be eradicated."

The bag on the empty chair next to Liam moved, and all eyes turned to watch as Ella emerged from her nest.

"And who is this?" Gryffid asked as Ella fought her way out of the carrying sack to fly around Liam's head twice before landing on his shoulder.

"*M Ella,*" she announced to the wizard.

"Greetings, Mistress Ella." Gryffid looked at her carefully.

"Aren't you a little young to be gallivanting about on your own?"

Ella shook her head, her long neck making it almost comical. *"Mama said could go with Leem. Had to get bad mage."*

"Ah." Gryffid nodded. "I assume Leem is her way of saying your given name?" One of Gryffid's bushy eyebrows rose in Liam's direction, and he nodded.

"Yes, milord. Liam seems to be beyond her abilities at present." Liam rubbed Ella's head as she butted it against his hair.

"It all begins to come clear. The mage was from Elderland, and this virkin chose to travel with you. I have no doubt that her goal was always to find that mage that had betrayed the virkins' trust and end him," Gryffid surprised them all by stating. "Virkin are highly magical, as you probably know by now. Occasionally, they will adopt a human, and if the man or woman is so inclined, the virkin will show them a thing or two about magic. Ninety-nine times out of a hundred, the virkin judge correctly and give their knowledge only to those with pure hearts. But, every so often, there's a mistake. People change. Someone who started out on the right side turns to evil for whatever reason. That's when the virkin go on the hunt. As Ella went with you to hunt the mage who was helping Fisk."

When Gryffid said it, it all made sense, but the idea was still a bit fantastical to Rivka. How could Ella—or Ella's mama—know that Liam would be the one to track down not only Fisk, but the mage who was helping him?

"Can they see the future?" Rivka asked as the thought occurred to her.

Gryffid beamed at her deduction. "Yes. Some virkin have been known to have the gift of foresight. Perhaps Ella's mother was one of these gifted creatures. Or maybe it is Ella herself. Or both. Virkin will not always tell you these things. You will have to discover them on your own as time goes on."

"We've already seen some of that," Liam said. "Ella seems

to have a tremendous capacity to heal. She saved a lot of lives in a town that had been raided by the pirates."

"How interesting," Gryffid looked at Ella again, seeming to take her measure. "And she seems devoted to you, Captain." He smiled at Liam. "And you, to her."

The tops of Liam's ears turned red, but he didn't gainsay the wizard.

CHAPTER 22

After dinner, the wizard invited Liam to sit with him while musicians started to play and many of the fair folk amused themselves by dancing. It was a party atmosphere, and Liam felt caught up in it to the point that he found his toes tapping along to the music.

It wasn't long before some of the more daring males came over to ask Rivka to dance. She complied, laughing at the outrageous compliments they were paying her, one after the other. Liam was content to watch the dancing and not participate. Gryffid had made sure to sit right next to him, so it seemed the wizard probably wanted to talk. Liam wouldn't pass up an opportunity to speak with the only wizard left in existence. Such chances did not happen every day.

"I wanted to talk to you about your virkin friend," the wizard said, surprising Liam with the topic. "She is very young, but at some point in her life, you will have to bring Ella back to Elderland to see if she can find a mate. She is a brave lass, and such traits would be good to pass along to a new generation."

"When, milord? When would be a good time to take her? I mean… I don't know much about how long virkin live or any of that," Liam admitted.

"Oh, they are very long-lived. That's part of why

Dranneth based his dragons on them. That, and he had a few clutches of very adventurous virkin who wanted to be bigger, and do bigger things, as they put it. Dranneth helped them get bigger with each generation until they evolved into the dragons you know today with his help. They are as much magical as miracle, if you ask me," Gryffid added with a chuckle. "Beautiful creatures, but quite different from my own gryphons. I took two animals and put them together. The virkin—as you know from your dealings with Ella—are not, strictly speaking, animals. Not in the sense of the lions and birds I used, who have little self-awareness in their original states. Dranneth was tinkering with intelligent beasts. I started with wild animals, and true intelligence came after much input on my part. Dranneth's dragons were smart from the beginning."

Liam was fascinated by the wizard's words. Dragons came from ancient virkin? He'd had no concept of such an idea. He'd bet even the dragons didn't know, based on how they reacted to Ella.

"I should think your Ella might start seriously considering mating in about fifty years, give or take. You should plan to bring her back to her homeland then, and see if she goes for it," he advised.

Liam's thoughts ground to a halt. "Milord, I'm already middle aged for a human. If I make it another fifty years, I will be a very old man. Too old for a sea journey to Elderland."

Gryffid laughed, his eyes twinkling. "That is not the future I see unfolding before you, my good captain."

"I don't see how—" Liam began to protest, but Gryffid held up a hand to stop the flow of words.

"Did you ever wonder how dragons extend the lives of their knights?" Gryffid asked, surprising Liam with what appeared to be a slight change of subject.

"I wasn't really aware that they did," Liam admitted. "I am woefully ignorant of what happens between knights and dragons. I always had my eyes set on the sea and distant lands. I never thought I would get involved—or that my only daughter would get so deeply involved—with dragons and the people who work with them."

"I would advise you that it was somewhat shortsighted of you to avoid the creatures so completely. Especially when you are one of the rare ones who can hear them speak. Perhaps, deep down, you knew that that would make you eligible for choosing as a knight. Perhaps your thirst for the ocean was greater, and you were so determined not to be sidetracked by some flying lizard that you turned away from the topic completely," Gryffid mused. "But yes, it was shortsighted," he went on. "Dragons who bond with knights give some of their magic to their chosen partners. It just happens. And it extends the lives of the knights and their bonded mates for several centuries beyond normal human life spans. Of course, the knights lead dangerous lives. Not all make it to old age."

Liam's head was spinning. His daughter was going to live for centuries because she had married a knight pair? When was she going to tell him that little nugget?

"I can see a bond has already formed between you and your virkin friend. Remember, her kind is the ancient ancestor of the dragons. If Ella stays with you—and I see no reason why she wouldn't—she will definitely have an effect on your lifespan," Gryffid opined. "Now, if, perchance, you were to bond to a dragon in addition to the bond you already share with Ella, that would increase the magic flowing into you, thereby increasing your life again."

"But Skelaroth is a sea dragon. He will not take a knight the way the land-based dragons do," Liam said.

"Ah, yes. But I sense he has already bonded a bit to you, as well. Captain, you are like a magnet for these deep bonds that can only benefit you in the long run." Gryffid chuckled at his own words. "You may have run the other way from dragons and their magic all your life, but you have not escaped. They've found you anyway."

Gryffid paused a moment while he laughed. Liam didn't really see the humor, but he kept his peace, not wanting to argue with the wizard.

"And that includes, by the way, the beautiful lady who arrived with you," Gryffid added, gesturing toward where Rivka was smiling and laughing. She was dancing with one of the fair folk warriors who had found the courage to ask her to dance.

"Rivka and I…" Liam didn't really know what to say, and his words trailed off awkwardly.

"Yes, Rivka and you," Gryffid repeated in a significant tone of voice. "You are a good match, my boy. Though I know you both bear scars on your hearts. You humans love fiercely, but often in vain. But Lady Rivka is only half-human. If you mated with her, her dragon side would extend its magic to you, as well. She is strong. Stronger than any human female. She would not leave you, and she is very hard to kill. You could take a chance on loving her, if you're brave enough to try."

*

Gryffid had invited them to stay the night in his keep. They would go back to the mainland in the morning, though how they would travel remained in question, since Skelaroth had taken off soon after greeting the wizard and had not been seen since.

Rivka had danced with many dashing fair folk males, but she really only had eyes for Liam. The dark and brooding sea captain had captured her heart entirely. Drat the man.

Gryffid left the great hall at one point, though the music continued. The evening was winding down, and the music reflected that, getting slower and softer. No more rambunctious reels or line dances. The dancing now, was more intimate.

Rivka didn't want to dance so close to any of the fair folk men who had led her through the country dances. No. She only wanted to be in Liam's arms.

As if he heard her thoughts, he appeared behind her,

holding out his arms for her to step into. Without words, she did just that, and he swept her around the dance floor in perfect time to the music. Liam, surprisingly, was a wonderful dancer, and she would hold this memory close to her heart forevermore.

A magical night in a wizard's castle with a band of the finest musicians in all the lands playing just for them. Or, so it seemed. Rivka had found her home in Liam's arms.

After a few songs, they went upstairs, hand in hand, to the suite of rooms that had been prepared for them. Their packs were already in the drawing room and two chambers were open off of the central sitting area. Without words, they chose one, and both went in. There would be no need for that second room tonight. One room. One bed. Two bodies and two hearts. That's all they needed.

Ella had flown into the suite with them but chose a soft chair to make a nest. They were in their own private little world in the beautifully appointed bedroom. The bed itself was huge and hung with golden draperies. A fire was laid in the hearth, but they would make their own heat.

If they woke cold in the nighttime, Rivka could always get the blaze going with little fuss. Sometimes, it was handy being a dragon.

"Someone's thought of everything," Liam murmured as he glanced into the large bathroom that was situated between the two bedrooms in the suite.

Rivka walked over to where he stood by the door and looked in. The wide tub was half-filled with steaming water. A few rose petals floated on top, sending up a gentle scent.

"That looks inviting," she mused. "Want to share it?" She gave him a flirty sidelong look.

He nodded, and she went into the large bathing chamber, undressing as she went. Liam followed her, doing the same. Her mouth watered as he lifted his shirt over his head and his muscles rippled. He was built on the large side, and every muscle was sculpted to perfection by the physical lifestyle he led. He might be the captain of his ship, but he didn't shirk hard work, and his fighting skills were sharp. Nobody stayed that good with a blade without constant practice. She knew that from first-hand experience.

She undressed and placed her clothing on the bench that ran along one wall. As she straightened, Liam's arms came around her waist, tugging her back against his hard body. He was as naked as she, and she felt the evidence of his desire against her backside as he lowered his head next to hers to nibble on her neck. Shivers of delight went down her spine, and he turned her in his embrace so that they faced each other.

His lips found hers, and the next moments passed in a fog of pleasure as the moist air in the room began to feel sultry and the subtle scent of the flower petals complimented their languorous kiss. When he finally ended the kiss and pulled back, Liam picked her up in his strong arms and walked the few steps to the large tub, setting her down gently. He let her dip her toes into the water and kept watch over her with gentle care that was altogether endearing.

"Too hot?" he asked.

Rivka chuckled. "I'm a dragon, remember?"

Amusement washed over his face, and he chuckled with her. "All I see, right now, is a luscious woman I want to make love with."

Touched, she reached up to cup his rough cheek in her hand. "That's the sweetest thing any man has ever said to me."

His gaze darkened for a moment. Was it the reminder that she had known other men? Surely not.

"I can see I'll have to think of sweet phrases to get you used to loving words. You're a beautiful, sensitive woman, Rivka. Any man who doesn't treat you like the princess you are isn't worth your time." Now, he sounded almost angry, but she thought she understood. He...cared.

The thought floored her. She'd thought he was too wrapped up in his own grief and the woman he'd lost, but maybe—just maybe—there was a little bit of room in his battered heart left for someone else. Oh, how she wanted it to be her!

"You've been so good to me, Liam. I'm glad I met you," she told him honestly.

He kissed her once more before lowering her completely into the steamy tub. Then, he knelt beside it, trailing his fingers over the surface of the water as she got comfortable. The hot water against her sore muscles felt like bliss. The only thing that would feel better was if Liam's hard body was in the water with her, sliding against her…and inside her.

"I'm glad I met you, too, princess. The last few days have changed my life forever," he admitted.

"Me too," she whispered back. The steamy room seemed suddenly filled with intense intimacy. The flickering flame of the lamp that provided the only illumination made the large space feel smaller than it was, as if there were only they two in the entire universe. "Come into the water, Liam," she invited, wanting to touch him body to body more than anything in that moment.

He ran his fingers over her shoulder, his gaze boring into hers for a long moment before he complied. He stood and, with an economy of motion, slid into the water next to her in the wide tub. She immediately went into his arms as the water sloshed around them. Some wise soul had only half-filled the tub. With both of them in there, the water level rose to cover them nicely in its warmth. Liam just held her for a long moment as the hot water relaxed her muscles.

"This feels so good," she told him, feeling the warmth penetrate her overused shoulder joints.

Seldom did the strain of flying so much carry over to her human form, but she'd flown farther and harder in the past few days than she ever had in her life. Now that they had time to rest and recover, she was becoming aware of all the aches and pains she'd dismissed while the quest was still uppermost in her mind.

"Mm," he agreed, his arm around her shoulders as they lay side by side, soaking.

"You're not going to fall asleep on me, are you?" she asked, only half joking. Sleep sounded so good to her, right then, but making love with Liam would feel even better, she knew.

"Never," he responded quickly but quietly. "Just enjoying the moment." He tugged her closer to his side. "I've experienced so many new things with you, princess. You're a special woman."

Aw. Now, that was sweet, too. Why was he suddenly saying things that stole her breath and made her feel all mushy inside? Where had her tough-as-nails, take-no-prisoners sea captain gone? Not that she was complaining. She liked this side of him, and as a woman, she was somewhat starved for compliments from a lover. She'd just expected he would draw away and distance himself from her, now that the quest was done, but he seemed to be doing the opposite. Dare she hope…?

No. She was being ridiculous. She shouldn't get her hopes up that he could change the habits of decades and make room in his heart—in his life—for a difficult woman like herself. Though, just thinking about a possible future for them together nearly took her breath away. It would be so amazing to be in Liam's life on a long-term basis. He was such a considerate, passionate, intelligent man. He was perfect for her, really. In every way that counted. If only he could see that.

"Come here," he said, surprising her out of her thoughts as he wrapped one arm around her middle and tugged her over him.

The buoyancy of the water aided her as she flipped around to face him, her legs naturally straddling his middle. She felt the hardness that hadn't abated rubbing lightly between them. Her mouth went dry as she looked deep into his eyes and saw the flames of desire reflected there. He might not be a dragon, but Liam had a fire within him that felt familiar.

"Do you want to ride?" he asked, a devilish hint of a grin lifting one corner of his mouth.

He was in a playful mood, apparently, which suited her. Rivka reached between them and took him in her hands. He was ready. She was more than ready. No sense playing around. She positioned him and began a slow, torturous descent, watching his face as she teased him into submission.

When she finally had him fully inside her, she stopped, allowing the water to cradle them both, enjoying the sensations. "Is this what you had in mind?" she asked him with a hint of challenge.

"A little more motion, perhaps," he rasped out, strain making his voice rough.

"All in good time, Captain. Have a little patience. I assure you, I'll make it worth your while," she promised him. And then, she began to move, riding him gently at first, with scant motion that barely rippled the water around them.

The walls of the tub were high enough and the water level low enough that she didn't worry too much about swamping the room around them as she slowly increased her pace. Liam's hands cupped her hips, guiding…encouraging. But she needed no real encouragement to take the pleasure he offered so freely.

Little by little, increment by slow increment, she increased her pace until she was riding him like a racehorse at full gallop. She moaned as he hit spots within her that drove her wild. He gritted his teeth and tried to hold out against her increasing passion, but when she cried out and came hard, he joined her a split second later.

The water around them rocked and rolled with their speeding hearts as they clung to each other in the slippery tub. When they finally disengaged, cleaned themselves up and stepped out of the tub together, only a little bit of water had escaped to wet the tile floor. That was somewhat miraculous given her loss of control toward the end, but at least the tiles would dry on their own. They'd already pulled the plug in the drain, and the water was sliding away, emptying the large tub.

Liam lifted her into his arms, again, surprising a small squeak out of her as he carried her into the bedroom. He lay her gently on the soft bed and came down next to her. She expected, based on their past experiences, another bout of lovemaking, but he seemed quiet, and it looked like he was searching for words.

That was new. They hadn't talked that much during their intimate times, so far. Was he going to try to let her down easy? Was he going to end things between them? Her heart clenched in her chest as she waited to hear what he would say.

CHAPTER 23

"I have to be honest with you," Liam began, not sure what he was going to say until the words came out of his mouth. "I don't really know what I'm doing, anymore. My life has turned upside down. But I've come to realize one thing. I don't want to lose you, princess."

She was looking at him with such wide eyes. He didn't know if she was happy or disgusted by his admission, but he went on anyway.

"My wife is long gone, though I held to her memory longer than most men would have, I'm sure. Now that justice has been served and Fisk is dead, I feel finally at peace with her passing. I think it was the need for vengeance that kept me going for so long," he admitted, laying it all on the line. "But that's over now, and I'm not sure where I go from here. I just know my life would be poorer if you weren't in it. I..." He hesitated but figured he had nothing left to lose and a great deal to gain. He had to be brave. "I've come to love you, Rivka."

"You have?"

Was that a smile turning ever so slightly at the corner of her lips?

Liam nodded solemnly. "I love you."

"Oh, Liam!" She reached for him, and he took her happily

into his arms. "I love you, too."

"You do?" He was stunned. He'd hoped, but he had tried not to have any expectations. "When did that happen?" he mused, running his lips along her temple in tender kisses.

"Almost from the first," she admitted, raising her head a trifle to find his lips with her own. She kissed him soundly, pouring all the love she had just declared into the tender assault. He was completely charmed and utterly destroyed by the honest passion in her kiss.

When they broke apart, gasping for air, he met her gaze. "There's just one last thing I need to know..."

He stroked a stray curl away from her cheek, loving the feel of her skin against his fingertip. Loving *her*. With every fiber of his being. This was a grown-up love. A mature love. It didn't diminish what he'd felt for Olivia, but it was as different from that young love as day is from night. Both beautiful in their own ways, with their own mysteries.

"What's that?" she asked, breathless. Whether that was caused by their kiss or anticipation, he wasn't sure.

"Will you marry me, Rivka? I want us to be a couple in the eyes of the world. I want you to be my family... My love... My wife." He held his breath, waiting for her answer.

"Well, there is one slight complication," she told him, though her eyes were full of mischief, which gave him hope.

"And what's that?" he asked, hoping she was just teasing.

"You know I'm Jinn..." she said, trailing her words off tantalizingly.

He nodded. "I do."

"I simply cannot marry a man who is not also part of the Brotherhood."

Liam's heart sank. What did she mean? Would she not marry him because he wasn't Jinn?

"What can we do about that? I wasn't born Jinn," he reminded her, hoping she had an answer to the problem.

"It's very simple, really," she replied, his spirits rising a bit at her casual tone. "You need to be adopted into my Clan. It would be a good move all around, actually," she told him as his spirits soared, once again. "We Jinn could probably make good use of your fleet, if you were willing to allow a few well-placed spies aboard your ships. You know our first allegiance is to Draconia, so you'd be in favor with the crown, as well. Win-win."

"While I applaud your efforts at recruitment and I have no objections to your plan, the only thing I really want to win is your heart," he told her. "Please stop torturing me and say you'll be mine, princess." He kissed her again, and when he drew back after some minutes, her eyes were dazed. He liked putting that look on her pretty face. He smiled at her, and she smiled back.

"I was yours from the first time we made love, Liam. Of course, I'll marry you."

He rolled them so that he could make love to her again, to celebrate their newly declared commitment. He couldn't remember being this happy in a very long time. Rivka had done that. She'd brought the joy back into his life.

She was a fierce woman with whom he could share his adventures. Sure, there might still be a few details to work out, but the main thing was that they loved each other and wanted to be together. The rest would sort itself out as they went along. For now, his heart high in the heavens, lighter than air with happiness. The happiness Rivka had given him…along with her heart.

When Liam and Rivka went down to the great hall that morning, just after dawn, Gryffid and some of his people were already there. It wasn't the crowd of the night before. Just a small gathering around three tables. All the other tables and chairs had disappeared from the room, as if by magic.

It probably was, Rivka mused. Gryffid probably snapped his fingers, and all the furniture had rearranged itself to suit his needs. She smiled at her own thought as they entered the hall. She and Liam had to walk some distance before they reached the massive hearth on the other side of the room, around which the long tables were clustered.

Gryffid sat at one of the tables, in a simple chair like all the others. He didn't go in for thrones or setting himself apart among his people. His staggering magical presence did that well enough without needing any outward physical signs. Rivka could feel the impact of his notice from across the wide room.

Certainly, all the fair folk seemed to have some innate magic of their own, but Gryffid's power was like a polished diamond glittering in the sun next to the lesser jewels—most of them neither cut nor polished—of his fair folk friends. Liam probably couldn't see it, but to Rivka's dragon side, the difference was clear. Gryffid was a *power*, in and of himself.

"Good morrow, my friends," Gryffid said when they approached his table to make their greetings.

"Good morrow, milord," Liam said politely. He had an aura of happiness about him this morning that was hard to miss. Rivka supposed she did, too.

"You two look happy," Gryffid mused. "Please. Sit with me and tell us your news." He gestured to two empty places across from him and slightly down one side of the table. The fair folk seemed intrigued by Gryffid's words and looked at them with interest.

Rivka hadn't really thought about announcing anything regarding their plans, but Gryffid was too keen-eyed. She should have realized he would spot the change in their manner. They hadn't talked about it. She wondered if this would make Liam uncomfortable. She looked up at him, and to her great relief, he looked proud rather than annoyed.

He reached over and took her hand in his—a clear sign to any who were watching—and escorted her the few feet to the seats Gryffid had indicated. Liam pulled out her chair for her, acting every bit the attentive suitor, and made certain of her comfort before taking his own seat next to her.

"Lady Rivka has consented to be my wife," he said, once they had settled in their places.

A round of congratulations came from all those at the table. Rivka and Liam thanked them all for their good wishes.

The fair folk peppered the couple with questions about where and when they would have their marriage feast and where they would live once married. Things they hadn't yet discussed. Liam looked at Rivka for answers, and they came up with a few on the fly.

"I think the marriage feast had better wait until more of my Clan can gather. Liam needs to be accepted among the Black Dragons first, of course, but there is no question he has what it takes to become part of the Brotherhood," she said, beaming at Liam while the others listened.

"Ah, so the fleet you have built will be put to good use, then," Gryffid said, speaking for the first time since they'd sat down. "I'd wondered what would become of it. Very clever. Putting it in service to Draconia under cover of the Jinn, who are themselves under cover, of course. Very sneaky. And, I suspect, this will turn out to be very profitable for you both. Your ships can continue trading—now with access to all the information of the mighty Jinn Brotherhood. Such knowledge of what cargo to take on and where best to take it will be invaluable, I suspect."

"I…" Liam stuttered a bit, seeming only to just realize what aligning himself with the Jinn could mean for his shipping empire. "I hadn't really thought that far ahead."

Gryffid gave him a wide smile. "So much the better. That means your thoughts are where they should be—on Rivka—and not on trade."

Liam ducked his head, and Rivka was charmed by the way he seemed slightly embarrassed not to have put two and two together before now.

"I confess," Liam said, "I have thought of little else besides my personal happiness in this matter. But, now that you've pointed it out, I'm almost frightened of what Jinn involvement might do to the business." He was chuckling as he said it, clearly amused rather than scared. Rivka had to laugh, too.

"Oh, if you give the Clan an inch, they'll return a mile," she assured him. "Let them use their network to help guide your ship captains and cargo masters, and your already profitable business will turn into something even bigger. We Jinn help each other." She sobered a bit. "But we also serve a higher purpose. We serve Draconia. The dragons and people who live in this land are our primary concern. Make no mistake—when you join the Brotherhood, there will be expectations that you'll end up with a certain number of spies on your ships. Good spies. Spies for our side," she assured him.

"I can live with that," Liam answered, taking her hand in his. "What I can't live without is you by my side," he added in a much quieter tone that was just between them.

Ella chose that moment to fly into the great hall and flutter over to perch on the back of Liam's chair. She had been gone from the suite of rooms when Rivka and Liam had awakened, but they hadn't worried. The virkin was nothing if not resourceful. She had probably wanted to look around at the island a bit on her own. Or, maybe, she'd gotten hungry and decided to hunt for mice or other prey. Whatever it had been, she was back now, and the subject of more than one interested glance.

"You know," Gryffid said, looking at Ella consideringly, "I find it significant that the captain's virkin companion chose to bond with him. That, more than anything, indicates he is quite special among humans."

"Oh, I knew that already," Rivka replied, giving Liam's hand a loving squeeze.

Breakfast was almost over when Gryffid broached the subject of their journey home. He first brought up the curious presence of Fisk's flagship, anchored just off the small cove where they were building a Lair for dragons.

"I have been over every inch of that ship, and whatever magic was being used aboard it has dissipated to safe levels. It is just a ship, now. Nothing magical about it," Gryffid told them. "You would be doing me a favor by taking it away from the island, since I have no use for such an infamous vessel. Perhaps you could add it to your fleet," the wizard suggested to Liam. "It might make any enemies think twice to see the flagship of your worst enemy now in your service."

Liam had to shake his head at that thought. "I'm not sure I want such a bloodthirsty reputation. After all, Fisk was the pirate. I'm merely the man who hunted him."

"You're the man who *caught* him," Gryffid corrected him. "It would be good if others had proof of your success there. The ship says it without having to utter a word."

Liam considered. "You're right, of course. And if, perhaps, a few of your folk would be willing to help me sail her back to the mainland, I would be happy to take her into my fleet."

"You know, now that the island is no longer hidden by magical means, more than a few of my friends who live here have expressed an interest in traveling to the mainland and back again. Perhaps we could discuss adding an occasional stop here for one of your ships to help bring that about," the wizard surprised Liam by saying. "You must have one or two trustworthy captains that could be given the mission."

"Aye," Liam replied, already thinking of the men he had in his fleet. "We could set something up, if it would be of help to you."

"And we have trade goods we'd like to find a bigger market for," Gryffid added, sweetening the deal. Liam had seen some of the beautiful things Livia had brought back with her from the marketplace here on the island. Not only could he help move the people of Gryphon Isle, but also their goods, which would be very profitable for all concerned.

"I'll set something up as soon as we get back," Liam replied, trying not to sound too eager, and probably failing miserably. This was too good a deal to pass up.

A gryphon consented to fly Liam over to the other side of the island later that day. It was both similar and different to ride on the back of a furred and feathered creature, but Liam enjoyed his short time in the air with the magnificent gryphon.

Rivka flew beside them, in her black dragon form. When they landed on the beach, Liam was surprised to see dragons in the cove. Not Skelaroth, but surely, these were some of his kin. Sea dragons. They had the right coloring and build, and there were no knights with them.

There was a longboat tied to what looked like a newly-built dock off to one side of the cove, near where the gryphon had landed. Liam unloaded the packs the gryphon had carried and thanked the creature for bringing him here before the gryphon took off again, heading back the way they'd come. Rivka shifted into her human form as she walked toward him.

No matter how many times he saw her do it, he was still enchanted by the thought of that fierce little black dragon turning into such a lovely, capable woman. A woman he loved.

That thought, too, was new and utterly amazing. His battered heart had been broken for so very long. It had taken a magical woman to weave it back together. Rivka. A woman he never expected but was so very thankful had come into his life.

She walked into his arms, and they shared a kiss, there on the beach. Now that their relationship was out in the open, they seemed to feel a mutual need to touch and kiss whenever possible. Being with her felt fresh and new. Different from how he'd been with Olivia, but just as pure and good.

"Sorry to leave?" she asked, her head resting on his shoulder as they looked out at the ship in the distance a few minutes later.

"I'm only sorry we won't have a chance to say goodbye to Skelaroth," Liam told her. "Certainly, I'd have liked more time to explore this magical island, but I don't want to overstay my welcome, and I suspect, someday, we might be invited to return. Especially if we manage to set up regular—if secret—service to the island."

"Skelaroth has been away from his fellow sea dragons a

long time," Rivka mused. "I'm sure he's very busy seeing to their needs. He is, after all, their leader."

"I know, but I've come to think of him as a friend. A really good friend," Liam admitted. "I'll miss talking with him."

Rivka rubbed her hand along his back in a comforting way. "We may see him again, someday."

"I truly hope so."

He would have said more, but a flight of gryphons appeared over the cliffs and began an orderly descent. Each gryphon carried passenger. Fair folk, with packs slung over their backs. Perhaps this was the promised crew.

Sure enough, when they had all landed, they introduced themselves as able seamen who had volunteered to help get the ship back to the mainland. At that point, they assured Liam they each had plans about where they would go and what they wanted to do. A few spoke to Rivka about her Jinn contacts, and Liam noted a few musical instrument cases among the personal effects being carried to the longboat.

They made the crossing from the cove to the ship under the watchful eyes of several sea dragons, but none of them was the one Liam hoped to see. Skelaroth was long gone, and Liam would just have to get over it.

Then there was little time to think as he familiarized himself with the ship, and the small crew of fair folk set about the task of making her ready to sail. They had just enough people aboard to manage it, and within an hour, they were heading out into the deep blue sea.

It took considerably longer to sail back to Dragonscove than it had to fly, but Liam and Rivka didn't mind. They spent the nights in their stateroom, enjoying each other and the motion of the ocean. Their days were spent pitching in with the small crew to make ship life enjoyable. Rivka helped with the food preparation, and Liam took a turn at the rigging, as he hadn't for many, many years.

The fair folk were pleasant companions, and there was

music every evening. Music that rivaled, and surpassed, the best Liam had ever heard. He got to know some of the men and women who had volunteered to leave their homeland for an adventure abroad. They were magical, certainly, but when it came down to it, they were people like most others, with stories to tell and family concerns.

Liam offered them every hospitality his company could provide once they reached the shore. A few of them took him up on the offer, taking rooms in the inn his fleet often used when spending time ashore. Most of the fair folk dispersed when they reached Dragonscove a few days later, taking their leave while still aboard ship and then fading into the harbor bustle the moment they were off the ship.

CHAPTER 24

After the formalities of docking and making contact with the manager who was looking after his ships in this port, Liam left the ship, escorting Rivka to his house. The house they had stayed in before leaving for Gryphon Isle. The house they had agreed to live in—at least for now—while all the other logistics of their new life together were settled.

Livia took the news better than he'd expected. He'd sent a messenger up to the Lair, telling her he was back at the house and saying he'd like to speak with her. She arrived that very afternoon with Sir Gowan and his dragon partner, Lady Genlitha. The dragon sunned herself in the courtyard while Gowan and Livia came into the house.

Liam got the impression that Gowan was there to protect Livia, though she hardly needed protection from her own father. Part of him was appalled at the very idea while another part of him applauded the man for having the balls to face Liam down in his own home and look after the woman he claimed to love.

Rivka had arranged for lunch to be delivered, along with a supply of groceries to restock the larder, so there was plenty of food to share when the younger couple arrived just as their elders were about to sit down to eat. Rivka became the gracious hostess, inviting the others to join them and producing more food out of the kitchen with Livia's help. Liam was amused to see his new lady in such a domestic role.

Rivka was more likely to use her sword than a bread knife in most instances, but she was adaptable. As he was. They would share the domestic duties, they had decided, but today, Rivka had insisted on seeing to their food supply while Liam dealt with the business end of his fleet.

In the end, when Liam finally got the words out to tell Livia that he was remarrying, the result was unexpected. He had thought his daughter might be upset by the idea of a new woman in his life. He'd hoped for eventual acceptance, not the immediate congratulations and true happiness he read on Livia's open features. She jumped up from her chair and came right around the table to hug first Rivka and then Liam.

Gowan was more subdued in his congratulations, but Liam felt they were real, nonetheless. Livia began talking about how they would celebrate, and Rivka joined in, mentioning her connection to the Jinn and how her Clan would be the ones hosting the party. Gowan asked a few pointed questions about what it would mean, marrying into a Jinn Clan, but the reaction of both Livia and one of her mates was all Liam could have asked for, and more.

"I need to say one other thing," Liam told them as the conversation naturally came to a lull. "I've been unreasonable. I see that now. I have had a very hard time accepting Livia's decision to marry into the Lair and that way of life." He cleared his throat, buying time to find the right words. Ultimately, it came down to one very simple fact. "I'm sorry."

"Papa..." Livia started to say, but Liam held up one hand, asking without words for her to let him finish.

"I've been blind and foolish for a very long time. Vengeance ruled my life, and I allowed it to take me away from the most important thing. You, Livia. I left you alone too long, and for that, I can only blame myself." He shook his head as regret filled him. "I missed most of your childhood, seeing you only occasionally. That wasn't right. And, in my mind, you remained that small child I left behind, even though there was much evidence to the contrary. The way you stepped in to help run the fleet. The way you solve problems and found new markets for our goods. All of these things should have convinced me, long ago, that you were an adult, fully able to make your own decisions. I just didn't want to see it."

Rivka reached out and took his hand under the table, offering silent support. He clutched at her kindness, taking her hand gently in his own. She was such a good woman. Too good for the likes of him, but he could not let her go. Not in this lifetime.

"And so, I apologize to you, Livia. And to you, Sir Gowan. If Seth was here, I'd say the same to him. I was wrong." Liam didn't like the taste of such words in his mouth, but he knew they had to be said. "It was pointed out to me that I had long shied away from learning anything about dragons, knights, and the ways of life in their Lairs. This was, perhaps, because I didn't want to be distracted from my own narrow vision. All I could see was my need for justice and my desire for vengeance. I've had it now, and I'm not sure it was all worth it in the end. I missed a lot, and I have been foolish. I see that now. It is my hope that, in time, you can forgive me."

There. That ought to make his feelings clear enough. He only hoped Livia would be as kind-hearted as her mother had been and forgive his foolishness. He had a lot to make up for.

Rivka let go of Liam's hand when, for the second time, Livia rushed around the table and threw her arms around her father. She certainly was an emotional girl, Rivka thought with an inward grin. Or maybe… Rivka sent a little tendril of her magic out to touch Livia and realized something wondrous.

Livia was pregnant. Suddenly, a fierce dragon presence made itself known in Rivka's mind.

"Black dragon you may be, but if you do not retract your magic from my friend, I will have something to say about it."

Rivka moved the little wisp of her own magic from Livia to the dragon basking in the courtyard. A female. A pregnant female.

"*Both of you?*" Rivka could hardly believe her senses. "*You're both pregnant?*"

"*We are,*" Genlitha confirmed with a mental huff. "*Now, I will thank you to stop probing either of us magically.*"

Rivka immediately removed her magic. "*My apologies, Lady Genlitha. We are going to be family, you and I, and I would not have you think less of me. I was merely wondering why Livia was so...*"

A dragonish chuckle sounded through Rivka's mind. "*Such an emotional mess, you mean? We have both been in a bit of a state since we discovered our interesting condition, just after you left for the wizard's island. That's why Gowan came along. One of the men has been shadowing her every move since they found out.*" The dragon sounded truly amused. "*Please don't tell her father yet. It's taken a long time for him to come around, and the others are afraid this might set him off again. Plus, Livia probably wouldn't want to steal your thunder. The focus, right now, should be on you two and your announcement. We'll have months to get used to our expected arrivals.*"

Rivka thought about that. She didn't like keeping secrets from Liam, but this was in a good cause. Livia had the right to tell people—including her father—when she felt it was the right time. This was not Rivka's secret to share.

"*I will abide by your wishes, Lady Genlitha, though I should warn you that I won't, in general, be keeping secrets from Liam in the future. We are going to be married, and I want total honesty between us. I can't expect it of him if I won't give it in return.*"

Genlitha was quiet for a moment before she finally answered. "*I understand. And I applaud your sensibilities. I think, if you continue on that path, you will have a truly happy life together.*"

Genlitha said no more, and Rivka was able to focus on Liam and his daughter. Livia had forgiven him tearfully. Rivka just shook her head, amused and indulgent. Pregnant females were always quite emotional. She expected that, if she ever was blessed with a child, she would be the same. And that was another thing they hadn't discussed. Liam wasn't an old man, though by human standards he was approaching middle age. Still, with all the magic they would be sharing, he would live much longer, now that they were joining their lives together.

Rivka would be able to have children for at least two centuries, if her Clan-mates were anything to go by. She would have to break the news to Liam and see if he was receptive. She'd like to have a few offspring, but only if he was willing. And she suspected he would be, given that he regretted missing Livia's childhood. He could start over, now. This was his second chance. Rivka knew he wouldn't mess up this time. He'd learned his lesson on that score, she was certain.

After Livia and her entourage left, Liam and Rivka worked to make the house more livable. It had been shut up for weeks, and they decided to open the windows and air everything out. They scrubbed the kitchen, side by side, reminding Liam of his younger days of swabbing the decks on his first ship.

He sent out for items they would need and brought in a few people who had worked for him before. A few young lads from the office to carry messages and run errands, a housekeeper and cook to help look after the place. He would add more staff, as necessary, until he had made his house a home in which Rivka and he could be comfortable.

After the work of the day, they decided to have dinner at an inn then take a walk down by the water. Liam had a private dock and boathouse behind his home, and they went down there. He'd had some benches built into the dock, just so he could sit down there at sunset and watch the water. It was one of his favorite parts about his home in Dragonscove, and now, he was able to share it with Rivka.

They were enjoying watching the sky change colors in the west when a disturbance in the water nearby captured Liam's attention. As he watched, a dragon's head emerged from the water.

"Skelaroth!" Liam said the sea dragon's name even before he realized it.

"I regret I could not see you off when you left Gryphon Isle," Skelaroth said into both Liam and Rivka's minds. *"There were some issues with my fellow sea dragons that needed sorting out."*

"We figured as much," Rivka said. "It's good to see you again, milord."

"I was wondering… If it's not too much of an imposition… If I could, from time to time, take refuge in your boatshed," he asked, flooring Liam with the hesitant request. *"I found it most comfortable, and I seem to have developed a taste for flying in the air."* The dragon sounded bemused by his own discovery. *"I also have to admit, I like land food more than I thought I would, and now, a diet made up mostly of fish seems rather bland."*

Liam didn't even have to think about it. "You are most welcome at any time to the boatshed, the courtyard, anyplace I can offer you where you will be comfortable. I hope you don't mind when I say that I consider you a friend, and I have missed your company. I would value any time you cared to spend here and welcome you with open arms."

Skelaroth's head dipped in a way that seemed to indicate he was touched by Liam's words. Liam had gotten so much better at interpreting dragon movements and what they meant over the past adventure. Such knowledge would come in handy when Rivka was in her dragon form, so he had better observe and learn all he could.

"I am honored by your words of friendship, Captain. I have never really been friends with a human before. Not the way we are friends. I will call you Liam, if you don't mind, and you should call me Skelaroth, or even just Skel, as your virkin friend does."

Liam sensed it was a big deal for a dragon—beings known for their love of formality—to invite him to use his name and drop the honorific. Liam bowed his head. "It is my great honor to call you friend, Skel. I'm really glad you came back."

"Where is Ella, I wonder?" Skelaroth asked out of the blue.

"She said she wanted to explore and took off early this

morning," Rivka told the dragon.

"*Then, she is staying with you?*" the sea dragon asked. "*I thought she would.*"

"Gryffid said she had bonded to me and would likely stay with me as long as I remained worthy of her regard," Liam told Skelaroth with a wry expression.

"*Then, it is likely she will stay as long as you live,*" Skelaroth told him with a little bow of his head.

"I can't say I'd mind. I like having her around," Liam replied.

"*There is another reason I would like to continue our association, Liam,*" the dragon admitted. "*I believe it is a disservice to all sea dragons if I remain unaware of what goes on here on land. We've discussed it, and most of us feel that the time for our isolation in the sea has come to an end. Not that we'll all be moving on land in the foreseeable future. The Island Lair is enough for now. Some of my folk who want to be more involved with people will be frequenting the Lair as it grows. But, as leader of my kind, I need to be more aware of what goes on in the wider world.*"

"I can understand that," Liam answered.

"We can serve as a conduit to you of the important events on land, if that is your wish," Rivka put in. "As you know, I am Jinn. Liam will be brought into the Brotherhood when we wed, and he has his own extensive network of trade ships that bring news from all over. It will be a formidable network when combined. I think we would all welcome an alliance of sorts with you for the sharing of information so we can avoid trouble like the kind Fisk caused."

"*That is exactly what I was hoping to hear,*" Skelaroth said, sounding eminently pleased.

"I think, given the scope of what we're bringing together here, we should probably consult with Prince Nico at some point in the near future," Rivka added. "Of course, Drake at the Lair will likely help with that." She seemed to contemplate her words as Liam began to get an idea of the kind of network the Jinn had.

Liam knew his own sources of information were as wide

and varied as the routes over which he sent his ships. It started to dawn on him that with the addition of the sea dragons, he and Rivka would soon be at the center of a web of spies and intelligence agents unlike anything the lands had ever seen.

Suddenly, he was looking forward to the challenge coordinating such a thing would pose. He would run his fleet, and Rivka would help him learn how to be Jinn. Between them, they would serve the crown and all people who sought to do good in the world. They could really make a difference on a large scale.

"Please allow me to congratulate you both on your engagement," Skelaroth said, bringing Liam's thoughts back to the really important thing—his love for Rivka. Without which, the bright future he had just been contemplating would not exist.

"Thank you," Rivka said quietly, snuggling into Liam's side. They were still seated on the bench built into his dock, Skelaroth floating in the nearby water. "As soon as we figure out where the marriage feast is going to be held, we'll let you know. You are, of course, invited," Rivka put in. Liam hadn't thought that far ahead, but he really liked the idea of having Skelaroth at the celebration. After all, the big sea dragon was one of the few friends Liam had.

"I would be honored to attend," Skelaroth answered promptly. *"And I wish you both many centuries of happiness."*

"Centuries?" Liam couldn't quite wrap his mind around that concept.

"Liam," Skelaroth's tone was chiding. *"You are marrying a dragon."*

Amazing as that thought was, Liam couldn't help thinking about the warm woman tucked into his side. Yes, she might also be a dragon, but she was *his* dragon.

EPILOGUE

In the far, far North, Loralie cast the bones and tried, once again, to foresee her own future. Once again, the bones told her of a dragon. Was he to be her doom, then? She had foreseen his coming for many years, but she had no indication of when he would arrive and if he would bring her freedom or her death, which was freedom of another sort, she supposed.

She looked closer. Something was different, this time, in the way the bones had landed. It showed the dragon, yes, but also a slight indication that he was getting closer. Thanks be to the Mother of All! Finally. Finally, some movement after all these years of servitude and disgust for the way her powers were used against her wishes.

Loralie went to sleep that night with a slightly lighter heart. Whatever was going to happen, would happen soon. She wasn't afraid. She had long been reconciled to her own death, if that's what it took. She just had to be certain of her child's freedom, and then, she would go to her fate with a quiet heart.

She slept easier, and she dreamed... For the first time in

too many years to count, the sorceress dreamed of a man with dark hair. A dragon. Fire and flame. Passion and fury.

She dreamed of a dragon…and a man…

#

ABOUT THE AUTHOR

Bianca D'Arc has run a laboratory, climbed the corporate ladder in the shark-infested streets of lower Manhattan, studied and taught martial arts, and earned the right to put a whole bunch of letters after her name, but she's always enjoyed writing more than any of her other pursuits. She grew up and still lives on Long Island, where she keeps busy with an extensive garden, several aquariums full of very demanding fish, and writing her favorite genres of paranormal, fantasy and sci-fi romance.

Bianca loves to hear from readers and can be reached through Twitter (@BiancaDArc), Facebook (BiancaDArcAuthor) or through the various links on her website.

WELCOME TO THE D'ARC SIDE…
WWW.BIANCADARC.COM

OTHER BOOKS BY BIANCA D'ARC

Brotherhood of Blood
One & Only
Rare Vintage
Phantom Desires
Sweeter Than Wine
Forever Valentine
Wolf Hills*
Wolf Quest

Tales of the Were
Lords of the Were
Inferno

The Others
Rocky
Slade

String of Fate
Cat's Cradle
King's Throne
Jacob's Ladder
Her Warriors

Redstone Clan
The Purrfect Stranger
Grif
Red
Magnus
Bobcat
Matt

Big Wolf
A Touch of Class

Grizzly Cove
All About the Bear
Mating Dance
Night Shift
Alpha Bear
Saving Grace
Bearliest Catch
The Bear's Healing Touch
The Luck of the Shifters
Badass Bear
Loaded for Bear
Bounty Hunter Bear
Storm Bear
Bear Meets Girl
Spirit Bear

Were-Fey Love Story
Lone Wolf
Snow Magic
Midnight Kiss

Lick of Fire Trilogy
Phoenix Rising
Phoenix and the Wolf
Phoenix and the Dragon

Jaguar Island (Howls)
The Jaguar Tycoon
The Jaguar Bodyguard

Gemini Project
Tag Team
Doubling Down
Deuces Wild

Guardians of the Dark
Half Past Dead
Once Bitten, Twice Dead
A Darker Shade of Dead
The Beast Within
Dead Alert

Gifts of the Ancients
Warrior's Heart

Dragon Knights

Daughters of the Dragon
Maiden Flight*
Border Lair
The Ice Dragon**
Prince of Spies***

Novellas
The Dragon Healer
Master at Arms
Wings of Change

Sons of Draconia
FireDrake
Dragon Storm
Keeper of the Flame
Hidden Dragons

The Sea Captain's Daughter
Book 1: Sea Dragon
Book 2: Dragon Fire
Book 3: Dragon Mates

The Captain's Dragon

Resonance Mates
Hara's Legacy**
Davin's Quest
Jaci's Experiment
Grady's Awakening
Harry's Sacrifice

StarLords
Hidden Talent
Talent For Trouble
Shy Talent

Jit'Suku Chronicles
Arcana
King of Swords
King of Cups
King of Clubs
King of Stars
End of the Line
Diva

Sons of Amber
Angel in the Badlands
Master of Her Heart

In the Stars
The Cyborg Next Door
Her Warriors

StarLords
Hidden Talent
Talent For Trouble
Shy Talent

* RT Book Reviews Awards Nominee
** EPPIE Award Winner
*** CAPA Award Winner

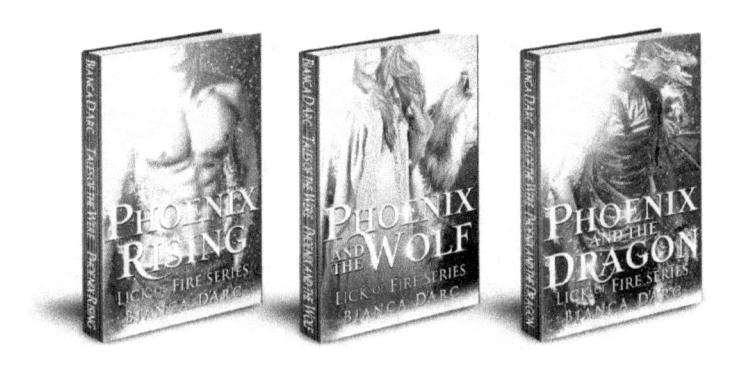

Phoenix Rising

Lance is inexplicably drawn to the sun and doesn't understand why. Tina is a witch who remembers him from their high school days. She'd had a crush on the quiet boy who had an air of magic about him. Reunited by Fate, she wonders if she could be the one to ground him and make him want to stay even after the fire within him claims his soul...if only their love can be strong enough.

Phoenix and the Wolf

Diana is drawn to the sun and dreams of flying, but her elderly grandmother needs her feet firmly on the ground. When Diana's old clunker breaks down in front of a high-end car lot, she seeks help and finds herself ensnared by the sexy werewolf mechanic who runs the repair shop. Stone makes her want to forget all her responsibilities and take a walk on the wild side...with him.

Phoenix and the Dragon

He's a dragon shapeshifter in search of others like himself. She's a newly transformed phoenix shifter with a lot to learn and bad guys on her trail. Together, they will go on a dazzling adventure into the unknown, and fight against evil folk intent on subduing her immense power and using it for their own ends. They will face untold danger and find love that will last a lifetime.

Lone Wolf

Josh is a werewolf who suddenly has extra, unexpected and totally untrained powers. He's not happy about it - or about the evil jackasses who keep attacking him, trying to steal his magic. Forced to seek help, Josh is sent to an unexpected ally for training.

Deena is a priestess with more than her share of magical power and a unique ability that has made her a target. She welcomes Josh, seeing a kindred soul in the lone werewolf. She knows she can help him... if they can survive their enemies long enough.

Snow Magic

Evie has been a lone wolf since the disappearance of her mate, Sir Rayburne, a fey knight from another realm. Left all alone with a young son to raise, Evie has become stronger than she ever was. But now her son is grown and suddenly Ray is back.

Ray never meant to leave Evie all those years ago but he's been caught in a magical trap, slowly being drained of magic all this time. Freed at last, he whisks Evie to the only place he knows in the mortal realm where they were happy and safe—the rustic cabin in the midst of a North Dakota winter where they had been newlyweds. He's used the last of his magic to get there and until he recovers a bit, they're stuck in the middle of nowhere with a blizzard coming and bad guys on their trail.

Can they pick up where they left off and rekindle the magic between them, or has it been extinguished forever?

Midnight Kiss

Margo is a werewolf on a mission...with a disruptively handsome mage named Gabe. She can't figure out where Gabe fits in the pecking order, but it doesn't seem to matter to the attraction driving her wild. Gabe knows he's going to have to prove himself in order to win Margo's heart. He wants her for his mate, but can she give her heart to a mage? And will their dangerous quest get in the way?

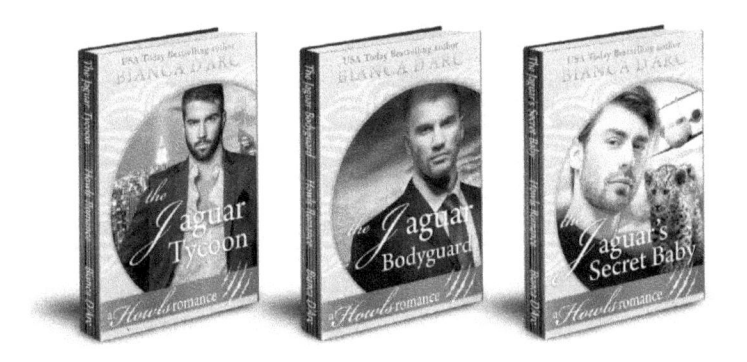

The Jaguar Tycoon

Mark may be the larger-than-life billionaire Alpha of the secretive Jaguar Clan, but he's a pussycat when it comes to the one women destined to be his mate. Shelly is an up-and-coming architect trying to drum up business at an elite dinner party at which Mark is the guest of honor. When shots ring out, the hunt for the gunman brings Mark into Shelly's path and their lives will never be the same.

The Jaguar Bodyguard

Sworn to protect his Clan, Nick heads to Hollywood to keep an eye on a rising star who has seen a little too much for her own good. Unexpectedly fame has made a circus of Sal's life, but when decapitated squirrels show up on her doorstep, she knows she needs professional help. Nick embeds himself in her security squad to keep an eye on her as sparks fly and passions rise between them. Can he keep her safe and prevent her from revealing what she knows?

The Jaguar's Secret Baby

Hank has never forgotten the wild woman with whom he spent one memorable night. He's dreamed of her for years now, but has never been back to the small airport in Texas owned and run by her werewolf Pack. Tracy was left with a delicious memory of her night in Hank's arms, and a beautiful baby girl who is the light of her life. She chose not to tell Hank about his daughter, but when he finally returns and he discovers the daughter he's never known, he'll do all he can to set things right.

BIANCA D'ARC

WWW.BIANCADARC.COM

CPSIA information can be obtained
at www.ICGtesting.com
Printed in the USA
LVHW031701061220
673493LV00014B/1451